Moving Target

by

Desiree Holt

Guardian Security Book One

Moving Target

Contact Information: info@thewildrosepress.com

Cover Art by *Diana Carlile*

The Wild Rose Press, Inc.
PO Box 708
Adams Basin, NY 14410-0708

Visit us at www.thewilderroses.com

Publishing History
First Scarlet Rose Edition, 2017
Print ISBN 978-1-5092-1595-9
Digital ISBN 978-1-5092-1596-6

Published in the United States of America

Praise for Iona Morrison

THE HARVEST CLUB was #1 in Ghost Suspense on the 2015 bestseller list in the Kindle Store.

~*~

"The mysteries are engaging, the characters worth meeting, and her writing eminently readable. If you are looking for a new set of fictional friends to entertain you, check out Iona's stories...I highly recommend them."

~James Switzer

~*~

"This story...grabs you in the first chapter and doesn't let go until the end. A romantic mystery. I think men as well as women will enjoy it."

~Sheila Dwyer-Hemingway

~*~

"There are heroes, heroines, bad guys, good guys, everything that goes into writing an entertaining and exciting book!!" 5 stars

~Doris L Vandruff

~*~

"Everyone wants a grandmother like Sadie! Let's not forget Radar! Can't wait to read more Jessie, Matt, and Katie and Jeremy!"

~Natalie Acosta

A bullet splintered the bark of the tree

where she had been standing. Jessie ran. She could hear someone crashing through the brush not far behind her. Another bullet missed her, hitting a little to the right, kicking up dirt and leaves on the ground. She ran faster. Up ahead, she could see a branch hanging low, and she did what she had done many times as a kid. She reached out, grabbed it as she ran by, and swung herself up into the tree to hide. She got a foot on a low branch and climbed up further, out of sight, her dress snagging on twigs. Her feet screamed in pain, her palms were slick with blood. Be silent! She crouched, one arm around the main trunk, trying to stifle her breathing. Her heart pumped hard, her ears strained for any sound. She took her gun from the holster, but her hand wouldn't stop shaking. A branch snapped, and she jerked. Quiet! She covered her mouth with her hand. He was still coming, the hunter hunting his prey. He wasn't trying to be quiet. Branches snapped, and she heard the thud of running footsteps. Jessie clung to the trunk, still as a piece of tree bark.

**The only friends she had were trying to kill her.
No place was safe. But maybe…**

"Did we… I mean, last night…"

"If you're asking if we had sex, the answer is no. You were hurting, Kate, and vulnerable." Quinn gave a rough chuckle. "I'd think I have a little more class than that."

"Ohmigod." Kate wanted to hide under the covers.

"Shh." His soft Texas drawl was so soothing. "It's all right. Whatever it is, I promise I can help make it better."

The warmth of his body was seeping into hers, chasing away the cold that lay inside her like a block of ice. The same sense of cold living inside her since the night she fled Peter's office. What would it be like to just say the hell with everything and let this man take away her pain?

"Quinn?" She had to ask. "What are we doing here?"

He sighed. "Damned if I know."

"I was hoping maybe one of us did," she told him, her breathing unsteady.

Get up, Kate. Move away. Don't do anything stupid.

"Kate?" Fingers stroked her rib cage.

"Yes?"

"I haven't wanted a woman in four years, and we haven't known each other long enough to even have a meal together. But if you don't want to get us both in trouble, you'd better get up. Quick."

Wetting her suddenly dry lips with her tongue, she tried to find what was left of her brain. This was *so* not like her. At least not like Kathryn Burke. She hadn't been Kate Griffin long enough to make judgments.

She drew in a shuddering breath. "And if I don't want to move?"

"You don't know how much I want to make you feel better. A lot better. I want to chase away those shadows in your eyes if you'll let me. But more than that, I promise you, if I don't move right now, my brain is going on vacation."

Dedication

To my daughter, Amy Nease,
who held my hand and talked me through
it when I first began to write this book.
This one's for you.

To my team, without whom
nothing would be written—Margie Hager, Janet
Rodman, and Joseph Patrick Trainor.

Chapter One

"Kathryn will be dead before the weekend is out. You have my word on it."

Kathryn Burke froze at the entrance to the suite of offices, keys in hand. The voice sounded just like Peter, her fiancé. He was somewhere in the suite, loud, confident, and unmistakable. No, she was wrong. He wouldn't be saying that so calmly. She must have heard wrong.

His next words dispelled that notion, blindsiding her and stealing her breath.

"Relax, Miguel. It's almost over. I'll get rid of Kathryn this weekend, and then we'll be home free."

She rubbed her forehead. Two days ago, she'd finally stopped taking the little white pills he kept giving her, pushing herself out of the fog she'd been living in. Was she having a hangover from the aftereffects? An auditory hallucination?

The meeting with the insurance adjuster had upset her, and she wanted Peter to help her push the matter.

"Let's have dinner," she'd begged. "I need your help."

She wanted more investigation into the fire that killed her parents. The adjuster wanted her to take the settlement check, telling her the arson investigation was closed. Peter had soothed her, telling her he had a late

1

client meeting and they could discuss it when he got home.

Irritated and frustrated, she'd finally dumped her frozen dinner in the trash, got in her car, and drove to the offices of Burke, Fleming and Associates. Peter usually locked the doors when he had late meetings, but she still had her father's keys. She was going to slip in unannounced, not give him a chance to turn her away.

And she'd walked into that frightening declaration.

God, how could he say it so calmly? This was the man she was supposed to marry.

Another voice spoke up, an unfamiliar one, lower, deep, and edgy with a Hispanic accent. "You'd better be right. Disposing of the girl is a priority."

She wanted to clap her hands over her ears. Icy fingers of terror danced on her spine, urging her to back out into the corridor and run like hell.

Get away from here. Now.

But like some evil magnet, the conversation pulled at her, dragging her farther into the suite of offices. Easing the key from the lock, she guided the door to a soundless close and moved softly into the darkened reception area. Slipping off her shoes with shaking hands and stuffing them into her purse, she forced herself to tiptoe down the hall, her footsteps silenced by the thick carpet.

Pulse racing like a Formula One engine, her stomach trying to claw its way up into her throat, she moved nervously forward until she peered around a corner into the largest office. Once it had been her father's. Now he was dead, her Uncle Merritt gone also, and Peter ruled the law firm from behind the massive desk.

The office was empty, dark except for a tiny desk lamp casting a narrow pool of light. The voices came from the small adjacent conference room. Swallowing her fear, Kathryn eased behind the connecting door that was open a few inches. She flattened herself against the wall, her heart beating a tattoo so loud she was sure they could hear it.

Maybe she'd misunderstood what they said. Of course. That had to be it. Her hearing was playing tricks on her or she'd imagined it.

"I'm telling you, Miguel." Peter's voice was confident. Arrogant. "You can relax. I have it under control. Blink your eyes, and she'll be gone. Dead. It's a done deal. Life will continue without a ripple on the surface."

Kathryn thought she might pass out. She hadn't been wrong. They were planning to kill her, Peter and this other man. Miguel. Who in God's name was he? And why did they want to get rid of her?

"We can't afford any mistakes with this." Miguel's voice again. "You've dragged it out long enough. If she decides to snoop around we're all in trouble. Get rid of her. Now."

"I told you, I have it under control." Peter's tone was defensive. Almost hostile.

Miguel's next words stunned her even more. "Until then, keep her away from the office. We can't take the chance she'll see or hear something."

Kathryn frowned. What on earth could she possibly see? Since her father's death, she only came by rarely, and then just to meet Peter.

"I'll make sure of it."

God, he was so smug. So assured. Had he always

sounded like that and she'd just been so besotted she hadn't noticed? What an idiot she was.

"We're out of time." Miguel reminded him. "I have orders from the top. Get rid of her at once or we'll do it for you."

"I understand. Believe me, no one will be happier to see her dead than me."

Her body shifted into full panic mode, the pulsing of her blood boomed in her ears. Dead. She still couldn't process it.

"And your arrangements won't trigger anything?" Miguel's skepticism was obvious.

"No. I promise you. I'm taking her away this weekend for a change of scenery. As far as anyone knows it will be to help her get over her depression. It's common knowledge she's been living on those pills. When she takes a few too many, who will think twice about it?"

Take a few too many?

Surely no one would buy that. Did anyone who knew her really think she'd kill herself? She tried to swallow, but her mouth was drier than Arizona. A hysterical laugh threatened to explode, and she forced it back.

None of this made sense. Why was it so important to get rid of her? What was it about the firm she wasn't supposed to know? She felt like Alice Through the Looking Glass, needing only the White Rabbit and the Mad Hatter to complete the crazy picture.

Peter—*her* Peter—wanted to kill her. How insane was that?

God. Peter. She closed her eyes, and his image swam before her, tall, muscular, handsome with his sun-bleached blond hair and laser blue eyes. Except now the face that had seemed so caring was stamped with evil. What an act he'd put on, and she'd been dumb enough to fall for it.

A wave of lightheadedness swept over her. She realized she'd been holding her breath and forced herself to exhale slowly. She was pushing her luck staying here, and she knew it. Any minute, they could discover her. She started to move away from her hiding place, but the next words she heard chilled her blood.

"I'm just telling you, Peter, this better be handled right. We were fortunate with the other deaths. We can't push our luck."

Other deaths? Had they killed someone else? Who?

"I'm taking care of business," Peter protested. "I got rid of the parents without any problems, didn't I? And despite all Kathryn's weeping and wailing, I convinced the investigators to rule it an accident and close the case."

Oh, my god. My parents. The fire. I knew something was wrong. That damn adjuster. I was right to be suspicious about the "accident".

She still remembered that night in painful detail. If she hadn't been tired and left early after dinner with them, she'd be dead, too. Was that the plan? But why? What was it that made her family targets for murder?

"John brought it on himself." Peter's voice had a strident quality. "He was about to do something foolish. I dealt with him, and I'll deal with Kathryn.

"Too bad John developed a conscience. Just like his brother, Merritt, or they could both be living the good life."

Her father? Her uncle? Kathryn's mind couldn't

process the implications.

"Yeah, too bad." But there was no remorse in Peter's voice.

"They should have remembered we can reach out anywhere in the country—in the world—to find out what we want. To find anyone. Anything. Anywhere." He paused. "You would do well to remember that, too."

"I'm not going anywhere."

"Just call me when it's over," Miguel told him, "so I can pass the word."

Alarm bells were screaming in Kathryn's brain. Get out! Get out! Get away! Her panic meter shot to a new high, the darkened room around her reduced to a swirling fog. Hysterically, she realized this was the most she reacted physically to anything in weeks. Maybe months.

Feeling dislodged from any kind of reality, she squeezed her eyes shut, hard, then opened them again and tried to focus. She had to get a grip here. *Slow breaths. Stay calm. Don't do anything to give yourself away.*

"Just deal properly with the officials." Miguel again.

"I'm not concerned. We've spread enough money around, have enough people we've paid off wherever we do business to take care of that. Cops, prosecutors, government agents, whatever, everyone has a price. It's all a matter of finding it. I can make anything go away, no matter how high up I have to go."

God, it got even worse. Peter had paid people off? If she got away, where could she go that she'd be safe? Nowhere.

"And our records?" Miguel asked. "Are they up to

date?"

"I'm going to enter the latest transfers tonight," Peter went on. "Everything's saved on the flash drive so there's nothing on my computer. It's plugged in and ready to go. As soon as we're finished here, I'll lock it up in its usual place."

"You leave it lying around like that?" Miguel's voice was sharp with irritation. "So carelessly? Don't you think that's irresponsible on your part? Everything about us is on there."

"For God's sake." Peter sounded exasperated. "I told you. There's nobody here but us. I locked the outer doors. And no one else is coming here tonight. Not even the cleaning crew."

"If that drive fell into the wrong hands, we would be out of business."

"Relax. No one's going to get their hands on it."

"You'd better be right."

Flash drive. If she could get hold of that…

Her eyes skittered wildly around the office. Could she make it across to Peter's desk without being spotted? Quietly, crouching down, she moved behind the desk and eased open the door where the laptop was. There, just as he'd said, plugged into the USB port. A desperate voice said *Take it.* Something this important could be her best insurance. If God forbid they found her, maybe she could bargain for her life with it.

Just let me get this and be out of here, she prayed. With hands that were far from steady, she reached for the tiny object and shoved it into her pocket. As she turned to move away from the desk her arm caught a stack of folders on the corner, knocking them to the floor with a thud. She froze.

"What was that?" Miguel's voice. Sharp. "Did you hear something?"

"I'll look," Peter said, "although I can assure you there's no one here but us."

They were coming! They'd find her! *Go, go, go.*

Propelled by a greater fear than she'd ever known, Kathryn raced down the hall, through the outer doors, down the stairs, and into the parking garage. Gasping for breath, she nearly leaped into her car.

Her hands were shaking so badly she needed both of them to get the key in the ignition. Heavy feet pounding down the stairs warned her to hurry. Finally she shoved hard, the key slid in, the engine started, and she threw the car into reverse.

The door from the stairs to the parking area banged open, and Peter and another man came barreling through. She slammed her foot on the accelerator and sped out toward the street, tires screeching, rainwater splashing against the doors. In seconds, she lost herself in the rat's nest of traffic on Dale Mabry Highway, Tampa's busiest major thoroughfare.

Weaving back and forth in the lanes, her view distorted by the rain that had not let up all day, she prayed harder than she'd ever prayed in her life.

Please don't let them be able to follow me, find me.

God, what a naive simpleton she'd been. What a dense, gullible fool.

Her chest felt so constricted she could barely breathe. Her heart still raced wildly, beating in cadence with the raindrops thrumming against the windshield. Fighting to get herself under control, she gripped the steering wheel so hard her hands were cramping.

Despite the inner chill that invaded her body, she

was sweating heavily. Her long hair was coming loose from the clasp that held it away from her face, and her once-neat tailored pants suit felt sticky and uncomfortable. Her hands were slick with sweat, slippery on the wheel.

"Damn it! Get out of the way," she swore at the cars in front of her. "Move, move, move."

She could still hear the voices, so cold and matter of fact.

...kill her...kill her...kill her...

And the swooshing of the inner door to the garage just as she had backed her car out, tires screeching. The panic as she listened for another car engine to start.

The tiny silver rectangle was tucked in her bra, its touch almost burning her skin. God, if only she hadn't been so clumsy and knocked those files to the floor. If only she'd been faster down the stairs.

If only...

OhGodohGodohGod. They're going to kill me. I have to get away.

Shut up, Kathryn, and think. This is no time to fall apart.

There it was, up ahead. The on ramp to the interstate. But which way to go? Which way? Which way? She took the northbound ramp, the first one she came to, and became lost in the lanes of speeding cars.

She drove through the rain, forcing herself to think. In an instant, her life had turned upside down. She could never go back. She'd be dead if Peter got his hands on her. But where could she go? What could she do? She had no one to turn to. And the little data storage unit was burning a hole in her pocket.

There was really only one thing she knew for sure.

Somehow, some way, she had to disappear.

****

"God damn it, Miguel, I don't know what she was doing here."

Peter ground his teeth in frustration.

His immaculate office looked like the aftermath of a tornado, with papers and files scattered everywhere. Frantic was not a normal part of his personality, but right now he was as close to it as he could get. He picked up the folders from the floor, dropped them, shoved others aside as he scoured his desktop for the precious storage.

"Bitch! Bitch! Bitch!" Each word was punctuated by the pounding of his fist on the desktop. He dropped into his chair and raked his fingers through his hair. Anger tightened every muscle in his body.

"It seems she's not quite as manageable as you thought," Miguel Osuna snapped.

"She assured me she was staying home tonight." He pulled out drawers, dumped their contents on the floor, and dug through them.

Miguel paced, something Peter knew he rarely did, hands in his pockets, his face set in angry lines. "It seems she changed her mind."

"Kathryn never changes her mind."

"It seems she did so at least twice in her life," Osuna pointed out, his voice lethal-sounding. "The night she was supposed to be with her parents and again tonight."

"I can't begin to think why she did." Furious, he swept a pile of papers aside, tumbling them to the floor to join the rest of the chaos. "Damn it. The flash drive isn't here."

"You assured me the office was locked up. How did she get in?"

"I don't know." He avoided Miguel's stare. "I guess she still has one of her father's keys. I thought I'd collected them all."

Peter knew he was in big trouble here. The air in the office was thick with tension and rage. And something else. For the first time in his adult life, Peter Fleming knew what fear was.

"You've put us all at risk." Osuna's voice was hard and cold. "Not just our little corner of the world, but Carlos as well, and our entire operation. I cannot believe how careless you've been. Now you know why leaving that thing out was a mistake."

"Damn it, Miguel. She never, ever comes here unexpectedly. Certainly not like this. Why should I expect she would tonight? Of all nights?"

"In our line of work you must expect the unexpected. Your lapse in judgment will cost us dearly. You won't like the reaction from the top, I promise you."

Peter scrubbed his hands across his face. "I was ready to make the new entries right after our meeting. There was no risk. No one was supposed to come near this place."

"You should consider yourself lucky she didn't take any of the hard copy files with her. Unlike the ones on the flash drive, they aren't encrypted."

"I don't know why she took anything, for God's sake." He slapped his hand on the desk. "I'll find her. Count on it."

"We need to make some arrangements." Miguel pulled a cell phone from his pocket. "I'm not sure after this we can trust you to handle things by yourself."

"What does that mean?" Peter curled his hands into fists.

"It means I'm going to use our available resources. As soon as I make a phone call, our men will start looking for her." He punched in a number and in a moment began speaking in rapid Spanish. When he paused, he looked at Peter. "Give me that picture of her on your desk."

"Picture?" Peter frowned.

"Never mind." Miguel Osuna picked up the framed head shot himself and snapped it with the camera in his phone. A few more sentences, and he disconnected his call. "They have her picture and general description. People will start looking at once."

"She can't have gone far," Peter told him. "She hasn't the experience or the guts to figure out how to hide herself away."

"Do you think after what happened tonight I'd put any confidence in your assessment of Kathryn Burke?" He was interrupted by the ringing of his cell phone. He listened for a few minutes, then hung up without saying a word. "She's not at the condo. There's no sign of her car, and we know she hasn't had enough time to get there and leave again. Wherever she went, that wasn't it."

"I can't believe she'd just drive off into the night with nothing," Peter said, his jaw set in frustration. "That isn't her style."

Miguel skewered him with a murderous look. "It seems there's a lot you can't believe, unfortunately for us. Especially unlucky for you."

Peter tried furiously to think of what to do next. He

looked at his computer, snapped his fingers, and in a moment his hands were flying over the keyboard. "Money. She'll need cash. She never carries much with her."

"What are you doing?" Miguel asked.

"Checking her bank accounts. Maybe she used her ATM card. It will tell me where she's been, anyway." He sat back and watched while information scrolled across the screen. When it stopped, he leaned forward. "There it is." He shook his head.

"What did you find?" Miguel demanded.

"She's hit some machines in town, pulling money out. But not enough. My guess is she's still running. When she thinks she's far enough away, she'll hit the ATMs again or cash a check. But the pattern shows us she's heading north."

"Where would she go?"

"God knows. I don't think she'd call any of her friends, and she has no close relatives left."

Miguel stabbed a finger at Peter. "I hold you completely responsible for this. There will be consequences. You know I'll have to make a rather unpleasant phone call tonight to report everything." He was gone before Peter could frame a reply.

He slumped back in his chair, rubbing his temples. Hell and damnation. He'd planned so carefully for everything. How had it fallen apart like this?

Where are you, Kathryn? When I find you, you'll be begging me to kill you before I'm finished.

Chapter Two

Charlotte, North Carolina

Kathryn didn't think the rain would ever stop. The storm followed her up the east coast, getting worse the farther north she went. She tried not to startle every time lightning streaked across the sky and thunder boomed in her ears. It was bad enough that she was afraid every car pulling close to her carried Peter or his friends.

The storm was behind her and the sun full up when she pulled off the Interstate into Charlotte, N.C. She was exhausted from tension and the long distance driving, stoked only by industrial strength coffee from two gas stops, and she was about at the end of her rope. This needed to be the end of the line for Kathryn Burke, but she had some things to care of to make that happen.

Peter would be tracking her, which meant her credit cards were useless. She had stopped at an ATM before leaving the city to pull out her daily maximum of cash, emergency money just in case. If Peter, with his skills, discovered it, he'd hopefully think she was still in the city. She'd put the check the insurance adjuster had thrust on her in her purse, thinking to discuss it with Peter before cashing. Now it could be her lifeline.

She'd have to be careful how she handled it, though. She was sure Peter wouldn't put a hold on her accounts, thinking to use that as a way to track her.

She'd write a check that didn't raise red flags with the bank and make that last withdrawal while still in the city, then get the hell out of Dodge. With money in her wallet, she could figure out what to do next

Yes, Kathryn, exactly what would that be? Think, think, think.

She also she needed to change her method of transportation. She could ditch the car, no problem, leaving them at least a temporary dead end. That would also give her some extra cash, although she'd get the short end of the stick in that deal. But airplanes were out because they required identification. A Trailways bus blew past her at a light and she took that as a sign. Buses were very innocuous.

At a diner, she ordered coffee again and a sweet roll and asked for a telephone book. She easily found the listing for the branches of her bank—having one that operated nationwide would make this easy. The book also had a map of the city. How lucky could she get? She picked a branch way out of the way and cashed a check for an amount that wouldn't throw up red flags. She felt a little more secure financially. Although the money wouldn't last forever, but it gave her a lot of breathing room.

Finished with her stops, she left her car parked on a side street and called a cab to deliver her to the bus terminal. She did her best to blend in with the people entering the building. She was sure Peter was checking her banking every five minutes, and she had no idea how long it would be before they had someone on her trail here. He was smart enough to guess she'd ditch the car and that the bus would be the only anonymous way out of town short of hitch hiking.

"We pay off everyone—cops, prosecutors…"

Was that brown sedan at the curb the same one she'd seen at the diner? What about the gray one sliding down the street? And the cop car idling at the light?

Stop it. He can't catch up with me that fast. I hope.

Inside the terminal she bought a ticket for the next bus out of town, leaving in an hour.

Too much time. Peter will be tracking my bank account and see the ATM withdrawals. Hurry, bus. Hurry, hurry, hurry.

For most of the hour, she huddled in a corner of the room, making herself as inconspicuous as possible, hoping her fear didn't emanate from her like a visible cloud. Every time someone came through the doors, she tried to make herself as inconspicuous as possible. She clutched her purse, with her money and the flash drive, as if they were a lifeline.

The hour was almost up when she saw them. She knew in her gut they'd come from Peter. Or his friend, Miguel. They had an air about them—quiet, methodical, deadly-looking. They probably had people checking the airport, too, just in case. Good thing she was staying away from planes.

The men searched the big waiting room quietly and methodically, glancing from their cell phone screens to the faces of every woman in the in the waiting area. The frightening realization that whoever Peter was involved with had tentacles everywhere and unlimited resources to seek her out nearly paralyzed her, but she had to get away.

Picking her moment, she eased her way down the hallway where the rest rooms were and out the side door. Her bus was just pulling up at the curb. Looking carefully to make sure the men were still inside, she blended in with the line of people waiting to board.

They were thirty minutes out of Charlotte before her breathing slowed.

****

Tampa

"What do you mean, they lost her?" Miguel raged as he paced Peter's office.

"We covered everything," Peter told him. "Airports, car rentals, the bus terminal. I called our contact there, and he sent out several teams. *Nada.*"

"She won't rent a car or take a plane, you idiot," Miguel stormed. "She can't use her ID. That means buses. You had people on it right away. So where did she go?"

"Calm down." Peter searched for calm himself. He'd been popping antacids like candy. "She'll show up. Maybe she got on a bus before they got there. Maybe she was somewhere else in the area."

"I'll calm down when I have her and that damned flash drive in my hands. Are you still tracking her bank accounts?"

"Of course."

"She didn't get enough money to do anything with. She'll need more. I want people on it the minute the hit pops up."

Peter tossed another antacid pill in his mouth and tapped his keyboard.

****

Los Angeles

A snippet of the conversation Kathryn had overheard flashed back to her.

"They should have remembered we can reach out

anywhere in the country—in the world—to find out what we want. To find anyone. Anything. Anywhere."

Her stomach hurt, her head ached, and her rear end was practically numb from riding one bus after another. Once, she'd been a totally different person, eating lunch at trendy cafes and expecting a marriage proposal. That was a person she no longer recognized.

She had become someone else. A new person who thought life at the moment really sucked. Her food came from vending machines and fast food restaurants, and she hopped from one bus to another, praying her so-called lover didn't find her and kill her. And her vocabulary was now sprinkled with language she'd picked up from her travels. Words like crap, damn, shit, fuck. Language foreign to Kathryn Burke, who she was beginning to realize had been a very uptight broad.

She was getting much better at this, surprising herself. The night she'd fled Peter's office in such terror the panic had almost incapacitated her. At first, she was on autopilot, knowing only that she had to get away. Somewhere. Anywhere. And hide where they couldn't find her.

She knew she was out there alone. No one was going to save her but herself. She couldn't contact her friends or her boss. Peter would be watching them. The urgent need to stay alive forced her to think and plan. And somewhere, on her crazy bus odyssey from city to city and state to state, strength she didn't know she had welled up from inside her.

The metamorphosis had begun. Goodbye, Kathryn Burke. Hello, Kate Griffin.

The fear hadn't disappeared, just been pushed to a place where she could manage it. Kathryn would have let it consume her to the point of helplessness. Kate used it to stay alert as she rode the edge of danger.

Kate. It took some practice, but she'd finally gotten used to her new name.

By now the bus terminals had all begun to look alike, the only difference being size. This one, in Los Angeles, was the largest yet, and she blended easily into the mixture of people. They were all sizes and shapes, enough of them in clothes as scruffy as hers that she didn't stand out.

Shielded by the protective bill of the gimme cap she'd picked up at a truck stop, Kate's eyes never stopped moving, scanning every inch of the waiting area, registering the crowd filling the benches, standing against the walls, reading, using their cell phones, napping, listening to iPods.

She'd learned to be extra careful, to watch everything that was happening, to study the scene before ever making a move. When she was sure no one was paying attention to her, she slipped into the line at one of the ticket windows.

"That bus outside?" she asked when it was her turn at the window. "Where is it going?"

"Albuquerque." The bored ticket clerk didn't even look up at her.

"When does it leave?"

"About forty-five minutes. You want a ticket?"

Make up your mind, Kate.

"Okay. Yes."

"One way or round trip?"

"One way."

She glanced around as she waited for her change. Was that grubby individual off to her left looking at her for too long? Who was he calling on is cell phone? God, was she seeing shadows everywhere?

She fidgeted while the clerk, with slow, unconcerned movements, completed the transaction. Grabbing the ticket and stowing it in her pants pocket, she found an end seat on a bench and scrunched into the corner. Fatigue pulled at her, but she willed her eyes to stay open.

She was so tired, more than she'd ever been in her life. Too many hours of hyper-awareness and too little rest. Keeping her guard up, trying to ignore the itch between her shoulders as if someone's eyes were pinned to her. And fighting the panic that always threatened to overwhelm her. She clenched her fists around her duffel, willing the fear to disappear, forcing back the sound of the voices in her head.

God, what if she hadn't decided to surprise Peter at his office? What if she hadn't overheard that conversation?

Who were these people he was involved with? What kind of resources did they have that they could reach out anywhere? Unconsciously, she rubbed one hand against her stomach, feeling beneath her jacket and shirt for the fanny pack where her money was safely tucked away in tight little rolls.

Along with the all-important flash drive nearly burning a hole in the cloth. Her only bargaining chip, providing she lived to use it. What a stroke of luck that had been, even though she'd almost been caught. Seconds. That was all that had separated her from capture, all that had allowed her to get away.

Reading the files might give her some leverage, although she didn't know with who. But she was fully aware what a pipe dream that was. She'd tried library computers at a couple of places between buses, but as expected, everything was encrypted and password-protected. She needed to find someone with the software to decrypt it. But who? She certainly couldn't go to the police.

"I'm not concerned," Peter had said. *"We've spread enough money around. You know that. There are enough people we've paid off everywhere to make them look the other way. Cops, prosecutors, government agents, whatever. It didn't take us long to learn everyone has a price. It's all a matter of finding it."*

Shivering as she remembered the words, Kate stole a glance at the clock on the wall, willing the minute hand to move faster.

Come on! Come on!

Idly, she wondered what Albuquerque would be like. Could she fade into obscurity there, or would it just be another place to change buses again? God, if she could just get out of L.A. before Peter's *friends* showed up, she was ready to find a hole and go to ground. Someplace to sleep for more than an hour. Take a shower, even eat a real meal. A day. Maybe two. Maybe even a whole week in one place.

Her eyelids drooped, and she sagged against the bench. Something plucking at her jerked her awake. An old woman's claw-like hands were tugging at her duffel. Heart racing, Kate yanked the bag closer to her body.

"What are you doing?" She tried to scoot away from the skinny hag. "Let go."

"Dear, you're dropping your bag."

"Don't touch my things." Kate forced herself not to shout.

"Well. Excuse me," the woman sniffed. "You were falling asleep and your bag was about to drop."

God, how had she let her eyes close? It seemed like only seconds since she'd sat down. What if this had been Peter pulling at her or someone he'd sent?

The old woman stared at Kate, her pinched face accusing. "I just didn't want you to lose it. Next time, I won't bother."

Kate slid her arms farther through the duffel straps and hugged it closer to her body. She was beginning to hate buses and bus terminals. If only she hadn't had to ditch her car. Instead, here she was, among the great unwashed, piling up frequent rider miles.

See America First.

How many states had she already passed through since that night, getting off one bus, boarding another, not even caring about the destination? How many more would there be on her trip to nowhere before she found someplace safe.

Safe!

She nearly laughed. What a fairy tale that was. She had a feeling whatever Peter was part of, there didn't seem to be any place they couldn't reach out and touch her. Hopefully, he and his *friends* would think she'd disappeared into Middle America somewhere, but she had a feeling they'd cover all bases. Did they have a network they could send her picture out to? Pay people to locate her? She'd read enough stories in the newspaper and online, seen enough on television to know people like the ones Peter was mixed up with could reach out anywhere they wanted. Her stomach heaved as the thought cycled through her brain. She had to be on the alert at all times.

Biting hard on the inside of her cheek to keep herself awake, she watched the minute hand on the wall clock crawl by at a snail's pace. Thirty minutes since she'd purchased her ticket, time inching along like cold molasses. Still fifteen minutes until her bus left.

She felt rather than saw the old lady sneaking curious glances at her every few seconds, but she deliberately ignored her. Pulling her cap even lower over her face, she continued scanning the room, always alert for anything out of the ordinary.

So far, so good. Nothing seemed to set off alarms in her head. Too much coffee eating away at the lining of her stomach served to keep her awake.

As she shifted in her seat, her glance was caught by a woman two benches away. The woman sat ramrod straight, clutching a large purse to her side as if it contained buried treasure. Long, thick chestnut hair was clipped back at her neck. Tailored pants suit, inexpensive but classic. Low heels. Tote bag hooked over one shoulder.

She could have passed for me a month ago.

Not now, of course. One layer at a time Kate had buried Kathryn Burke. Jeans and a T-shirt replaced the pants suit. A shaggy, self-styled cut now tucked up into a gimme cap took the place of the long hair that had been her trademark. Dirty tennis shoes and an ugly nylon jacket with coffee stains completed the outfit. Whenever she looked in a mirror, she realized the metamorphosis from Kathryn to Kate was complete.

She hoped—*prayed*—that Peter would think she didn't have sense enough to change her appearance.

Her name. Anything.

Looking at the clock once more, she thought it impossible that only two minutes had passed since the last time she checked. Her stomach was doing funny thing, which she hoped was due to the rotten coffee and not her newly-developed early warning system.

And then she saw them entering the terminal, two men who could have been clones of the ones in Charlotte. The same deadly air, the same carefully blank faces, the same hunter's gleam in their eyes as they surveyed the waiting area. The image of the grubby thug making a furtive call on his cell phone popped into her brain. Every one of her senses told her she was their quarry. Bile rose in the back of her throat as nausea swept over her, and she swallowed hard against it.

She watched them as they moved through the terminal. They spoke in quiet tones into the cell phones they carried, every few seconds checking the screens.

"See that," the old lady squeaked to the man next to her. "I'll bet they're police, after some criminal."

When the man ignored her, she turned back to Kate again. "Who do you suppose they're after?"

Me. They've got a picture on their cell phone screen and they're looking for me. Adrenaline pumped through her veins, accelerating her heartbeat. Her pulse was beating a fierce tattoo, and a thin trickle of sweat ran down her spine.

Thankfully the picture they had couldn't bear much resemblance to her now. In Peter's arrogance, he would never consider she'd have sense enough to change her appearance. Still, who knew what could give her away? She had to get out of here.

Choking back the scream blossoming in her throat, she forced herself to move, rising as casually as possible from the bench. More than anything she wanted to run, but she made herself move slowly, one step at a time.

Miss Pants Suit rose and started toward the rest rooms. Kate saw the men spot her and, keeping their cell phones open, move in her direction.

They think she's me. God, that poor woman.

As Kate moved away from the bench, the men came abreast of the unlucky Miss Pants Suit, boxing her in between them. Each of them took one of her elbows and the one on the left leaned over and said something in her ear. Kate saw the woman try to jerk her arm away and open her mouth to scream.

"My wife," the man said apologetically to the curious crowd. "Given to unpredictable mood swings. Come, sweetheart, you need your medication."

Kate saw the desperate movements as the woman struggled to free herself. Her head whipping back and forth, she was yelling "Help me" to the people around her. Instead, they uncomfortably averted their eyes.

Watching as she slithered toward the exit, Kate saw one man put his mouth to the woman's ear and say something. The one word she caught chilled her. Kathryn. Then his hand moved, and in seconds Miss Pants Suit was limp in their arms. They moved away with her, the man who'd pretended to be her husband arranging his face in a sad expression.

Kate nearly passed out. For a moment, she almost screamed out, "Leave her alone." She was sick at the thought of what would happen to this woman whose only crime was to look like Kathryn Burke. It wouldn't take long for them to figure out they'd made a mistake. Maybe once they figured out she was the wrong woman, they'd let her go. She prayed that's what would happen.

But she had to get out of here, and she couldn't wait any longer for the Albuquerque bus. She needed to get away now.

Anywhere. I don't care. Just as long as it gets me away from here.

A city bus was idling at the curb, riders jostling each other in their haste to board. Kate pushed her way in front of everyone, fear making her aggressive. Any second she expected to feel a heavy hand on her shoulder, yanking her back onto the sidewalk.

"Do you mind?" a girl in Goth makeup and spandex spat as Kate shoved her way onto the vehicle.

"Sorry," she mumbled.

She dropped coins into the receptacle and made her way to the far corner of the bus, slumping into a seat as her rubbery legs gave out. Peering out from under the gimme cap, she watched to see if the men had realized their mistake yet and come looking for her. She held her breath, waiting for them to rush out to the sidewalk. When no one appeared, she released the pent-up breath with a *whoosh*. Good. Still occupied with Miss Pants Suit. She was safe for the moment.

Her heart still thundered like a jet, and she gripped her duffel hard to control the shaking in her hands. They didn't just want to kill her. That would come later. They were after the drive. The damned flash drive. If they got their hands on it she was history.

The bus rumbled along, pulling up at a stop to let passengers off. Through the window Kate's eye caught the sign for Highway Harry's Used Car Lot—Try 'Em and Buy 'Em. Okay. Time to change transportation again. She hopped off the bus before the doors closed, shifted her duffel to a more comfortable position, and strode into Highway Harry's.

"She don't look like much," the oily salesman told her, patting the hood of an aging sedan, "but she'll get you where you want to go."

Yeah, right. As long as I don't want to go too far. "If you say so."

At least at Harry's, they didn't ask for any identification, and Harry was eager enough to take her cash.

"You might want to check the oil after a little while," he said, handing over the pink slip and the keys. "We gave her a good tune-up, but you know how these old babies are."

I'll just drive it until it falls apart and find something else. Just let it get me out of here.

"I'll keep that in mind." Did he even notice the sarcasm in her voice? "I probably won't keep it that long, anyway."

"Well. She's all yours now."

In thirty minutes, she was on IH 10 heading west out of L.A. But to where?

Chapter Three

Texas, the Hill Country

"Damn!" Kate slammed the hood of her car shut and pounded it in frustration. Well, she'd told the disgusting salesman at Highway Harry's she'd drive the car until it dropped. She just hadn't expected it to happen at night in Texas in the middle of nowhere.

Driving steadily since leaving L.A., fueled by gallons of coffee, she'd allowed herself only a few hours rest at a cheap motel. Her nerves were raw, she was riding a caffeine high, and now here she was, stranded and exposed on a highway somewhere in the middle of Texas.

Her head throbbed, every bone and muscle in her body screamed for relief, and the hamburger from the drive-through hours ago still sat like lead in her stomach. More than anything she wanted to curl up in a corner somewhere and hide from everything.

All her life she'd allowed herself to follow what other people had decided for her and look where it had gotten her. She'd mistaken her father's obsessive attitude for one of protection and Peter's attentions for affection and safety. Look where that had gotten her.

She stared at the car.

God, could things possibly get any worse?

She'd kept it together day after day, even during those narrow escapes. She couldn't believe the ease with which she'd created her new identity. All it took was watching enough television and having a little ingenuity. Was it all going to fall apart now because of this stupid car? She'd hoped to get as far as Houston or Dallas. What a pipe dream that was. The last sign on the highway said San Antonio was forty miles away, but it might as well be a thousand.

On top of it all, her body was coming down from the adrenaline high that had kept her going after L.A. and fatigue was weaving its way through her system. She was hanging on by a thread, and this latest disaster was threatening to snap it. She bit her lip so hard she wondered why she didn't draw blood.

Reaching into her car, she pulled out her throwaway cell phone but stopped before she could punch in any numbers. Who did she think she was going to call, anyway? It wasn't as if she had road service, for crying out loud. She didn't even have a clue where the closest town was between here and San Antonio.

Cars whizzed by her on the highway in both directions. Kate didn't know whether to be glad or mad no one stopped. She didn't think she'd left any leads for Peter to pick up, but after Los Angeles she wasn't counting on anything. She swallowed the panic that kept clogging her throat. Here she was, out here in the open, vulnerable to anyone—

A blinding flash of headlights and the crunching of tires on gravel startled her, freezing her in place. Her stomach clenched, and the familiar taste of fear crawled up her throat as a door slammed and a tall figure outlined in the lights moved toward her. God, could they have found her this easily? No, stop and take a breath, dummy. They've had all the miles since L.A. to catch her. Why wait for now?

Then who had stopped? Someone just as bad?

Kate looked frantically around her for a place to hide.

Too late. Here he came, whoever he was, a dark shadow moving toward her with panther-like grace.

"You look as if you could use some help." The disembodied voice was deep, rusty, as if it wasn't used much, and she detected a hint of a drawl.

Then he was in front of her, materializing like smoke out of the blackness of the night. Kate took a deep breath. Her heart was banging against her ribs like a jackhammer and not just from fear. The unexpected visceral punch of his powerful male presence caught her totally off guard.

It was the fatigue. It had to be. She hadn't felt sexual awareness in more months than she could count, but *now*? Now, when she was in the worst jam of her life, her body stood up and shouted hurrah for a stranger? She actually had to squeeze her thighs together to still the tingling in her belly, even as she wondered if this man meant her any harm.

I have truly lost my mind.

"Sorry I scared you." His voice was deep and gravelly, the sound resonating through her. "I spotted you over here on the side of the highway and figured you had car trouble."

"Y-Yes." She cleared her throat. "Yes, I do." As he came closer and the truck's headlights shown on him, she got a better look.

Holy Mother!

When was the last time in the mess her life had

become that a man had affected her this way? He was tall and lean, a black T-shirt and worn black jeans molding his body, outlining every muscle. The jeans brushed the tops of scuffed western boots. Thick dark hair, just a little bit long and so inky it barely reflected the headlights, accentuated a lean face full of sharp planes and angles. She had an almost uncontrollable need to reach up and run her fingers through it.

Dark stubble shadowed his jaw, and deep lines bracketed his mouth and the corners of his eyes. Not the face of someone who smiled often. His black eyes, looking out from beneath thick, dark lashes, were like coal that had been chipped from the earth.

Why wasn't she running from him, scared to death? Why was she trying to imagine what he looked like without those clothes? She had truly lost her mind. What was wrong with her hormones, anyway?

"Let's see what kind of problem we've got here." He looked her over from head to toe with a critical eye, then started toward her car. Two steps, and he was right next to her, all that masculinity overpowering her and crowding her space. The faint scent of sandalwood and man tantalized her nostrils.

"I'm fine," she said, backing up to the side of her car, desperately needing to put space between them. "Nothing I can't handle."

Right. Who am I kidding here?

"I'm pretty good with engines," he said, as if she hadn't even spoken. "Move over and I'll take a look."

When he put his hands on her arms to shift her out of the way she jerked as if he'd touched her with a match. Heat traveled through her, liquefying her muscles.

31

"I'm sorry." He studied her face, frowning. "I just want to pop the hood of your car, and you're standing in the way."

She rubbed her arms nervously. This man was all rough edges. Take it or leave it, his attitude said. She didn't want to take it, and she was afraid she couldn't leave it. She had managed to get herself in a stupid predicament, leaving herself exposed not just to Peter and his hunters but to any predatory male who came along. Was that what this man was? A hunter?

She sucked in a huge breath and somehow pulled herself together. "Oh. Okay."

He took a cautious step forward again. "I'll see if I can find out what's wrong here."

"I-I hate to bother you," she stammered.

What if her car really wasn't broken and he did something to it? What if somehow he was...no! She had to wipe those crazy ideas from her mind. She was seeing demons where there weren't any. Except that was how she'd been staying alive, watching every corner for shadows.

"It's no trouble." His voice was flat, neither friendly nor unfriendly. She could have been a telephone pole he was talking to. "Anyway, I'm already here, so let me eyeball this. Maybe I can spot something and fix it easily."

"All right." She backed up, needing to put space between them. Her skin still sizzled where he'd touched her, and her pulse was still thumping erratically. "Thank you."

His gaze raked over her face, something indefinable flashing briefly in his eyes. Then he blinked, and it was gone. Whatever it was, she was sure she'd imagined it.

He turned back to the car, popped the hood, and looked inside. In just a few minutes, he closed it again, shaking his head. "I don't know where you got this piece of junk, but I hope you didn't pay too much. You can't drive this anywhere tonight."

All her carefully constructed defenses were beginning to fall apart, and the effect of this man on her senses wasn't helping. She tightened her hands into fists, desperate for some shred of control. Now was not the time to lose it. She'd known the car would die sooner or later. She'd just hoped it would be later, and not in the middle of no place without any other options.

"Are you positive it won't move?" She shoved her hands into her pockets, knowing how stupid the question sounded. "Maybe you missed something?"

He looked at her, his eyes now like black ice, so intense she shivered slightly.

"Believe me," he insisted, "I'm sure. I know cars. The carburetor is a mess, and I think the engine block's cracked. Neither of those are good."

"You're kidding." *Crap.*

"Unfortunately, I'm not. Do you by some chance have anyone you can call?" He looked at his watch. "Because at this hour every garage close enough is closed. You're at least an hour from San Antonio, and unless you've got some kind of road service you'd have a hard time getting anyone out here this time of night."

"N-No road service," she told him, feeling more and more like an idiot. But running for your life didn't allow for amenities or anything that would leave tracks for people to follow.

He studied the car. "Those plates are from

California. Did you drive from there in this piece of junk?"

"It's...just temporary. I'm traveling." He had to know she was lying. God, maybe she'd be better if he just went off and left her.

No! That would leave you with no options at all.

The look he gave her seemed to see right into her. "Not in this car you're not." He kicked at a front tire. "I'm surprised you made it this far."

"It's what I have," she said with what little bit of defiance she could muster. "I just need to figure out how to fix it."

Again he stared at her with that penetrating look. "I don't suppose this happens to be the area where you were heading, is it? Maybe you have some friends around here you can call?"

The only 'friends' I have right now are busy trying to kill me. I don't think I'll be calling them.

She wet her suddenly dry lips with the tip of her tongue. "No. There's no one."

He slammed the hood shut. "Whoever you are, this vehicle isn't going to move and you sure as hell can't sit here on the side of the road. Too many predators out there. Come on." He touched her arm, lightly, as if expecting her to jump away. "I'll take you somewhere safe."

"Take me somewhere? Why would I just go off with you?" She yanked her hands from her pockets and wrapped her arms around herself, her body quaking as the full impact of her situation hit her.

"You're trembling." There was a faint note of surprise in his voice. "I'm sorry. I didn't mean to frighten you, but this is a ridiculous situation. You can't stay out here, and I can't go off and leave you like this. The next person who comes along here might not be as harmless as me."

Harmless. Right. Wrapped in a blanket of pure sexual masculinity.

When she still didn't move, he drew in a deep breath and exhaled slowly. "Look. I'm just worried about you, okay?"

"Why? I'm no one to you. Besides, where would you take me?" More crap. Just what she didn't need. "I mean, I don't know you. Why should I trust you? And what am I supposed to do with the car?"

"You can't drive this thing so you'll need to get it towed and—"

"Towed?" The word stuck in her throat. "Who would I call to tow it? You said yourself everyone's closed around here."

A muscle jumped in his cheek. "I can help you with that if you'll let me finish here."

"Okay. I'm sorry." Did her voice sound as shaky to him as it did to her?

"I have a friend who'll do me a favor on the tow, and there's a place you can stay for the night. Like a motel," he explained with exaggerated patience. "Lucky for you there's one just a few minutes away. I'll drive you there. Okay?"

"A motel?" *God, I sound like a moron.*

"Jesus. Yes. A motel. You know. Where people rent rooms and go to sleep? Which, by the way, is something you look like you haven't done for a long time." His eyes scanned her from head to toe. "Can you even afford a room? Maybe we should think of something else."

35

"I can handle it. No problem. I have money."

She forced herself not to touch the fanny pack where she'd stashed all her cash rolled up in tight bundles, along with the all-important flash drive. Hidden beneath her shirt, the pack burned against her skin like live coals.

He waited the space of one heartbeat. Two. "That answer all your questions? Can we go now?"

The calm, reasonable tone in his voice washed over her, taking the edge off her anxiety. She had to trust someone. She couldn't keep running aimlessly around the country with death breathing down her neck. Minutes ago, she'd prayed for someone to help her. Here he was, and in a minute, he'd decide she was too much of a pain in the ass and leave her stranded. It would serve her right.

"This isn't an open-ended offer." Irritation was obviously getting the best of him. "If you want to just hang out here on the highway, be my guest. But it's late and I'm tired, so what are we doing here? You staying or coming with me?"

For the first time, she noticed the fatigue shadowing his eyes and deepening the grooves in his face. He'd stopped at this late hour to see if she, a total stranger, needed help, yet here she was, giving him nothing but grief. He had no way of knowing why she was so terrified and that trusting him would be a real leap of faith for her.

But it wasn't so much whether she could trust him, as whether she could trust herself *with* him.

At that moment, as if to underscore the tenuousness of her situation, fat raindrops began to splatter everywhere—the shoulder of the road, the highway, her rattletrap car, and most of all, the two of them.

"Oh, great," she muttered, shivering as the density of the rain increased. In a moment, she was soaked, rubbing her arms to chase away the chill.

"Okay. If you want to stay out here in the rain, fine by me, but I've got better sense than that." He started to turn away.

No. Don't go.

She almost shouted the words. She sure didn't have a lot of choices. It was either stay here like a stupid fool catching pneumonia in wet clothes or take a chance with a complete stranger. A complete *sexy* stranger.

"O-Okay." The rain was coming down more heavily, and her clothes were plastered to her. "Th-Thank you."

"The first thing to do is get you out of this rain and dried off. Come on." He held out his hand and reluctantly, she took it. They jogged to his truck, a black leviathan as dark and dangerous-looking as he was. He opened the passenger door and practically threw her inside.

Guiltily she realized he was as drenched as she was.

He opened the back door of the dual cab and pulled out a torn towel and an old blanket.

"I always carry odds and ends," he told her. "Dry yourself as much as you can with the towel and wrap the blanket around yourself. Do you have anything you need in your car?"

"A duffel. A tote bag. Oh, and my cell phone."

"A cell phone." He grunted. "At least you have *one* necessity. I'll get them and be right back."

Kate didn't argue with him. She had no desire to

get out in the rain again, and there was nothing in the car that could give away her real identity or she'd never have let him near it. She was scrupulous about not leaving anything lying around that could identify her or scratch at someone's curiosity.

She blotted the rain on her clothes and hair, then wrapped the ragged blanket around her shuddering body. She was huddling into it when the door on the driver's side opened, the man climbed in and tossed her tote and duffel in the back seat. Digging around, he pulled up another towel that he used to wipe himself off as best he could.

"I'll turn on the heat in a minute," he told her, "and see if we can ward off pneumonia."

Suddenly, she was so tired she could hardly keep her eyes open. "Where did you say this motel is you're taking me to?"

"There's a little town where I live just off the next exit. The motel's on the main street. You'll be safe there."

No place is safe for me. But maybe...
Okay, here goes nothing.

Silently praying she'd made the right decision, she wrapped the blanket more tightly around herself...and was immediately hit with another problem. He must have slept on this at some time or wrapped himself in it, because a distinctive, tantalizing male scent clung to it. And in the unexpected intimacy of the cab, this dark and mysterious man was having a sudden effect on her. There was an air of raw sex about him that stole her breath.

Great. She was exhausted, terrified, soaking wet, and hanging onto the end of a frayed rope, and *now* her hormones decided to wake up. She inched as close to the door as her seat belt would allow.

When he started the engine and pulled out onto the highway, she cleared her throat. "Excuse me, but I don't even know your name."

He glanced sideways at her but said nothing.

"This isn't a trick question," she pushed. "You do have a name, don't you?"

After another long silence, he spoke. "Quinn. My name is Quinn."

Chapter Four

Tampa

Peter was in a rage. Too many days had ticked away since the night Kathryn made her unexpected appearance at the office and disappeared with the key to his life. Two very long weeks, and they were no closer to finding her and the tiny memory stick.

He looked up at Miguel Osuna, the ever-present reminder of his situation, and slammed his hand on his desk. "God damn it, I don't know what she was doing here that night. I've told you that again and again. She was supposed to be at home."

That was the unanswered question. Why had Kathryn decided to show up with no warning? Whatever the reason, she'd run smack into a conversation not meant for her ears. Because of that a copy of the entire operation was now missing.

Every day Miguel materialized at his office to ride his ass about Kathryn' disappearance and the loss of the flash drive. The daily process never varied. The questions. The accusations. The threats.

Peter ground his teeth in frustration. Frantic was not a usual part of his personality, but right now he was as close to it as he could get. Running the business operation for the powerful Osuna cartel had its benefits but also put him in a vulnerable position.

"Most unfortunate that she heard us discussing her

future," Miguel pointed out yet again.

"Or lack of it," Peter said, tossing a pencil he'd been fiddling with onto his desk.

Miguel raised an eyebrow. "The fact she also heard us mention the flash drive and made off with it is what makes this whole situation so volatile. A woman whose life is in jeopardy will use any advantage that comes to her. And unfortunately for you, we gave her one as a gift."

"I shouldn't have waited to get rid of her." A muscle jumped in his jaw. "You were right about that."

Miguel's face was like stone. "That's correct. I urged you to get it done and over with."

"You know the reasons for it, though," Peter reminded him. "So many deaths, coming one right after the other…"

"Nevertheless, you have made an unforgivable error, Pedro. And because of that Kathryn Burke has disappeared with something that could destroy us all. If we hadn't heard her and chased her to the garage, we might never known she has it. You'd find it gone, and we'd all be screwed. Unfortunately, she was too quick for us and now she's gone."

"We'll find her."

"You'd better be right about that. You know what's on the line."

Peter dropped into his chair and raked his fingers through his hair. Rage at the situation Kathryn had put him in surged through his system. "I'll kill that fucking bitch when I get my hands on her."

"*If* is the operative word," Miguel snapped. "Not *when.* I wouldn't count on anything at this point. It seems Miss Burke isn't quite as manageable as you thought. And how did you not know she still had a set of her father's keys?"

"It never came up. I thought the set I took from her was the only one." Peter grimaced as he forced out the words. He hated admitting failure of any kind.

"Your lapses in judgment will cost us dearly. You have much to answer for." Miguel's voice had the sharp sound of the executioner's axe. "You've put us all at risk. Our entire operation. This is the result of stupid carelessness."

The air in the office was thick with tension. For the first time in his adult life, Peter Fleming knew what fear was.

He scrubbed his hands across his face. "At least the files on the flash drive are encrypted."

"And a damn good thing. Consider yourself lucky that she didn't take any of the hard copy files with her, which aren't so protected," Miguel pointed out.

"I'll find her. Count on it."

"*We'll* find her." Miguel pulled a cell phone from his pocket.

Peter stuck his jaw out belligerently. "What does that mean? Your men missed her twice already. What more do you think you can do that I can't?"

"I'm calling in my contacts everywhere. Everyone who owes me a favor. It's time to pay up. I want every corner of this country searched." He punched in a number, and in a moment began speaking in rapid Spanish.

"She can't have gone far," Peter told him when he hung up. "She hasn't the experience or the guts to figure out how to hide herself away. Luck. That's what she's had. She'll run out of it sooner or later." He tried furiously to think of what to do next.

Miguel stabbed a finger at him. "I hold you completely responsible for this. There will be consequences, once I report everything."

Then, thankfully, before Peter could frame a reply, he was gone with his bodyguards closing ranks behind him. Peter slumped back in his chair, rubbing his temples. Hell and damnation. He'd planned so carefully for everything. How had it fallen apart like this?

****

Somewhere in Texas

"Quinn what? Is that a first name or last?" Kate tried to keep her gaze away from his thighs and the muscles flexing under the soft denim.

"Just...Quinn. That's good enough." When she didn't comment, he said, "Well?"

"Well, what?"

"When someone tells you their name, it's customary to give them yours." A tiny rough edge of humor colored his words.

"Oh." She twisted her fingers together. "I'm Kate. Kate Griffin."

"Well, Kate Griffin, you'll be a lot better off at this motel than out on the highway. As soon as you get inside take a long hot, shower. Do you have anything warm to wrap up in?"

"Um, I think so." Actually, she was shivering so badly she could hardly think at all.

"You have to get warm, or you'll get sick. While you register, I'll call my friend Mike to tow your car to his garage. Tomorrow, we'll see what needs to be done."

"Exactly where am I, anyway?" she asked. They'd

43

exited the highway and were driving into a small town.

"Welcome to Windswept," Quinn said, sardonic humor edging his words. "People say one day the wind swept through and when it left, there was the town."

Kate stared out the window, but it was dark and she was too fatigued, waterlogged, and cold to make much sense of anything. In a few minutes, Quinn wheeled the truck up under the archway of a two-story limestone building. A sign hanging from it had the legend "Windswept Inn" sandblasted into it.

"Must be a busy place," she commented. The parking area was filled with cars, pickups, and motorcycles.

"The Inn's been around a long time," he told her as he jumped down from the truck. "They have a lot of repeat customers."

He jogged to the passenger side and opened her door. She clung to the blanket as he helped her down. When his hand touched hers, the strangest feeling stole through her.

Safe.

She mentally shook herself because, really, no place was safe, but when he dropped her hand the feeling didn't disappear. Her mind was turning somersaults. What was happening here?

"I need my tote bag," she told him.

He handed it to her, and she followed him toward the entrance, feeling like a leftover from a cat fight. Her clothes were still damp, but warmed by the heater in the truck, they stuck to her like a second skin. Her hair, cut more for serviceability than style, straggled around her face. She used the fold of the blanket to cover the fanny pack, which the shirt in its bedraggled condition could no longer disguise.

"I have to know about my car," she reminded him.

She was already feeling helpless and vulnerable, the panic working its way through her again. She couldn't just hang around to see what happened. Give Peter time to root her out.

"I said I'll take care of everything," he told her, "and I will. While you get registered, I'll get that pile of junk towed. Then you need a hot shower and a good night's sleep. Which it doesn't look as if you've had for a while, by the way."

Sleep. He was so right about that. For days she hadn't closed her eyes except for brief periods. Even when she napped on the bus, she was never fully at rest, and it was catching up with her. The fatigue that had grabbed her on the highway washed over her again. A full night's rest beckoned so invitingly.

Wait! Was she crazy, trusting this complete stranger? She'd just spent days running away from the last man she trusted, a man she knew a lot better than this one, and look how that had worked out.

She nibbled her lower lip. "I'm not sure…"

Not sure she should put herself in the hands of a stranger? He couldn't be any worse than someone she knew.

"Jesus." He rubbed his hand over his face, as if wiping away his own weariness. "Are you for real? Can we please not argue about this anymore?"

"You're right. I'm sorry. Let me go take care of business." The last thing she needed right now was for him to get mad at her. She was disintegrating bit by bit. The necessity of staying alive and keeping ahead of the hunters had been the glue that held her together, had formed who she was now, Kate Griffin, and Kate Griffin didn't come undone. Couldn't afford to.

The minute they entered the lobby, Kate was slammed by a blast of frigid, artificially-cooled air, and she began shivering harder.

Quinn cast a studied eye at her and pulled the blanket tighter around her. "Come on. I'll talk to Anna for you."

The motel lobby was small but neat and clean. Leather furniture was scattered over terra cotta tiles, and two tall cactus plants guarded the entrance. The woman behind the counter smiled as they approached.

"Brought you a stray, Anna. Got a single she can have?"

"I think I might just have one tucked away," she grinned. "It's Key to the Hills Race Week, and everyone's jammed, but I always hold one or two rooms back."

"Great. We'll take one."

Kate, who had been standing next to Quinn shivering in her damp clothes, turned as the door to the lobby swished open, and nearly fainted. Oh, Holy Mother, they can't have found me again. So soon. In this godforsaken place.

Two unsmiling men, dressed in jeans and T-shirts rather than suits, were advancing on the desk, eyes focused on her. It didn't have to be them. It could be just two strangers here to see the race, but she couldn't take any chance.

"I have to get out of here," she whispered to Quinn. "Right this minute."

He looked at her and raised an eyebrow. "Get out of here? Why?"

"I just do. Please. Don't ask any questions." She tugged on his arm and headed to the hallway off the lobby. "And don't leave me, okay?"

"Kate, what's going on?" He hustled along with her.

She literally ran for the truck, threw herself inside, and locked the door.

"Lock your door, too," she told Quinn as soon as he climbed inside. "Can we get out of here? Right now?"

She was shaking so badly she could hardly get the words out. He turned on the ignition and flipped on the heater again, then sat behind the wheel staring through the windshield at the rain dripping off the motel. There was tension in every line of his body.

He's probably wondering why the hell he ever stopped in the first place, trying to figure out how and where to dump me.

"Can we just go? Please?" *Before those men come back out here.*

Quinn looked at her once, then cranked the engine and backed out of the parking lot.

"You want to tell me what this is all about?" he asked when they were back on the highway.

"I...I thought I recognized those two men. I-I'm trying to get away from a bad situation and I thought...someone...had sent them." She hugged her arms around her body, the chill still knifing through her.

Bad situation. Boy, that's the truth.

Quinn sighed. "Okay. The next town's only thirty miles away. It's bigger so they'll probably have a room."

Thirty miles away. With no car. Her own about to be towed to some stranger's garage. And who was to say they couldn't follow her there.

"Are you married?" she asked.

The look of pain that flashed briefly across his face stunned her, but he shook his head. "No. I live alone."

"Then will you take me home with you?" The words were out of her mouth before she could stop them. How insane was that, asking to go home with a man she'd known for five seconds. And she didn't even know where he lived.

But there was something so solid about him, so strong. Not a man to be cowed by Peter's thugs. She didn't know how she knew that, but she did. She held her breath as she waited for his answer.

"You want to tell me exactly what kind of trouble I'd be bringing into my home?"

"It's a long story." She sighed. "Very long. But if you can just give me a place for tonight and help me with my car tomorrow, I'll be out of your hair and you'll forget I was even here."

The next five minutes stretched out like hours for Kate as Quinn drove in silence, not answering, but glancing at her now and then.

"All right, look." She cleared her throat. "That was presumptuous of me. Asking you to take me home with you. I realize that. If there's a bus station anywhere around here, you can just drop me off there. They have great benches to sleep on."

He swiveled his head to look at her, the outside lights of the motel reflected in the inky blackness of his eyes. "Been doing a lot of that lately, have you?"

"No. Yes. I mean…" If possible she gripped the

blanket tighter, holding it around her like a shield. "When I was a kid…"

One eyebrow lifted. "Your parents let you sleep in bus stations when you were a kid?"

"No." She bit her lip in frustration. "I've…just had experiences with them."

"I'll bet. And speaking of parents, maybe this would be a good time to call them. Let them know you're stranded."

I'm not stranded. I'm running for my life.

"M-My parents are dead." The hot, prickly feel of tears pressed against her eyelids, and she blinked them rapidly.

More silence. Then he turned onto a two lane highway, still not answering her.

"W-Where are we going?"

"My house. You wanted me to take you there, so all right, I'm doing it. But as soon as you get your shit together, you're going to tell me what the hell this is all about."

Kate nearly sobbed with relief. She wanted to throw her arms around him and kiss him, but she didn't think he'd like that too much.

"I have empty bedrooms that no one sleeps in. You can even lock the door if you want to, since you seem so jittery."

Heat rose in her cheeks. "I didn't mean to imply—"

"No, that's okay."

He unclipped his cell phone from his belt, pressed a number on speed dial, and began speaking in low tones. Kate didn't even try to hear what he was saying. She knew better than to relax or trust a total stranger.

That could lead to death. Hers. So what was she doing in this truck, letting a man she'd just met take her to his house—wherever that happened to be. Of course, how much worse could it be than putting herself back out there in worse shape than before for Peter to find? Quinn No-Other-Name didn't seem like a killer to her, but one never knew.

She huddled into a corner of the seat. Right now, she just wanted to be warm and dry and fall asleep.

****

Well, shit.

Quinn gritted his teeth so hard he was afraid he'd grind off the enamel. How the hell had he let himself get into this mess? Of all the stupid things in the world to do.

Stopping like he had was a stupid thing to do. He'd been almost home after a long, draining evening, and was ready for a hot shower, a cold beer, and a soft bed. But there she was, stranded on IH 10, looking like a refugee from some Third World country.

Baggy jeans and a shirt ten sizes too big, looking as if she'd slept in them for a year. No makeup, no jewelry. Her small frame too slender, the kind that came from not eating properly. A wild mop of curls framing a thin, pale face dominated by sad and frightened eyes. Terrified and trying not to show it.

The car was such a disaster he couldn't believe she'd gotten five miles in it, much less all the way from wherever in California she'd picked it up. One look at her, and he felt as if someone had baited a hook and reeled him in.

He'd let himself be talked into taking her home with him? He had to be out of his mind.

She was trouble. He could smell it a mile away. And not of the usual kind, either. He'd seen all the signs of trouble like hers before, and he didn't need to get involved in it. If she wasn't running from the cops—and his gut told him she wasn't—then the people after her were of the worst kind. What the hell could someone like her get herself into, anyway? She looked like the worst thing she'd ever done was return a library book late.

But somewhere, somehow, she'd gotten crosswise of someone who was on her tail, people Quinn was sure weren't the kind you invited home for dinner. Whatever they were, it was easy to see she was about to lose it altogether. So terrified of something, her fear was like a living thing wrapped around her. And apparently no one to help her and no resources but her own wits.

Yup, Miss Kate Griffin was carrying a hundred pounds of trouble around with her, and he had a feeling he'd just picked up part of the load.

Dumb, Quinn. Dumbass dumb.

Only what else was he supposed to do with her? He couldn't just dump her. Whoever those two men were, they'd obviously scared the shit out of her. And what was *that* all about?

He slid a glance at her. The rain hadn't helped the situation. She sat pushed into a corner of the cab, bedraggled and shivering, wrapped in his ratty old blanket, looking for all the world like someone had thrown her away.

Double shit!

Worse than that, though, was this unexpected chemistry that exploded out of nowhere the minute he touched her. Back there on the highway, they'd nearly gone up in flames. He could see it shocked her as much as it had him. It was more than he wanted to handle. Safety in solitude. That had been his mantra ever since that awful bloody day. Now here he was, dragging trouble into his house. Into his carefully guarded life.

Four years had passed since Lisa and Nikki died, years in which he'd withdrawn more and more into himself. Memories of his dead wife and child twisted painfully inside him, images that he worked hard to keep at bay. He'd never forgiven himself for what happened to them. His work had put them in harm's way, and he'd failed to protect them. The pain of losing them still wrenched his heart.

He'd managed to keep everyone at bay since then, jumped into a hole and pulled the dirt in after himself, yet one look at this ragamuffin and he wanted to do everything to her. Touch her everywhere. Plunge himself into her every place he could. Keep her safe, even though he didn't know yet from what.

Was this a sign from the gods? His chance for salvation? For redemption? If he could save Kate Griffin from whatever was chasing her, maybe he could finally go to sleep at night without the image of those blood-covered bodies burned into his eyes.

The rain had stopped as suddenly as it started. Maybe it would wash out the confusion in his brain as it had washed the streets and roadways. He sure hoped so.

Chapter Five

She must have dozed, fatigue wearing her down, because she was suddenly aware of the truck slowing down. Looking out the window, she saw only the black night, the moon casting enough light to show her they were climbing a long driveway, at the end of which was a very large house.

The smooth glide of a garage door sliding up sounded over the truck's engine, and in a moment they were inside, the darkness lit by the overhead light. By the time Kate managed to get her seat belt unfastened and unwrap herself from the blanket, Quinn had her door open and was helping her out. She felt a hundred years old, her limbs stiff and aching, the cold still penetrating to her bones. Her head ached, her eyes burned, and her stomach felt like a foreign object in her body.

Carrying her duffel and her tote, Quinn led her through a utility room into a short hallway and flicked a light switch in a darkened room. Immediately, a bedside lamp came on, casting its soft glow over the big queen-sized bed and the night stand and reflecting the patina of the polished wood.

He set her things on a bench at the foot of the bed and pried the blanket loose from her fingers.

"Shower's right next door," he told her in a gentle voice. "Is everything you need in that duffel bag?"

She nodded, speech suddenly deserting her.

"Okay. Come on, then."

The bathroom was done in rich tones of terra cotta and had a separate tub and shower. Quinn put her bag on the vanity, reached in a closet next to it, and pulled out fluffy burnt orange towels. Reaching into the shower, he turned on the water and stood there testing it until he had the right temperature.

"I'm going to take a quick shower myself," he told her. "Turn right out of here to the kitchen when you're finished. I'm going to fix us something hot to drink.

Again, she nodded. Quinn gave her a searching look, then closed the door and left her to the steam-filled room.

The hot water felt incredibly good. It reminded her that she'd had little chance for proper hygiene on her odyssey to nowhere. There was soap in the shower soap dish, and she scrounged the tiny bottle of shampoo she'd bought at a convenience store, hoping to have a chance to use it.

She had no idea how long she stood under the shower, lathering and rinsing, letting the hot spray beat down on her, blanking her mind to everything but the here and now. Eventually, the chill faded from her bones and her skin took on a rosy glow, but even the hottest water couldn't do anything about the cold pit of fear still lodged in her stomach.

For the first time in days she realized just how hopeless her situation was. Peter was still out there somewhere, relentless in his pursuit. She'd been lucky so far, sharpening her wits with each near miss, but sooner or later her luck would run out. She couldn't keep running forever, but when she stopped, then what? And where would that be? She wanted to curl up in a ball, hide, and release the tears she'd been holding back.

The conversation that night still replayed over and over in her head, like a stuck CD.

"Relax, Miguel. It's almost over. I'll get rid of Kathryn this weekend, and then we'll be home free."

And then…

"I'm taking her away this weekend for a change of scenery. As far as anyone knows it will be to help her get over her depression. It's common knowledge she's been living on those pills. When she takes a few too many, who will think twice about it?"

His words, said so callously, still rain through her brain like individual cuts of a knife. A shiver of fear skittered over her spine. There were killers after her and *that's* what she needed to keep focused on.

A knock at the door startled her from her unpleasant reverie.

"You about done in there?" Quinn's rusty voice called. "I've got hot drinks out here."

"Give me a minute," she answered.

She towel dried her hair as best she could and ran a comb through it, thinking one of these days she'd treat herself to a professional cut. Then she pulled out the long night shirt that she'd bought in caseshe ever had a chance to sleep in a real place. It wasn't until she looked at herself in the mirror that she realized just how revealing soft cotton could be.

Shrugging mentally—her choices were limited; this or nothing—she hung up the damp towel, stuffed everything including her fanny pack into her duffel, and opened the door. From the room he'd given her, she followed the short hall, which opened into a wide room that appeared to be the center of the house—living room, dining room, and kitchen all in one, with huge windows and a high ceiling. The wood floor felt smooth under her feet.

Folding her arms across her chest to conceal the outline of her breasts as best she could, she climbed up on the bar stool Quinn indicated at the long counter. He slid a mug toward her.

"Hot tea with lots of sugar and bourbon. My mother always swore it could cure anything. You need it after tonight's soaking."

She wrapped her fingers around the steaming mug, letting the warmth seep into her. "Do your parents live near here?"

His face closed up like a trap door. "My parents are dead."

Kate's heart felt as if someone had pinched it. She knew the feeling. "Mine are, too."

"Illness?" he asked after a moment.

She shook her head. "Accident."

"Mine, too." But there was something in the tone that said it might be a little more complex than that.

Kate sipped at the tea. The sugar and the whiskey jolted her system, wiping away the last effects of the rain and warming everything but that cold place that wouldn't thaw.

They sat in a silence, drinking from their mugs.

"Thank you very much," Kate said after a while. "For, you know, stopping to help me and bringing me here. I guess I don't know what I would have done otherwise."

"Tomorrow, we'll see what's what with your car and you can figure out what to do from there." His voice was flat and uninflected. "Are you in a hurry to get on the road again?"

"I-I think so."

"You *think* so. Okay. Whatever. But you'll need something a lot more dependable than what you had."

"I know."

More silence.

"Sleep as late was you want," he told her. "You look like you could use it."

She ran her fingers through her still damp hair. "I guess I've been pushing it a little."

Quinn collected their mugs, rinsed them, and put them in the dishwasher. He stood there, apparently waiting for her to head for her room, so she slid off the stool.

"Well, goodnight, then. Thank you again."

"Holler if you need anything."

As she rounded the corner of the counter, she stubbed her toe on the limestone facing and pitched forward. Quinn caught her before she could fall.

Her toe hurt, although not a lot, but it was the catalyst that broke the damn. The tears came flooding from nowhere, held back for so long they were fighting each other for release. Her tears soaked his clean T-shirt, and her entire body shook with the force of her sobs.

Quinn said nothing, just wrapped his arms around her and let her lean against his chest. His arms tightened around her, but nothing could quiet the strength of the storm raging throughout her body. All the gates were down, all the rigid discipline gone, the true reality of her situation smacking her in the face.

Even as the newer, stronger Kate Griffin, it struck

her that she hadn't thought beyond staying on the move, keeping ahead of the men tracking her. She had no destination, no plan other than what she'd been doing. And she couldn't do it forever. Sooner or later, they'd find her and it would all come crashing down.

The fact that she'd fallen apart in front of a complete stranger didn't even seem to enter into the equation. She just let the emotional hurricane rage over her until it was finally spent. Her throat was raw and her eyes felt like burning coals, but still the tears came.

She was barely aware of Quinn picking her up and carrying her into another room, laying her down in acres of bed and pulling her against him. His hand stroked her hair, and he murmured soothing, crooning sounds to her while her breathing steadied and the last of the tiny shivers died away.

Kate lay curled into Quinn's hard, muscular body, sheltered in the circle of his arms. She was too exhausted to even care that he must think her a nut case and be cursing his Good Samaritan tendencies. She only knew that this was the first time she'd felt really safe since she'd fled Peter's office.

She had no idea how long she lay there like that, Quinn's hand stroking her as one would ease a child, still murmuring to her. Eventually, her breathing evened out and she fell asleep.

****

Quinn hadn't known what else to do with her. The racking sobs that had ripped through Kate's body stabbed at him like tiny knives. There hadn't seemed to be any solace he could offer her, anything to ease whatever was driving her with such destructive force. At last, with gasps and shudders, the storm abated.

He lay on his bed with the slender body tucked against him, staring into the darkness. He knew nothing about this woman except that whatever was wrong had her completely terrified. From what little he'd seen of her behavior tonight, he was sure she wasn't a person given to hysterics. She'd apparently been holding herself together with spit and baling wire, and tonight her discipline had come to the end of the line, her collapse triggered by a reminder of what she was running from.

The two men? Quinn had watched carefully to see if they followed the truck, but miles down the road, there'd still been no sign of them. Or anyone else they might have contacted. No, they were probably just what they seemed—tourists here for the race. But to Kate, they represented something more terrifying. Now that she'd edged her way into his life, he felt a need to help her, but not until he knew what was going on.

He had the skills and the contacts to help her, but he had his own fears to wrestle with. Fear of letting someone into his life again. Fear of *feeling* again. Fear of pulling his emotions out of cold storage and having them ripped apart again.

Yet how could he turn her away, knowing he was throwing her back into the path of danger?

Finally, his head aching from the thoughts banging around in it, he shifted his body long enough to skin his jeans and T-shirt off. But when he lay back down, pulling the covers over them and spooning her against him, he realized stripping down to his boxers was a mistake. She felt too good next to him, her small body fitting his perfectly. She wore nothing under the soft fabric of the sleep shirt, a recipe for disaster. Her nicely rounded ass pressed against his groin, making him harden reflexively.

He banded his arm around her middle to keep her close and felt the softness of her breasts resting on him. She smelled clean and fresh and tempting.

How had he gotten to this point, anyway? All night, from the moment he saw her on the side of the road, he'd had an eerie feeling someone or some*thing* was pulling his strings. Maybe his hermit life was getting to him mentally. He didn't know. The only thing he *did* know was his common sense had just taken a nose dive. There was no way he was letting her leave. Tomorrow, he would find a way to get it all out of her. Make him tell her what was wrong. Then he'd put a plan together to help her.

"Are you satisfied?" he whispered to whatever unseen presence was screwing up his life.

Gritting his teeth to make his body behave, he finally fell asleep.

****

Kate woke slowly, still sluggish from sleep. When she tried to move, the first thing she discovered was a man's arm thrown around her waist, tanned skin covered with fine dark hair. One muscular leg was lying across both of hers. Behind her, male warmth cocooned her body. The delicious scent of soap and the outdoors teased at her nostrils and sent shivers through her body. She was in bed with a man?

She opened her eyes wider, looking around at an unfamiliar room. Sunlight poured in through a wall of French doors, casting shadows on cream-colored walls. The high ceiling gave the room an additional feeling of spaciousness. Across from the bed was a wall of bookshelves with a built-in entertainment center. This was a room for a man who liked his comforts.

Where was she and who's room was she in? Whose bed? Wearing only her night shirt, for god's sake. And totally naked beneath it. But when she tried to shift her body, the arm around her tightened.

"Mornin'," a warm male voice said behind her, soft breath tickling her hair.

And it all came flooding back. The car. The rain. The motel. The two men. Quinn. And that godawful breakdown.

She should move. Get up. Be embarrassed that she'd fallen apart so completely, that she'd taken comfort in a stranger's arms. Spent the night wrapped up with him in what was apparently his bed. But it felt so good where she was, wrapped up in his strength. So right. So *safe!*

"So…how goes it this morning?" he asked. "Feel better?"

Images and sensations of her gigantic meltdown flooded her again, and the heat of embarrassment bloomed on her cheeks. She was glad her back was to him as every detail replayed itself in stark clarity.

She cleared her throat self-consciously. "How did I get here? I mean, I know how I got to your house, but how did I end up in bed with you?"

"You pretty much came apart last night. It was the only thing that calmed you down and made you relax. Fall asleep."

Her cheeks turned even hotter. If only she could block her entire performance out of her mind. "I guess I pretty much made a fool of myself."

"No." He kissed her temple, a wisp of a contact

that sent unexpected shivers through her. "My guess is you're just exhausted running from whatever is chasing you—and please don't try to tell me nothing. I'd say it's pretty bad, enough to string out your nerves to the raw edge." She hadn't moved, and his head was right next to hers, the nearness of it warming her. "I'd say you probably needed the emotional release. I was just trying to keep you from totally self-destructing."

The smart thing would be to jump out of the bed as fast as she could, but it was impossible to think with his body molded so closely to hers. The feel of him was so good, his lips brushing against her neck teasing her, and there was certainly no mistaking his hot, hard, and obvious erection. Or the unexpected spikes of pleasure it drove through her.

Okay, any minute now, he would slide away from her, they'd get past the initial awkwardness, and she could try to figure out what to do next. Right?

Wrong.

Then another thought stabbed at her. Had they already… "Listen, Quinn. Did we… I mean, last night… That is…"

Why couldn't she just get the stupid words out? Because she didn't want to know the answer?

"If you're asking if we had sex, the answer is no. You were hurting and vulnerable. You needed some…human contact. But not sex. Just…holding. You were pretty much a mess." He gave a rough chuckle. "Besides, I'd like to think I have a little more class than that."

"Ohmigod." She wanted to hide under the covers. "I am so mortified. I can't…I don't…"

"Shh." His voice with its soft Texas drawl was so

soothing. "It's all right, Kate. Whatever it is, I promise I can help make it all right."

She buried her face in the pillow, trying to shut out the mess that was her life. "You can't imagine how *not* all right everything is. Or ever will be again."

"Maybe if you tell me about it, we can figure out a way to fix it."

If only.

The warmth of his body was seeping into hers, chasing away the cold that lay inside her like a block of ice. The same sense of cold living inside her since the night she fled Peter's office. What would it be like to just say the hell with everything and let this man take away her pain?

She shifted slightly. The arm holding her tightened even more, and she couldn't mistake his body's response. Well.

"Quinn?" She had to ask. Had to make sure she was misinterpreting this. "What are we doing here?"

He sighed, his chest rising and falling against her back. "Damned if I know."

"I was hoping maybe one of us did," she told him, her breathing unsteady.

Get up, Kate. Move away. Don't do anything stupid.

"Kate?" Fingers stroked her rib cage.

"Yes?"

"I haven't wanted a woman in four years, and we haven't known each other long enough to even have a meal together. I don't know if it's the circumstances or what, but if you don't want to get us both in trouble, you'd better get up. Quick."

Wetting her suddenly dry lips with her tongue, she

tried to find what was left of her brain. This was *so* not like her. At least not like Kathryn Burke. She hadn't been Kate Griffin long enough to make judgments.

She drew in a shuddering breath. "And if I don't want to move?"

"Then I think we both know what's coming. Crazy as it seems."

"Do we?"

"Please don't panic and leap out of bed when I tell you something, because this is completely out of character for me. But Kate? You don't know how much I want to make you feel better. A lot better. I want to chase away those shadows I see in your eyes if you'll let me. But more than that, I promise you, if I don't move right now, my brain is going on vacation."

And would that be so wrong? So maybe she didn't do this kind of thing. Maybe she knew diddly squat about this man. But she did know he'd helped her when he didn't have to and he hadn't turned her over to Peter.

In answer, she pressed back against his body. One big hand moved tentatively to cup her breast, and his mouth pressed against her ear. Oh god, it felt so good. When she didn't move away his hand tightened. A feathery kiss sent tremors skittering through her, straight to the spot between her thighs that seemed to get wetter by the minute. And for once, she wasn't thinking of Peter or anyone connected with him.

Quinn brushed her hair behind her ear in a gesture so tender it made her throat close. She couldn't remember the last time someone had touched her in such a way.

His thumb barely brushed her nipple. Even with such a faint touch, it plumped and beaded, threads of heat streaking to that hot spot between her thighs where her pussy suddenly throbbed.

Mistake! Mistake!

But in the next moment, her pulses went haywire and moisture seeped embarrassingly onto her thighs.

"I want you," he said, affirming his actions.

"I want you, too." Her words were barely a whisper.

This was so not her style. She had always been reserved sexually, but maybe that was because she'd never been with a man who lit up all her nerve endings like Quinn did.

I need this. So badly. Whatever happens next, happens. If I'm dead, none of this will matter anyway.

He kissed the tip of her ear, his hand kneading her breast with a gentle motion, and he buried his face in her hair. "Kate, listen to me a minute. There's something I have to tell you first."

Oh, God. Now what? Did he have something wrong with him? "Is...Is there a physical problem I should be aware of?"

"No. But I haven't...been with a woman in a long time. A very long time. You're the first one I've even had any desire for. It's a long story, one I'd rather we not get into right now. I'm only telling you because I'm afraid my technique is a little rusty."

She closed her eyes, tiny pinpricks of sensation spreading outward from where he was again working her nipples. "I'm not sure I'd know the difference," she told him in a tremulous voice, her painfully unexciting history flashing through her brain.

"Then we should make a good pair." His voice dropped, low and heated.

His essence, so clean and masculine, surrounded her like a tranquilizing aroma. His strength wrapped around her, bringing every nerve in her body to life. There was something so impossibly erotic about Quinn, the dark knight, that made her throw away all her inhibitions and safeguards, made her body respond with so little prompting.

Pushing away any lingering reservations, she wriggled back against him. His shaft hardened even more, pressing firmly against her buttocks.

Just get on with it before I explode.

Quinn rolled her over to face him. He looked even better this morning, sleep rumpled with a day's growth of beard, than he had the night before. No man should be allowed to look this sexy, she thought, just before he softly trailed his lips down to her mouth.

He stroked her hair, his eyes devouring her face, before he bent his head and touched his lips to hers. Feathery kisses that were both tentative and firm, searching, as if, like he'd said, he'd been out of practice for a long time and was relearning what to do and how to do it.

When he pressed his rough silk lips more firmly to hers, the kiss that began as a gentle connection soon turned heated and drugging. They were like desert refugees who could never satisfy their thirst. His mouth was hard and demanding as he pressed his tongue against the seam of her lips. She opened for him, inviting the intrusion, savoring the taste of him. He probed her mouth with a tongue that parried and thrust like a rapier, exploring, feeding. Heat swelled to every part of her body.

Time slowed as he traced the line of her cheeks and

eyelids with fingers that trembled slightly. Moving his mouth from hers he nibbled at her ear, licked the very sensitive spot behind her ear, and nipped at her ear lobe. Her breathing hitched, and her beaded nipples ached for his mouth.

She was liquid against him, resistance gone like a wisp of smoke. He cupped her ass, pulling her tight against him, pressing his cock against her with sudden desperation. It was so obvious he was hungry for the feel of her, wanting nothing more than to be inside her. And wherever he touched her, flames ignited, spreading directly her clit.

"I want to see you naked," he whispered, pushing the nightshirt over her head.

She was self-conscious at first, spread out for him like a meal before a starving man, his eyes devouring her naked body. But the heat and appreciation she saw in them wiped any misgivings away. And made her flame even hotter. Her pussy throbbed with need, the scent of her musk so strong it drifted on the air.

Fuck me, she wanted to shout, wondering where that word had even come from.

Then he whispered, as if he'd heard her words "I'm going to fuck you, Kate, hard and deep."

His hands drifted over her body, cupping her breasts, cradling them in his palms. He pinched each nipple in turn between thumb and forefinger, squeezing and tugging. Tiny shards of pleasurable pain streaking directly to her pussy where more of her cream slicked the tissues of her inner walls. He bent his head and took one darkened nipple into his mouth, sucking on it, grazing it gently with his teeth.

"Ohh!"

The exclamation whispered from her mouth as she arched up to him, threading her fingers through the soft strands of his hair to anchor his head in place. With every pull of his mouth, every little bite of his teeth, the pulse in her inner walls beat harder and more demandingly. The scruff on his face abraded her skin like some sensuous brush, making every nerve ending tingle and stoking the hunger flashing within her. Heat sizzled, snapping everywhere in her body, melting what was left of her brain as well as any reservations she might have had.

"You're so soft," he murmured, his voice thick with desire. "Your skin feels like satin."

His touch was like magic, drawing responses from her in places she'd never thought of as erogenous zones. She was floating on a cloud, her body both pliable and demanding, driven by his erotic touches. He laved and sucked until she was sure she would lose her mind. When he stopped, she moaned a protest, but then he shifted so he could take her mouth in a kiss of ravenous hunger.

When her lips were swollen from the kiss, when his tongue had scoured every inch inside her mouth, he cupped her head with his hands and trailed hot kisses from her chin down her neck and between her breasts. He stopped to swirl the tip of his tongue in the indentation of her navel before using it to draw a line to her mound.

She never thought to resist him when he bent her legs and spread them wide to give him unimpeded access. His thumbs, on the outer lips of her pussy, opened her, his breath making her flesh quiver with need. She closed her eyes and gave herself up to an intimacy that for whatever reason did not seem out of place with this man.

"So wet. Jesus, Kate. I have to taste you."

Again, he put his very clever tongue to work, lightly tracing her inner lips, then drawing a line the length of her slit. Up and down, up and down until she wanted to scream for more. He tormented her clit with his teeth and his tongue, now lightly, now harder. And when at last he slid one finger into her tight channel, it slipped in so easily she had to be soaked.

"Drenched," Quinn said as if he'd heard her thought. "Nice and slick. I love it." He placed a hot kiss right on the tip of her clit. "Jesus, Kate. It's been so long. Please tell me if I do anything wrong."

"So far you're doing it all right," she told him in a strangled voice.

He added a second finger and began working them in and out, the tips circling to scrape along her inner walls, hitting her sweet spot. Each time he touched her *there,* it set off a fresh wave of tremors inside her vaginal walls. Each time he withdrew and pushed in again, each time he pulled hard on her clit with his mouth, another wave of tremors overtook her until, without any warning at all, a climax roared through her like an onrushing wave.

She arched up to his mouth, pushing against the bed with the soles of her feet, shuddering at the wave of spasms rocking her. Her heart stuttered and her breath cut choppily into the air as the intensity of the orgasm eased. Kate lay there, trying to regain some sort of balance, but Quinn didn't seem about to let up.

She wondered hysterically if indeed he'd been without for so long he was trying to make up for it all in one night. He lapped slowly at her sex, slow languid swipes of his tongue against her very sensitive flesh. With his thumbs, he held her open while he took his time devouring her. The low moaning sound she heard was hers, shocking her that it came from her mouth.

Kate didn't know how long it had been since Quinn had sex, but for her, it was far longer than she wanted to admit, even to herself. Apparently her starving body was gripped by a voracious hunger. How else could she explain that she'd lost all her inhibitions with a man she'd just met?

The caresses with his tongue made her already sensitized nerves snap and crackle with need. Her inner walls pulsed and quivered, and she was almost embarrassed at how wet she was. Then she forgot all about being self-conscious as yet another orgasm rolled through her that quickly, just mere seconds after Quinn resumed his erotic caresses. The spasms were milder this time but no less gripping. She lay back on the pillow, panting, trying to pull the grayed edges of her brain together.

Quinn slid upward on her body, placing a kiss in the valley between her breasts. She felt the muscles of his cheeks pull as a smile curved his lips.

"I guess I'm not as out of practice as I thought," he joked. "And we're not even half done."

Your turn, she wanted to say. But she couldn't make her mouth form words. Instead, she tugged him upward and pushed at him until he lay flat on his back.

"I can't do what I want in this position," he protested.

"But I can," she told him, feeling more wicked than she ever had before and wondering where this nymph had come from.

She smoothed her hand over his chest, brushing against the thick, springy curls sprinkled over the hard wall of muscle. When her fingertips coasted over his hard male nipples, it drew a hiss of breath from him. Tracing the line of soft hair down his hard, flat abdomen, she slipped her finger beneath the waistband of his boxers until she reached the rich nest of curls at his groin and the thick, hard shaft rising from it.

Just touching him this way spiked her pleasure. She'd never wanted to feel every bit of a man the way she did with him. Whatever chemistry had ignited between them was beyond incendiary, threatening to combust and consume them completely.

He lay there, letting her explore him with her fingers, but she could tell the effort at control he was making. A muscle ticked in his jaw and his hands were clenched at his side.

"I'd love to tell you to take your time," he told her in a strangled voice, "but I think I'm getting close to the danger zone."

"You got to have your fun," she pointed out, amazed again at how bold and free she felt with him.

"And you'll get yours," he promised. "But darlin', you better have it real quick."

Wrapping her fingers around the thick stalk of his shaft, she slid them up and down, stroking the silky soft skin covering the steel length of him. Beneath her touch, the pulse of blood raced through the thick vein that roped around it. Impulsively, she lowered her head and swiped her tongue across the velvet head, lapping up the tiny bead of fluid that sat on the slit. This wasn't something she'd ever enjoyed doing before, but with

Quinn, the stranger who seemed more familiar than people she'd known longer, it seemed so natural.

He lay there, body rigid, while she explored and tasted him until suddenly his fingers clamped around her wrist and he tugged her hand away. She tensed, wondering if she was doing it wrong or if he'd decided he didn't like it.

"What—"

His smile was dark and ravenous. "I'm at my limit, Kate. I haven't been this aroused in I can't remember how long." He shifted her aside and swung his legs off the bed. "Don't move. Stay right where you are."

As if she had any intention of going anywhere, or even could.

He jogged into his bathroom, she heard him rummaging around, and then he was back, holding a string of condoms he dropped on the nightstand.

"I haven't needed one for so long my friends worry that the ones I had were out of date." He snorted. "They make it their business to keep me well supplied, just in case. Good thing I didn't throw these out." He saw her staring at them and chuckled. "I don't expect to use them all up at once. Don't worry." Then his face sobered, and heat flared in his eyes again. "But you never know, right?"

Then he was over her, guiding himself into her, the thickness of him filling her. He stretched her beyond belief. When he was fully inside of her he lowered his head and captured one of her nipples in his mouth. He worried it with his teeth, soothed it with his tongue, tugged on it with his lips until she was sure, as aroused as she was, she'd climax again just from that alone. When the sensation became almost unbearable, he moved to the other nipple and gave it the same attention.

Kate was strung tight as a bow, every fiber of her body screaming for release. But even as she strained toward him, one thought came out of nowhere and flashed in her mind—this was right.

This was not an accident of fate. This was where she belonged.

****

What the hell am I doing here?

The sudden flash of reality was almost like a dousing of cold water for Quinn. For one thing, he hadn't even thought about sex for so long he was afraid he'd forgotten how. He and his good right hand had become very close friends during his self-imposed solitude. And loneliness. Let's not forget that. But this woman…this waif…she pulled feelings out of him he didn't know still existed. And made him want things he thought were gone from his life.

And sweet Jesus, for another thing, he'd just met her. Somehow, he'd got caught up in helping her. That didn't give him a license to have incredible sex with her. In fact, it was probably the stupidest thing he could do. But it just seemed so…right. Yeah, that was it. It was *right*. Almost as if Lisa was hovering somewhere nearby, giving him a shove, pushing him out of his comfort zone and telling him to quit playing dead. *That* was the presence he'd felt. *That* was what had impelled him into this muddle of a mess.

He could almost hear *her* voice. "You're supposed to do this, Quinn. It's time now, and she's the right one."

And with that every nerve in his body snapped.

He had to grit his teeth to maintain any semblance of control. She felt like the purest silk around him, so tight he worried at first he'd hurt her. Then her muscles clamped down on him, and he forgot to worry. Sweat popped out on his forehead. He wanted this to last forever.

He paid homage to her nipples, little rosebuds that plumped in his mouth. She strained against him, so responsive that he could have sucked her forever. But his body argued with him, demanding movement, begging for release.

At last, he began a steady rhythm in and out of her tight sheath, his hips rolling and thrusting. His body was on fire with need, his lungs burning for air, as he pumped into her, harder and faster, his balls slapping against her thighs.

"Look at me," he demanded, needing to see deep inside her. To make that visual connection.

The familiar tingling tightened in his spine, and he grit his teeth so he could wait for Kate to get there. She matched his every move. The moment he felt her orgasm grip her he erupted, and they tumbled together over the crest into a space filled with bursting fireworks.

The last thought Quinn had as his body exploded was that this was where he belonged.

Chapter Six

They lay gasping for breath in a tangle of limbs. She could feel Quinn's heart thundering against hers. Long minutes passed before either of them could speak.

Finally, he shifted his head to look at her, his gaze locking with hers. "Please tell me you're not sorry."

Her smile came from deep inside of her. "Not even a little bit." Then the smile faded. "So what does that make me, falling into bed with a complete stranger?"

He traced her lips with his tongue, teasing her mouth, then he locked his gaze onto hers. His eyes had darkened to a rich ebony. "Do you believe in fate? That things happen the way they do for a reason?"

She swallowed before answering him, her heart still beating erratically. "I used to. Then fate played some very nasty tricks on me so I decided it was all a vicious rumor."

"Me, too," he told her. "But last night changed my mind again. I almost didn't stop when I saw you, but my conscience—or something—kicked me in the butt. If I'd just driven on home, we wouldn't be here together like this. I think some master puppeteer is pulling our strings, Kate. I don't know what your story is, but I can tell you mine is far from pretty. Maybe we were sent to heal each other."

She turned her face away, unwilling to meet his eyes. "My story would send you running for your life.

You wouldn't stick around long enough to do any healing." Reality had suddenly reared up to smack her in the face. What in hell was she doing here? She could not involve this man, put his life in danger. "This was great, Quinn, but—"

"Great?" he exploded. "It was a damn sight more than great. Look at me."

But she couldn't. She'd hug the memory of the night to her for a long time, because memory was probably all she'd ever have. "Quinn, you don't need the kind of trouble I'm dragging along with me. And I need to get out of here before you get sucked into it."

He refused to let go of her and let her get up. Instead, he feathered kisses over her face and brushed her hair back, tucking it behind her ears.

"Listen to me." He cupped her chin and turned her face so she was forced to meet his penetrating gaze. "I look in your eyes, and I see such terror it frightens me. No one should be that afraid of anything. You tell me your parents are dead, and you have no one. Whatever you're running from, you can't keep doing it alone. You're *not* alone anymore. So let me help you. Please."

Kate wanted so badly to say yes. To not be alone anymore. To have more of *this* with this man. She wrested her chin away and tucked her face against his broad chest, loving the feel of the soft curls against her cheek. Oh God, could she do this? If it was a mistake, it meant her life. And maybe Quinn's.

But what they had shared was…magical. So special she couldn't find words to describe it. And she wanted so desperately to hang onto him, to have him 'fix' this, so she could get her life back. With him, if it was meant to be.

"Kate?" he urged, kissing her jaw line, his warm hand cradling her still tingling breasts. "Listen to me. I've lived with emptiness for a long time. Suddenly, that hole inside me isn't so big anymore. You broke down at that exact spot for a reason. I stopped for the same reason. I want to see where this thing goes, what we have together. What Fate has in store for us. But in order to do that, we have to take care of whatever's wrong here."

What can I lose? I can only be dead once, right?

"All right." She touched her lips to his briefly. "But first I need a shower and coffee."

He held her so tightly she could barely breathe. "Good. We can do that." Then, as if repeating it to himself, "We can do that."

****

Kate insisted on showering in the bathroom she'd used the night before.

"I want you to move your things into my room," Quinn insisted.

"I will, but this way we can both shower at the same time."

He hardened as images of them in his big shower danced in his mind.

As if she read his thoughts, Kate grinned. "We can save that for later." Then her face sobered. "If you want me to tell you my story, I have to do it before my courage leaves me. So let's be quick, okay?"

He thought about the feel of her, next to him and around him, as he lathered and rinsed. The taste of her still lingered on his tongue, a taste so exquisite, the memory of it so erotic his dick instantly swelled and he turned the water to icy cold. She was a totally unexpected intrusion, but not, it seemed, an unwelcome one. Far from it.

He wasn't a big believer in ghosts, but he'd swear to anyone that Lisa was looking over his shoulder, telling him not to lose this opportunity. That it was time to wake up again. Join the living. God knows Jake and Nick had been after him long enough to forget about what they called "all this isolation shit" and get on with his life. But they hadn't felt the pain he had or his keen sense of loss, the feeling that life had permanently stopped for him.

"I don't know what I even have left to give anyone," he said, as if Lisa could hear him. "What we had was perfect. How can you improve on that?"

"Try," a voice whispered.

He looked around the bathroom, stunned, as if expecting to see his dead wife sitting on the edge of the bathtub.

"You're losing it," he muttered, but maybe it was just the sound of that high wall he'd built around himself beginning to crumble.

So. He'd find out whatever trouble Kate was in and help her take care of it. Whatever it was surely wouldn't be any worse than what he'd been through before. For the first time in four years, he actually had a purpose. A reason to get on with his life.

Dressed in his usual black jeans and T-shirt, he started the coffee maker in the kitchen and poured two glasses of juice. He heard Kate moving around in the other bathroom, the door finally opening. When she came into the kitchen, she was still carrying her tote.

He quirked an eyebrow at her with an uneasy feeling. Was she leaving? "Going somewhere?"

She shook her head, her face pale but determined, the fear even more evident in her eyes.

"No. I have some show and tell in here. But first could I have some of that heavenly-smelling coffee?"

"And juice." He handed her a glass.

He'd thought they'd sit at the counter on the bar stools, but it didn't seem a place conducive to the kind of talk they were about to have, nor did the dining table. Instead, he carried their mugs into the living room area and motioned for her to follow him.

She sat gingerly on the edge of the big couch, placing the tote bag on the floor between her feet. Her hand shook slightly as she picked up her mug, but the set of her jaw told him she was going to tell him what he wanted to know.

When she did, however, even he was unprepared for the story she laid out for him.

****

Kate sipped at her coffee, taking the time to pull her thoughts together. Her body still glowed from the early morning sex. Maybe that was why, for a change, her nerves weren't jangling like cowbells.

Sun poured in through the wide windows in the great room, casting its rays on the polished wood floor and highlighting the warm colors of the furniture. This was a house for joy, yet Quinn had obviously hidden in it with his pain. Now, she was about to dump her dirt all over it. For a moment, she thought about changing her mind.

S*afe!*

Out of nowhere the word jolted her.

Trust your instincts. But she'd trusted Peter and what a disaster that was.

Trust Quinn. Okay, she'd trust that inner voice and hope it didn't land her in a grave.

Nervously, she settled herself on the couch, the tote bag with the money and the flash drive nestled between her feet. She took a long swallow of her coffee, hoping it would settle her nervous stomach.

"It's not a nice story," she began, "and I warn you it's pretty bizarre. You may want to toss me back where you found me when you hear it. You may not even believe me."

"Whatever it is, we'll deal with it together," he assured her, his voice calm and steadying. "Nothing much scares me anymore."

She exhaled a long breath. "Okay. The first thing you need to know is my name's not really Kate Griffin. It's Kathryn Burke. But she's a person I'll never go back to being."

Quinn's fingers tightened almost imperceptibly around his mug. "And the reason?"

"Let's start with the law firm my father and uncle founded, Burke & Associates. It all begins there."

Staring into her coffee mug, refusing to look at his face, she laid it out for him. Choosing her words carefully. She'd thought to give him the bare bones version, but once she got started the words tumbled out, nearly falling over themselves in their haste to be heard. The law firm, Peter, her parents' deaths, the depression she'd fallen into, and Peter seamlessly taking control of her life.

When she told him about the conversation she'd overheard, her voice shook, but she swallowed hard and got through it. She left nothing out, starting with the escape from Tampa. When she finished, her body shivering from the memory of every frightening detail, she was almost afraid to look at Quinn. She waited a long breathless moment for him to say something.

Then he reached over and pulled her against him, brushing a kiss against her forehead. "Jesus, Kate. I have to say you have a lot of guts."

"And stupidity," she added.

"We're all stupid at some time, darlin'. The key is learning from it."

He gave her a tight hug, then sat her away from him and looked directly at her face. "Let's take one thing at a time. Okay?"

"Okay." She'd do whatever he wanted. He wasn't running away from her mess.

"What you did took guts. More guts than most people ever think of having. You are unbelievably brave and resourceful. There aren't a hundred people who could have done what you did."

"I think it was more fear than anything else," she told him.

"But you didn't let the fear defeat you." He pulled her against his body. "Fate hasn't been kind to me for a while, Kate, but I'm thinking last night was her way of making it up to me. So count on this. From now on, darlin', you're not alone."

Darlin'. The word warmed her and eased some of the tension.

"I can't believe what a fool I was about Peter." She twisted her lips in a grimace. "I really thought he cared about me. When he insisted the doctor give me something for my so-called depression, I just idiotically kept popping pills in my mouth." Her laugh had a touch of hysteria. "I think I was so spaced out on drugs the

Unibomber could have taken over my life and I wouldn't have noticed."

Quinn gave her one quick squeeze and picked up his coffee mug. "Exactly how much do you know about the operation of the law firm?"

She shrugged. "Not much. My dad pretty much kept business away from the family and Peter never discussed it. Why?"

"Because there has to be a reason why he wants you dead. There's something there they want to hide, something they're afraid you'll find out, and that made getting rid of you necessary. We have to find out what that is."

"I'm telling you." She dragged her fingers through her hair. "I never even met any of the clients. Dad was very careful to keep all of that separate. And Peter was even more secretive."

"The first sign that something isn't kosher," he told her. "But that also doesn't tell me why they'd send people to hunt you down. Not that aggressively."

She took in a deep breath and slowly let it out. "Okay. I may have the answers here." Reaching into her tote bag, she unzipped the fanny pack and took out the flash drive, holding it in the palm of her hand. She was trembling, knowing that if she'd misjudged this whole situation she was as good as dead.

Quinn looked at it. "A flash drive?"

"I heard Peter and Miguel discussing what was on it so I grabbed it as some kind of insurance or protection for myself." She shook her head. "I haven't even had a chance to see what's on it."

Quinn's face hardened, and his eyes turned almost black. "If what you heard that night is correct, this could hold every record of the firm's operation, whatever that is. Jesus, Kate. This thing could be dynamite. No wonder they're after you."

Without saying a word, she dropped it into his hand. "You take it. Maybe you'll know what to do with it."

"I won't do anything to put you in danger," he promised. "But we've got to figure out what what's on here or you'll never be safe."

She nodded, misery gripping her. "I know."

"First things first," he told her. "You can't just walk around with this. We have to lock it up until we can find out what the hell is going on."

"But where? I can't put it in a safety deposit box. I don't dare trust it that far away from me."

He rose and held out his hand. "Lucky for you, I have just the answer."

But she resisted when he tugged at her. "I have one more thing to show you that also needs safekeeping." Her hands shook as she took out the fanny pack and showed him its contents. His eyes narrowed, he glanced from the money to her and back to the money.

"Whose is it?" he asked, his voice flat.

"It's mine. Honestly." Quickly, she explained all about the deposit and the cash she'd taken out as her safety net.

And she'd made a mistake with that, wanting to increase her cushion of cash just in case. She'd found a branch of her bank on the road and cashed one last check. Stupid, stupid, stupid. That was how they'd almost caught her.

"Okay." He stood up, pulled her into his arms, and brushed a kiss over her lips, a silent promise. Then he grinned. "No more of that or we won't get anything done."

In his bedroom closet, he pulled out a drawer in one of the built-in dressers to reveal a safe sunken into the floor.

"Take whatever you think you might need for walking around money. You can always get more. Whatever you buy you'll pay cash for. I'll put the rest in here."

She grabbed a handful of bills before handing the rest over to Quinn, watching as he stored everything away.

"I'll write the combination down for you," he told her. "Memorize it and throw the paper away."

Her head was spinning as he led her back into the kitchen. So much, so fast. So…everything. A fresh mug of hot coffee settled her nerves but only slightly.

"At least I know why Peter and his men are so anxious to find you." Quinn reached a hand out and brushed her hair back from her face. "I know you're scared, but I'm going to fix this."

"How?" she cried, fear slamming back into her. "You keep saying that, but what if you can't?"

"I've been around the block a few times, darlin'." He gave her a half-smile. "I'm not without resources."

The knot in her stomach began to loosen, but then something else occurred to her. "Resources? What do you mean? You can't tell anyone about this. About me. Please. Promise me."

He took both of her hands in his, squeezing them gently. "I promise you that I won't put you in any danger. Can you trust me on that?"

Well, dummy, you dumped your whole story on him

84

and he didn't run to the phone and call Peter. Haven't you already made that decision?

She nodded. "I—Yes. I do. I will."

"Good." He brushed his lips over hers. I promise you I'm not going to let you down."

"So where does that leave us?" she asked.

"Right now, we're going to see about your car. Then I'm going to call a man who's my closest friend in the world."

She tensed. "But I said—"

"And *I* said to trust me. Okay? Kate. Darlin'. We can't do this by ourselves. We need information that I can't get without tapping into some connections. The first thing to do is find out if that law firm is on anyone's watch list. I can do that very cautiously."

"But—"

"I trust this person completely. If you look in the dictionary under 'honest,' you'll see his picture. Let me talk to him. Please, Kate. We need to get a handle on what's happening. If we're dealing with a big organization here, he'll know about it or at least be able to find information for me. And maybe give us some help."

Kate sighed and nodded. She hadn't thought he'd believe her, and now he was willing to stick his neck out for her. The sudden feeling of relief made her weak.

"This is all so insane," she said, trying to hold onto her control.

"Maybe we both need a little insanity in our lives." He stroked her cheeks with his thumbs, the roughened pads sliding over her skin. A single tear plopped onto his knuckles. "Don't cry, Kate. Whatever it turns out to be, I'll make it right. I promise."

She'd thought she was done with crying, but more tears were gathering, ready to cascade down her cheeks. "What if you can't?"

"I used to think there were some things so bad they could never get better. I've told myself that every day for the last four years." For a moment, a faraway look flashed in his eyes. "Then you fell into my life, and suddenly I thought I had a chance again. No matter how bad this is or what you've done or who's after you, it will be okay. I promise. We'll handle it together, and I'll keep you safe."

She wiped away what she hoped was the last of her tears. Leaning into his chest, she could only think how secure he made her feel. For the first time in days, she actually began to hope. Reaching up one hand, she touched his cheek. "Thank you. For…everything."

"Everything?" he grinned.

"Yes." She felt herself blushing and lowered her eyes. "You were pretty amazing."

"You get at least half the credit." He pulled her in for one last hug, then swatted her rear lightly. "Time to get dressed and see about your car."

Kate had a feeling that problem would be just as difficult to solve as everything else.

Chapter Seven

Quinn had wanted to feed her first, but Kate was too antsy about the car to eat.

"Later," she told him. "After the bad news, which I'm sure is what we're going to hear."

She got her first real look at Windswept as he drove down Main Street. She hadn't seen anything of Texas except what was visible from the Interstate, and she hadn't been interested much in the scenery. Limestone buildings lined both sides of the street, with crepe myrtles set in tubs along the sidewalk. Benches were placed here and there for people to sit and chat, maybe share a cold drink or a cup of coffee. Almost everywhere she looked, the Texas flag was displayed in some form.

She wondered what it would be like to live in a small town like this. No fears. No worries.

No Peter.

Mike's Garage was on a side street, a long cement building with five bays, all of them full. Kate figured the man had a lock on the town business.

Quinn made the introductions. Inside one of the bays, they stared at her car up on a hoist, then at the tools and parts scattered beneath it.

Kate's heart sank. "How long will it take to fix the problem?"

Mike shook his head. "I don't know who sold you

this hunk of junk, but I sure hope you didn't pay too much for it. You must have been desperate, is all I can say. Forgetting about all the other problems, the engine block's cracked and a new one would cost more than the car is worth. I can't guarantee it'll work even then."

Kate swallowed against the knot in her throat. "What you're saying is you can't really fix it, right?"

Mike shrugged. "If it could be repaired, I'm the man to do it. But this one's beyond even emergency care. Quinn, I thought you knew better than to let your friends run around in something like this?"

Quinn grunted. "I didn't have a say in this one."

Mike shrugged. "Whatever. So what are we doing here?"

On the short drive to the garage, she'd chewed on her situation. Could Quinn truly protect her the way he promised? What kind of 'resources' was he talking about?

Safe!

But how safe would she be without transportation, despite everything Quinn said? What if she needed to leave in a hurry?

"Kate?"

Quinn's voice jerked her from her internal discussion.

"I need to have a vehicle. No matter what, I can't be without wheels."

He took her arm and led her outside.

"Darlin', getting a new car is not important right now. Solving your major problem is. Are you planning to take off, is that it?"

She shook her head. "No. I'm not… No."

"Then you don't need to worry about wheels. If

something happens and you feel you absolutely have to have something, we'll take care of it then."

Kate swallowed and nodded. She was through running.

"Okay," she told him. "Let's forget about a new car, at least for now."

Quinn walked over to Mike. "Can you junk it for her?"

The man looked at Kate. "If you sign over the pink slip for this thing, I'll give you something for the parts. Every little bit helps, right?"

"Yes. All right. Thank you."

Kate signed the owner's slip, Mike gave her what she thought was more than a fair amount of cash, and Quinn hustled her out the door.

****

She was such an enigma. Feisty even while fear surrounded her. Wearing a coat of invisible armor but soft underneath it all. Oh, yeah. She was definitely soft. And he couldn't wait to feel more of her softness.

Quinn helped Kate into the truck, then unclipped his cell phone and dialed a number he hadn't used in a long, long time. He heard the shock in the voice that answered.

"I don't believe it. This is a true Jesus Christ miracle. Are you dead and calling from heaven? Oh, wait." A deep chuckle. "You'd be calling from the other place, right?"

Quinn chuckled, an unfamiliar sound but one he'd used a lot since meeting Kate last night. "Coming back from the dead to haunt you. How goes it?"

"The better question," the man said, "is how goes it with you?"

"I wondered if you had time for a drink this afternoon. Maybe around two o'clock?"

"You don't want lunch?" Jake Garza asked.

"Afternoon works better for me if it's okay with you. Two o'clock okay? The usual place?"

"Fine by me," Garza agreed. "The alcohol can help with the shock. Can I ask what this is all about?"

"You could," Quinn said. "But you won't get an answer. Not until I see you. And don't mention this to anyone, okay?"

He heard exasperation in the man's voice as he answered. "Business as usual, I guess. Okay. Two o'clock."

Quinn disconnected the call and climbed into the truck.

"Was that your friend you called?" Kate wanted to know.

"Yes. And before you say anything, I didn't want him to know I was with anyone. No information, right? Not until I talk to him and figure out what to do next."

"Are you going to see him?"

Quinn nodded. "This afternoon."

"He has to keep it to himself," Kate said nervously. "No one can know about this."

"Kate. Darlin'. You said you trust me. Then believe that I won't put you in jeopardy by going to someone I can't trust. Jake is good as gold, I promise you." He put his arm around her. "But if this turns out to be a barn buster, a lot of people will have to know. My responsibility is to keep you off the radar and out of the way of traffic."

"You know he'll have questions."

"And I'll handle them the best I can. But I don't

90

want you there. I want you hidden until I get a better handle on things. I also don't want to leave you alone at the house."

"Afraid I'll find a way to run?" she asked, her voice edgy.

"Not a bit, and don't even ask that. Call me crazy, but with this situation, I just don't feel good leaving you alone."

"Is there a big library around here?" she asked.

"Downtown. It's got everything you could want." He grinned. "Why? You have a sudden urge to do some reading?"

"No. As a matter of fact I thought I might do some searching on the Internet."

His hands tightened on the wheel. "Don't stick your nose into something that might bite it off," he warned.

"I won't. But my curiosity is in high gear about the law firm. I just thought I'd see what references I could find. Maybe print out some articles about it." She shifted in her seat to look at him. "Quinn, it stuns me that I know almost nothing about the firm my father helped found that paid for our lifestyle all these years. Whatever they do, they have a public face so there has to be something about them, right?"

"Yeah, I guess so." He didn't like the idea, but at least it was something she could do. And they did need to collect all the information they could. "Just be careful what you do."

She grinned. "I know how to be invisible in cyberspace. I used to do searches for our clients at my job without letting people know what I was looking for. I'm good at it, okay?"

He tried to swallow back his anxiety. The force of his feeling of possession shocked him. So much time had passed since anyone had meant anything to him. This relationship wasn't even twenty-four hours old, yet it had an incredible sense of permanence and intensity to it. He didn't want anything to happen to her.

"All right. Lunch first. Then the library and my meeting."

****

They ate quickly, then hit the Interstate, Quinn voicing his doubts one more time.

"I told you, I know how to cover my footprints out there on the Internet." She grinned at him. "It'll be fine. Honestly. Okay?"

"Just be careful out there in cyberspace." He pulled out to pass an eighteen wheeler. "I've got a hinky feeling about this."

"What time are you meeting your friend?" she asked.

"As soon as I drop you off."

He trailed his hand over her thigh, then squeezed it lightly.

Traffic wasn't too heavy on the Interstate, and in just over half an hour, Quinn pulled up in front of a large red brick building. "The natives call it the Big Red Enchilada."

She laughed. "As good a name as any."

"Listen." He frowned. "I'm not sure how long I'll be."

"Don't worry. I can keep myself busy."

"You want the fifth floor," he told her. "That's where they have the computers."

"You are coming back, right?" she joked.

"Will you make it worth my while?" he drawled seductively.

"I'll try." Heat bloomed on her cheeks at the images his words called up, but she gave him a mischievous grin.

"Anyway, I have big plans for tonight." He winked, then pulled out onto the street.

Kate stood looking after him, that same delicious shiver racing up and down her spine, then turned and walked through the building entrance.

The fifth floor was surprisingly quiet, almost hushed, despite the number of people working away at various desks and pulling reference books from the stacks.

"You can use any of these terminals over here," an accommodating librarian told her. "There's a common printer you can send your documents to. It's a quarter a page to print."

"Thank you."

All right, Kate. Get to it.

****

"I don't believe it. The hermit actually came down from the hills."

Quinn looked at the man waiting for him in the back booth at Miguel's, a quiet bar where they'd often gone to thrash out cases away from prying eyes and ears. He was tall, with the build of a former football player who kept in shape, which was exactly what he was. His masculine face, framed by unruly black hair and dark eyes, had unexpected dimples. But not to be fooled. Jake Garza had a commanding presence that made him hugely successful in the courtroom.

The two men had been friends for years. They'd

worked together for the United States Attorney for the Western District of Texas until Quinn's resignation four years earlier. Quinn didn't miss many people these days, but he did miss Jake. It had been far too long since they'd talked, more since they'd seen each other.

Jake had tried several times to get him out of his cave. Dinner. Drinks. Coffee. Anything. Quinn was always polite but aloof. And unbending. His life had ended, and he'd been passing his days until he stopped breathing.

But Kate had shone light into the darkness, found a way into his soul, and maybe, strange as it was to admit, with a little nudge from Lisa. Telling her everything had cracked the wall he'd built around himself and let his rusty feelings out to test the waters of life again. He hoped he'd made the right decision going to Jake. If not, he could lose both a friend and the woman he had just that quickly fallen in love with.

"Nice threads," he said, noting Jake's well-tailored suit and dress shirt with monogrammed cuffs. "Looks like the prosecutor business is paying well."

Garza laughed. "You know me. I always believe clothes make the man."

"Which female are you dressing for this week?" Quinn asked, grinning.

Jake smiled and winked at his friend. His reputation as a ladies' man was legendary in the legal profession, and he never lacked for female companionship.

They each ordered a beer and made small talk to cover the awkwardness of the unexpected meeting. Finally, Jake pushed his bottle away and leaned back. "Okay, I'm flattered that I seem to be the only person in

San Antonio you care to keep in touch with. Maybe in the state of Texas. But you don't make casual social visits so your call really intrigued me. Want to tell me what this is about?"

When the waitress collected their empty bottles, they switched to coffee. Quinn idly stirred in cream and sugar while he figured out how to ask what he wanted. He'd made up his mind on the way in not to give Jake any details until he knew the lay of the land. If he could keep Kate's name out of it, he would.

"Okay," he said. "I'm looking for some information, and I'd like to keep it just between us. For now, anyway. Until I find out what it's all about."

Garza raised his eyebrows. Quinn seldom asked favors. Usually, it was the other way around. "Well, you know I'll help you with anything I can. But what the hell could you be mixed up in, hiding in the hills the way you do."

He chose his words carefully. "Do you happen, just happen, to know anything about an attorney in Tampa named Peter Fleming? Or the law firm of Burke, Fleming & Associates? Are they flying anywhere on your radar?"

Garza looked at him carefully, dropping his eyes but not before Quinn caught a look of surprise in them. "Just how is it you're interested in them?"

Quinn took a sip of his coffee. "We've been friends a very long time, Jacob. We've trusted each other with our lives. Please, just for once, take off that official vest and answer me."

Jake fiddled with his coffee cup. "You're asking about a very heavy dude here, Ace. If you want answers, I have to know why." He held up his hand as

Quinn got ready to protest. "I trust you. That's not the problem. But I know you, remember? This question didn't come out of left field. You hit a bullseye without even aiming."

"I'm asking for a friend," Quinn said in a cautious voice.

Jake raised one eyebrow. "You have a friend who knows Peter Fleming? You're playing in a very nasty sandbox if you do."

Quinn pushed his cup away. "Okay. Thanks anyway. Nice seeing you." He started to slide from the booth.

"Okay, okay, okay." Jake shook his head. "I know I'll be sorry, but I can go this far with you. Only because it's you. Peter Fleming is the only surviving partner in the Tampa law firm of Burke, Fleming and Associates. The firm has one client, Trans Global Industries, which is really a front for a drug cartel run by Miguel and Esai Osuna. They make every other organization look like boy scouts. Nasty, nasty people."

An icy feeling raced down his spine and dread curled in his stomach, but he kept his face carefully blank. "You know about them."

"Know about them?" Jake's mouth twisted in a grimace. "The Department of Justice has been trying to build a case against them for two years. Our problem is we can only go so far. Fleming keeps them so low under the radar if you didn't know better, you'd think they were just another corporation." He drained his coffee cup and signaled for the waitress. "So let me ask *you*. What the hell are you doing mixed up with the Osunas? Especially after your last fiasco with drug cartels."

96

His last fiasco with the Osunas had been a tragedy that nearly destroyed him. He still had nightmares about the situation that had sent him running from his job and hiding in the Hill Country. He didn't think the pain would ever go away.

"You know me, Jake." He gave him a steady look. "I wouldn't call you after all this time and ask a question just to pass the time of day." He waited while the waitress refilled his cup. "I may have, let's say, stepped into something by accident, and I have to know how to handle things."

"*Compadre,* the Osunas are big time trouble. You don't even want to stick your nose in there."

Every muscle in his body tightened as past licked at him like the fires of hell. "What else can you tell me about them?"

Garza stared, curiosity stamped on his face. "Jesus, Quinn. How about *you* telling *me*?" He waited while the waitress refilled his cup and Quinn's. "If you have even the tiniest scrap of information, you gotta give it to me. We're desperate for anything to crack the wall around the cartel."

"And?"

"And what?"

"I know you're keeping something back so give. You told me this much."

Jake drummed his fingers on the table. "Okay. John Burke, the last of the senior partners, died in a house fire a few months ago. Word has it Fleming was set to marry the daughter. Then she up and disappeared."

"Disappeared?" *I'll say she disappeared. Otherwise, she'd be dead.*

"Yeah, and there's something funny about it. A lot more than some guy looking for his missing girlfriend."

Quinn frowned. "What do you mean?"

"The Osunas have a manhunt out for her of major proportions. They've called in favors every place they can. They want this broad badly. And I don't think they're looking to welcome her with open arms."

The flash drive. Of course. But why did Fleming want her dead to begin with?

"Is she suspected of being part of the organization?" He had to find out if Kate was in trouble on both sides of the problem.

Jake shook his head. "Not at all. Her father kept her pretty much separated from it, and Peter seldom brought her to the office. We think she was just window dressing for him. But wherever she is, she's got a big target painted on her back."

"Yeah? No idea why, huh?"

"No, but we'd sure like to talk to her. She may be able to give us information she doesn't even know she has that would help us take these guys down."

Quinn pushed away his rapidly cooling coffee. "So you're looking for her, too?"

Jake's eyes narrowed, comprehension bright in them. A muscle jumped in his cheek. "Shit, Ace. You've got the girl up there in the hills, don't you?"

Quinn didn't answer, just waited to see what Jake would say next.

"Quinn, she may be a material witness. Worst case, she has some very bad dudes wanting to wax her. How the hell did you get yourself in the middle of this?"

"Right now, I'm not in the middle of anything." He pulled a paper napkin from the dispenser on the table and wrote something on it. "Here's my new cell phone number. When you have more information on the girl, give me a call."

Garza lifted an eyebrow. "Give *you* a call? Are you joking? Here's a news flash for you. The Osuna brothers run the biggest drug cartel in the United States. Maybe on this side of the world. They are more dangerous than the *pendejos* you put away four years ago. And very different from every other cartel we've tracked. No street killings, no gang fights. Their enemies just disappear and are never heard from again. And you want to wait for a phone call?"

The coffee in Quinn's stomach suddenly turned to bile. "How do they get away with it? You've always been able to tag the cartels before."

"Because they operate like a corporation and the guy who runs the business is one cold-hearted bloodless bastard. The aforementioned Peter Fleming. Not someone I'd ever want to cross."

Only years of practice allowed Quinn to keep any expression from his face. "I'll keep that in mind."

"Ace, if you're mixed up with this female, she needs to come in. I told you they've got everyone and his uncle after her. I've never seen them go after someone like this before. Something's off kilter about this search. It's too intense. She could be drawing her last breath any minute."

"Thanks for the information." Quinn stood up and tossed some money on the table. "It was good seeing you."

"Yeah, yeah, yeah. I hope you live long enough for me to see you again. By the way, if you don't get yourself whacked, could I entice you into town for dinner once in a while when this is over? Maybe with a few old friends?"

Quinn's face tightened, and he shook his head. "Not my thing these days. You know that."

"Apparently something's your thing, or you wouldn't be here in the first place. All right, all right." He held up his hands, palms outward. "Just watch your back, please."

"Let's keep this between us for now, okay?"

"Ace, I don't know—"

"Just give me a little breathing room, okay? I promise to get back to you."

"Only because I've known you for so long. I can give you twenty-four hours. Hopefully, you and the girl will still be alive. But that's it."

"That's not very much time, Jake."

"It's more than I should give you. Besides, my boss would fry my ass if he knew I was doing even this much. Please. Don't make me get official here. I want us to stay friends."

Quinn nodded "Twenty-four hours." Not much time to convince a skittish Kate what she needed to do.

The men shook hands and walked out of the bar together.

Quinn watched Jake head toward the courthouse. The Osunas. Just the name scared him shitless. They'd destroyed his family and his life once before. Could he let them in to do it again?

Fuck. His nose had smelled trouble from that first minute on the highway. He'd never expected anything like this, that was for damn sure, but this was no longer an offer to help someone in distress. This was about Kate, who had suddenly become the most important person in his life.

He looked at his watch. Time to see if she'd found anything in the library that they could use and hope she hadn't tripped over anything she shouldn't. Then he'd have to figure out how to tell her what Jake had to say and try to convince her to give him the flash drive. It could be the only way to keep her alive.

Chapter Eight

"You lost her again?"

Miguel Osuna sat in the leather client chair, legs crossed, fiddling with an unlit cigar. He was, as always, immaculately groomed in a custom silk shirt and well-tailored slacks that did little to disguise the heavy body. The soft Hispanic accent belied the innate cruelty and anger Peter knew lurked beneath the surface. The fact that he allowed the intensity of his rage to creep into his voice was not a good sign.

Miguel and his ugly bodyguard had arrived unannounced, as usual, at the Burke-Fleming offices.

Why doesn't the man stay home where he belongs?

"I wasn't the one who made the mistake in identity." Peter fidgeted with his tie, knowing he was twisting the tiger's tail by pointing out whose men had screwed up. The chronic headache he'd developed the past few weeks set up a rhythmic banging behind his eyes.

"Are you implying that this is *my* fault?" Osuna's voice was soft and deadly. "You're the one who gave me her picture."

"Listen. The men told you themselves this woman was a dead ringer for Kathryn," Peter insisted. "She looked enough like her to be her sister."

"It didn't occur to you that she'd make some kind of effort to change the way she looks?" A sour look washed over his face. "I should have thought of this myself. This woman is not as stupid as you'd like us to think she is."

"At least we know she's taking buses, probably sticking to the big cities." Peter tried to meet Miguel's hard stare. "Airplanes would require identification, and there are hardly any trains any more. On top of that, she ditched her car. So what else is left?"

Osuna twisted his unlit cigar. "We know nothing, only that she accidentally left a trail of bread crumbs, and we didn't follow them properly. It's clear to me she's unpredictable and far more resourceful than any of us expected."

"We have our people out there everywhere now," Peter pointed out. "We'll catch her out." He picked up a pen from his desk and flipped it in his hands, something to ease the almost unbearable tension gripping his body. "What about the woman from the terminal?"

"Safely on her way to heaven. It will be a long time before they find the body." Osuna leaned forward in his chair. "Pedro, I can't tell you enough times. Leaving that flash drive out where anyone could get it is one of the more stupid things you've done. Maybe we misjudged your abilities all along."

"How many times do you want me to tell you? No one was supposed to be in the office that night except us."

"And I will tell you again, if the *policia* or the *federales* get their hands on it, we'll be sitting ducks." His eyes turned so dark the irises all but disappeared. "If I get my hands on that woman, I'll kill her myself."

Peter ground his teeth. "Listen to me. Those files are encrypted. No one can break the pass codes. I wrote them myself, and I'm the only one with the key. She'll be stymied."

"Don't delude yourself, Pedro. There isn't a code that's been written yet that can't be cracked by someone. The government employs people who do nothing but that kind of thing all day.

"Fine. You've given me my lecture for the day." Peter was getting tired of all this bullshit, and he hated it when they called him Pedro. He was doing what he could to track Kathryn down. Threats from the cartel didn't make things work any faster. No one wanted to find that bitch more than he did. "I'm on it," he repeated. "I'll get her. You have my word."

And I'll take her apart piece by piece when I do.

"If this organization is destroyed because of your carelessness and poor judgment, the results for you will be very unpleasant. That's my personal guarantee."

A tiny bead of sweat worked its way down Peter's spine. "We'll get her. That's a promise."

Miguel Osuna stared at him, unblinking. "Is it? My brother and I have come to believe we can't afford to count on your promises any longer. That's why I'm here today, to give you an...update. He and I are taking charge of this search. We have called in reinforcements, and the word is out. Wherever she is, someone will find her. When they do, they'll report to one of us."

"But—"

"No buts. You need to remember that your neck is on the line, too."

Peter swallowed hard against the nausea that rolled through him. "I understand. I will continue to pursue my own avenues."

"Fine. But we can't let her slip through our fingers

again."

Peter allowed himself to breathe a sigh of relief when Miguel and his bodyguard took their leave. Those two men could frighten the devil.

Shit!

He swept the papers on his desk aside in a gesture of frustration. Who would have thought dull Kathryn Burke, the quiet little mouse, could do him so much damage? If that flash drive fell into the wrong hands, he wasn't sure he could find a deep enough hole to crawl into.

How rosy everything had looked when the Osunas moved him into the law practice. They'd gotten rid of one brother. Now it was time to slide the other one out, they'd told him. And Peter, with his computer knowledge and extensive modern legal expertise, was taking the operation further and higher than either of the Burke brothers ever could.

But John Burke had been tougher than they'd expected. He'd finally had enough. He'd leave, all right, but he was taking his story to the feds. He was tired of being covered with the same slime as the cartel. When threats and pressure didn't persuade him to keep quiet, they got rid of him and his wife.

How unfortunate for everyone that Kathryn had left the house early that night. The plan was supposed to eliminate all of them at one time. Still, it hadn't taken long for him to bring her under his control.

Only he'd made the fatal mistake of underestimating her. Now a billion dollar organization teetered on the brink of disaster because of it. Life was full of surprises. Too bad for him not all of them were pleasant.

How many times could this scene repeat itself, Miguel invading his office with the same threats? But that was the man's habit. He used his threats like a hammer, and Peter could feel it banging against his brain. Well, it was working. He was consumed with frustration at his lack of progress. And fear. Yes, fear.

He'd better find her before the brothers did, or he would be in deep, deep shit. She couldn't disappear indefinitely. She had to leave a paper trail somewhere. And wherever it was, he'd find it.

****

The silence in the library was, as usual, so thick you could touch it. Kate's nose twitched at the familiar smells of printed pages and rubber stamps. People filled the room like ghosts, walking with whisper-soft steps and mouthing their words to eliminate vocal sounds. She shut it all out so there was just her and the machine.

Not knowing how long she had until Quinn returned, Kate didn't waste any time. Finding anything about either Peter or the firm was a long shot, but she had to try. Her lack of knowledge made her feel incredibly stupid. She wanted to be able to tell Quinn something besides, "I don't know."

Maybe she'd get lucky. "You can do this," she muttered as she flexed her fingers over the keyboard. "Just think. Blank everything else out of your mind. That's all you need to do."

Caution was important. She knew how to build layers of anonymous servers to hide the original source. In market research, clients often wanted their identity kept secret.

She began with the law firm, a more likely subject to find information on. But everything that came up was so innocuous she might have been reading about air. Burke and Burke was described as a quiet corporate law firm dealing in a few major clients. Although there were a number of articles, they told her almost nothing. There was a little background on her father and his uncle, but that was it. Still, she sent them all to the printer, figuring anything was better than nothing.

She got a little more when she did a search on her father's name, including social items that documented any entertaining they did. But nothing she wasn't already aware of.

She glanced at her watch, wondering just how soon Quinn would be back. Chewing her bottom lip, knowing Quinn would probably be angry but unable to kill her curiosity, she decided to see what she could find out about Peter.

The work was tedious and time consuming. She wanted to bang the computer in frustration every time a page opened only to have a message pop up that read, "Server Error. Remote server could not be accessed." Several times, she closed down everything, rebooted, and started again, but the same results stared her in the face. Something was wrong, and she couldn't seem to fix it with the skills she had. No matter how many times she tried, the results were always the same.

"Damn, damn, damn." She smoothed strands of her hair away from her forehead. "Who are you, Peter? Did you emerge one day from under a rock?"

In the end, she had little more than when she started—a bare bones profile, mostly gleaned from the UVA site where he'd received his law degree. Peter Fleming indeed appeared to have sprung whole from the atmosphere, with an undergraduate degree from

MIT, a law degree from UVA, and no family history. What the hell did that mean? Everyone had a family. Didn't they?

Tired and frustrated, she sat back and rubbed her eyes, trying to ease the strain of reading fine print for so long. Her head ached, her back was stiff from sitting hunched over the terminal, and she was irritated beyond belief. And what did she have to show for it? Little more than a big fat nothing.

She sensed Quinn's presence even before he spoke. Although he'd moved up quietly, in that stealthy, catlike way he had, she knew he was there. Her Quinn radar was fast shifting into overdrive.

"Find anything interesting?" His voice, that deep, rusty sound softened by the warm Texas drawl, floated in from behind her. "It's nearly three-thirty, and I'd like to get out of town before rush hour."

When he touched his hands lightly on her shoulders, shivers skittered along her spine. "Yes, I'm done. I'm sorry. Were you waiting downstairs all this time?"

"No. I just got here, as a matter of fact."

"How was your…meeting with your friend?"

He rubbed her shoulders, easing the strain. "Okay. We'll talk about it later."

"Oh-oh." A whisper of fear raced through her. "I won't like it, right?"

"Later," he insisted. "Meanwhile, let's get out of here."

Kate pressed the key to return the screen to the main menu and stood up. "Just let me get the sheets I printed out. I figured anything was better than nothing."

She felt the possessiveness in his touch as he gently

guided her to the elevator, his fingertips at her elbow, and she leaned into him. The lightest of touches, yet that surge of electricity kicked in again. Oh, yes. They were definitely connected. It seemed as if their relationships had existed for light years rather than hours.

The headache that had begun in the library was building steadily, a combination of the hours at the computer and the tension of waiting for Quinn's information of his meeting. She was happy to kick back as he guided them through traffic and back out onto the Interstate.

****

They'd been driving for about fifteen minutes when Quinn's cell phone rang.

"Yeah?"

"Can you talk or just listen."

"Uh-huh." Quinn hoped Jake caught onto the brief answer.

"Okay. Got it. Listen, then. When I got back to the office, Dean was waiting for me to discuss something about the Osuna case."

Dean Morgan was Jake's immediate boss, and once had also been Quinn's.

Damn you, Jake. You told him about our talk, didn't you. "Yeah?"

"And before you start chewing me out, I didn't give away any secrets, but he could tell I was holding something back. Jesus, Quinn. You have no idea how big this thing is.

"And how is our old friend?" Quinn asked, sliding a glance at Kate.

She was leaning back in her seat, eyes closed.

Maybe, hopefully, even dozing.

"I'll try to do this as briefly as possible, buddy," Jake said.

"That would be very good, since my patience is getting shorter by the minute."

"I'm going to give you a little more detail than I did when we met. Then you'll understand why I couldn't keep this to myself."

"Well, that's very nice of you," Quinn drawled, his voice edged with sarcasm. He glanced sideways again. Kate hadn't moved, her eyes still closed.

"Listen," Jake protested. "Friends or not, I have a job to do and a duty to perform. Even if you were my wife, I couldn't just ignore what I think is going on."

"If I were your wife, we'd *really* be screwed up. So give."

"Okay." There was one heartbeat of silence. "Here it is. Our office—especially Dean's staff—is part of a Strike Force involving the FBI and the Narcotics and Dangerous Drug Section of the Department of Justice. For more than two years, we've been after the Osuna cartel. Ever since a major dealer killed a DEA undercover agent, was careless afterwards and left a trail that led back to the Osunas. The DEA caught him and managed to flip him."

"Well, that's real interesting, buddy," Quinn drawled. "And how are those boys doing now?"

"Better than we are," Jake told him. "He told us the Osuna distribution center is here in San Antonio, which is why this is where they set up the Strike Force. But Miguel, the younger brother, runs the money operation from Florida where the law firm we discussed is located. That brings in the U.S. Attorney's office in

Miami."

"Well, sounds like all our old friends are having a great time." Quinn was trying his best to keep the edginess out of his voice. What the hell was Jake getting at here? "But what's going on? Are they having a party or something? You know I'm not much for socializing anymore."

"We've been stymied everyplace we tried to crack the wall. Electronic surveillance doesn't help us. Their computers have multiple firewalls, and their satellite phones use complex encryptions. We can't get evidence of anything. Nada. I'm telling you all this for a reason, you know."

"Who's that?" Kate stirred in her seat and looked at Quinn.

He pressed the cell phone to his thigh, blocking out the sounds in the cab. "The friend I met with this afternoon. He has some more information for me. This is part of what we need to discuss later. Meantime, darlin', just close your eyes again if you can." He put the cell back up to his ear. "So, Jake. Is there a point to this call other than shooting the bull a little more?"

"These people aren't just involved with drugs. You can add arms sales to terrorists, human smuggling, white slave trade. You name it, they do it. These are not nice people, Ace. If you've got John Burke's daughter tucked away somewhere, we have to talk to her. She could be our first break. This is critical, Ace, and that's no shit."

"Thank you very much for that report." Quinn was getting very impatient. "I'll see if I can find out anything to add to it. Oh, and Jake?" He couldn't keep the sarcasm from his voice. "Thanks for keeping the lid on things."

"Quinn, I don't want to come barging into your house looking for her. Give this some serious thought and call me, okay? And quickly."

"I'll get back to you." He snapped the phone shut, put it in the console, and reached for Kate's hand.

"It's not good, is it?" she asked, her eyes open her voice troubled.

"No, but we'll handle it together. When we get home we'll lay it all out and make some decisions."

"I'm scared, Quinn."

He felt her trembling beside him on the seat. "I know you are, darlin'. But the important thing is to get the right information in the right hands. And get these people off your back. Right?"

"I guess so." But her voice trembled and her hand clutched tightly at his."

"Then maybe I can think of something to help you forget about it for a couple of hours," he teased.

He was rewarded with another hand squeeze and a sliding glance at her saw her effort at a smile.

"Okay. I trust you, Quinn. I never thought I'd say that to anyone ever again."

"I promised you'd be safe with me, right? I don't intend to break that promise." He lifted her hand and kissed her fingers.

I hope I'm doing this right. God knows how close they are to finding her, especially with headquarters in San Antonio. But who the hell would look for her up here? The tough thing will be making Jake and the others understand that.

The worst part was, he knew in the end they might not have any choice except for Kate to talk to Jake. If

God forbid there was a leak in that office... No, he wouldn't think about that. He'd protect her whatever he had to do.

Chapter Nine

They finally left the worst of the traffic behind at the exit for Windswept. Kate straightened in her seat and fiddled with her seat belt.

"I hate to bring this up," she said, "but I really have to go shopping."

"Shopping?" Quinn pulled up to one of the few stop lights in town and looked at her.

"You know, like going to a store and buying things?" She almost giggled. "You should try it sometime."

"Very funny." He moved forward with the traffic. "So what kind of store do you need?"

"I've been traveling pretty light. I'm sure you know I don't have much with me, and there are some things I need. Clothing type things, toiletries, that kind of stuff." She fiddled with her seat belt again. "Is there a Wal-Mart in town?"

"That means you're staying for sure, right? Not trying to run off? Even after we talk?"

She sighed and swallowed the lump in her throat. "I'm through running, Quinn. For the first time in what feels like forever I feel safe. With you. And after…everything else that's happened, I really don't want to leave."

"I hope you still feel that way after you hear what I have to say," he said slowly. "Just remember, as long as you're with me, you'll be okay. Got it?"

"Got it. So about the shopping."

"All right, then. Wal-Mart, coming right up. I'm pretty short on groceries, too. This is a Super Wal-Mart so I can pick up some grub while you do your thing."

It seemed to Kate she needed everything. Her entire wardrobe at the moment consisted of what she could carry in her duffel. Everything else she'd had to leave behind. Not that she was looking for an entire array of clothing, but it would be nice to have some variety. And she discovered Wal-Mart even had some pretty sexy lingerie. She giggled as she tossed it into her basket, amazed that she could still laugh.

They met up at the checkout, then loaded all the sacks into the truck. Kate waited for Quinn to unlock the doors, but he startled her by pulling her into his arms right there in the parking lot and kissing her. It wasn't any little discreet peck on the cheeks, either. One hand molded to her head, and he pressed his tongue along the seam of her lips until she opened for him, then it swept inside.

His kiss made her weak-kneed and sped up her heartbeat. She pressed herself against him heedless of their surroundings, her breasts against the hard wall of his chest. When he fitted his groin into the notch between her thighs, his erection was completely discernible beneath the faded denim.

She was breathless when he released her, cheeks heated as she looked around and caught a few people staring at them. She was sure this was not the kind of thing Quinn usually did.

"I think people are staring." She glanced around, her cheeks hot.

"Let 'em watch." His voice was low and thick with hunger. "They probably think what a lucky bastard I am. Listen. I think we need to get something to eat so we don't have to worry about cooking tonight. How about I treat you to hot dogs and ice cream before we head home." His half-smile lifted a corner of his mouth. "I understand all little kids are crazy about it."

Quinn walked her over to a tiny restaurant with an outdoor patio. At the walk up window, he ordered them hot dogs fully loaded, which they ate sitting at one of the tables. Then he bought ice cream cones at a little stand two doors down. They sat on one of the sidewalk benches to eat them, people-watching. For a little while, Kate even managed to forget how and why she'd ended up here.

It didn't take long to unload their packages at home. Quinn showed her where to put everything in his closet and bathroom, then left her to it while he attended to the groceries. When she was finished, she wandered back into the kitchen. He was just opening two cold bottles of beer.

"Want to sit out on the porch and watch the sunset?" he asked.

"I thought you were going to tell me about your meeting."

"I am. Would you rather sit in here?"

She shrugged. "Outside is okay. No place will be good, so whatever."

When they were settled in the rocking chairs, Quinn's feet propped on the porch railing, Kate gripped her beer tightly and said, "Okay, let's have it. What did your friend tell you that's got you so uptight?"

"Not uptight, darlin'. Just very concerned. About

you." He took a large swallow of beer. "First I need to tell you more about Jake, so you know where he's coming from."

"All right." She forced herself to relax. How much worse could things be? "Tell me about Jake."

Don't panic until you have to.

He reached over with his free hand and enfolded one of hers, wrapping his fingers around it. "I met Jake Garza when I first graduated law school and we were wild-eyed young turks. We joined the federal prosecutor's office at the same time and were even on the staff. We became very close. Very good friends."

Kate nearly spilled her bear. "A federal prosecutor? Damn you, Quinn."

We pay them off everywhere...cops, prosecutors, even judges. Everyone's in our pocket. The vicious words rattled in her brain, and her heart was practically beating in her throat.

"Will you just simmer down a minute? Not every one of us is crooked, you know."

She tried to tug her hand from his tight grip, tried to get up from the chair and move away from him, but he held on tight. "What have you done?" She tried again to pull away from him. He wasn't letting go. "What on earth have you done to me? You went to a prosecutor. *A federal prosecutor.* I told you what Peter said."

"Kate—"

She was trembling all over. "You said you were going to see a friend. I had no idea...Damn it, I should have figured." She dropped back into her chair and smacked her forehead with a shaking hand. "Oh my God, Quinn. What have you done?"

"Shh, shh. Settle down, darlin'." He was out of his chair and kneeling in front of her, holding both of her hands and pressing his lips to them. "I told you we needed help with this, and I went to the best place to get it. These people aren't going to forget about you."

"Did you tell him…you know."

"About the flash drive? No. Not yet. I wanted us—you and me—to talk first."

"What if he knows…*them*, and he's on their payroll? What if he tells them about me?"

"Kate, listen to me."

"Jesus, Quinn, they want to kill me, and I don't even know why. This friend of yours could lead them right to me."

Quinn moved one hand to cup her chin, forcing her to look at him. "I told you this before. Jake Garza is the most honest person I know. He'd never accept a bribe from anyone. I swear to you on both our lives, there is no way he's on anyone's payroll except the U.S. government."

"You can't be sure about that," she protested.

"Yes. I can. I would never do anything to put your life in danger. Okay? Just listen to me. You have to know what you're facing. And you're right. These people have you targeted."

"Who are *these* people anyway? What kind of crimes are they into? How did my father get mixed up with them? And why did he bring Peter in as a partner?" She pulled her hands away and twisted them together. "I don't even know who the man was in Peter's office except for his name. Miguel."

"If you'll let me tell you, we can figure out what to do. Okay?"

"All right." A shudder racked her body. "I'll listen."

Quinn lifted her from her chair and settled back in his rocker, cuddling her on his lap. "Okay? Now just listen to me so you have a good idea of what you're facing."

"A-all right." She pressed herself into his body.

"I do want you to know I'm damn mad at Jake Garza for jumping the gun on this," he told her. "He promised me twenty-four hours. Although, if I were in his shoes, I'd probably do the same thing."

Her eyes widened. "What did he do?"

"Apparently, when he got back to his office, things were suddenly heating up again and the twenty-four hours deadline is off. And before you go jumping up again, no one actually knows you're here or anything else. He's kept that to himself. So let's get all this out in the open, and *then* you can scream and yell."

"What did you tell him?" The fear was ripe in her voice.

"I just asked questions, Kate. That was all. But asking him about Peter and the law firm, I unexpectedly tripped over something big they've got going. Jake's smart enough to follow the thread. Pretty much as we got into the conversation he figured things out. But I never confirmed anything."

"What did he tell you about Peter that's so awful? Much worse than him wanting to kill me? I can hear it in your voice. Please," she begged. "I have to know what he said.

"I'll tell you what I know," he soothed, "which at the moment isn't all that much. Let me just give you the bare bones. Which is pretty much all I have right now, anyway."

In a slow, calm voice Quinn laid out everything he'd learned from Jake, including what he'd added on the cell phone. "That's all I could get out of him. He really has to clear it with his boss to tell me anything else, and I didn't want to push the envelope." He reached for her hand again. "There's something else you need to know, but I don't want you to freak, okay?"

"Oh, God, what now?" Everything that Quinn told her made her sick with fear. She fisted her hands in an effort to stop her trembling.

What could possibly be worse?

"According to Jake, the Osuna cartel covers the entire Southern United States, with two major bases of operation. Tampa is only one of them. The other is here, in San Antonio."

Her skin was suddenly cold and clammy, her heart lodged in her throat. This couldn't be. It just couldn't be. She wet her lips with her tongue and tried to draw a steadying breath.

"You mean, all this running I've done, living on buses like some derelict, scared out of my mind, and I somehow end up in their back yard?" She felt the blood drain from her head and a wave of dizziness swept over her.

"Remember—" Quinn pressed his lips to her forehead "—the Osunas still have no idea where you are. And it's good to know the feds are already onto them and building a case."

"God, I think I'm going to be sick." She shook her head wildly, as if she could shake all the ugly information out of it. "Quinn, I just can't see my father or my uncle involved in something this illegal. This ugly."

"It's never easy to think people close to us can do something very bad, but you don't know the circumstances. That's something Jake might be able to explain to us."

"I know why Peter and his friends are after me now, but not why they wanted to kill me in the first place."

He shifted her on his lap. "Kate, there's something else we have to look at. Another reason why Jake doesn't think he can keep this to himself."

"What else could there possibly be?"

"The folks downtown have quite a file on everything to do with the Osunas and the law firm. And you're in it."

"Oh, God." She pressed her body to his, seeking his strength and his warmth.

"The feds don't think you're connected with the cartel," he assured her, "but they're wondering why the organization is conducting a manhunt for you out of all proportions to the situation."

"The flash drive," she whispered.

"Right on the mark. I know it's your insurance policy, but giving it to Jake could be our best move. They have people who can read it and decipher it."

"But we don't know who's on the Osuna payroll." She clutched at his shirt as if it was a lifeline. "Anyone in that office could be taking money from them.

We pay people off everywhere. Cops, prosecutors...

She believed it. These people were everywhere.

"I can guarantee you one thing. It's not Jake. He pretty much guessed you're the major part of the equation with me, but he didn't give it up to his boss. Or the Osunas, or else they'd be out here in full force."

She looked at him helplessly. "So now what happens?"

"You've probably got the one thing that could blow this cartel wide open. That could make the feds case for them. We have to do something with it. It won't help to keep hiding it in my safe forever."

"But I don't know who to trust," she blurted out. "Besides you, that is. What if…" She shook her head.

He stroked the side of her face, and Kate could tell he was being deliberately gentle. "You *do* trust me, don't you? No bullshit here, Kate."

She nodded. "Yes. I do." And that was no lie.

"I told Jake I'd call him back in the morning. I bought us at least that much time. I don't want him barging out here and taking control of the situation, which is always a possibility. Let's invite him out for dinner tomorrow night and tell him your story. He's doing his job, but he's also a reasonable man. And he won't want to put you at risk."

"As long as he doesn't think I'm part of this and throw me in jail."

"Not gonna happen. So is that okay? Will you talk to him? Let him help us?"

All she could do was nod her head. Yes. She wanted this nightmare over more than anything. But the knowledge of what she would be facing with Jake had the effect of pulling a plug. Tears pushed against her eyelids and cascaded down her cheeks. Every bit of strength she'd dredged up dissipated in a heartbeat, and she wound her arms around his neck, drenching his shirt with huge, unladylike sobs.

She cried until she thought she had no more tears, then cried again.

Quinn held her tightly, one hand caressing her back in a soothing motion, his voice soft as he murmured soothing sounds in her ear. When the worst of the storm had passed, he pulled out a handkerchief, mopped her face, and tucked her loose hair behind her ears.

When she raised her head at last, he looked down at her. "Better?"

"Yes." She sniffled, wiped her eyes on the handkerchief, and gave him a watery grin. "For the moment. I hope I don't start making a habit of this."

"Understandable after holding it in for so long. This is a scary situation for anyone, darlin'."

"You must think I'm the biggest mess in the world."

"I think you're a very brave, very gutsy lady who kept it together when most people would have given up."

Tilting her chin up, he kissed her, slow and sweet, a kiss meant to reassure, but their emotions were so high that it quickly turned hot and demanding. His hands slid under her T-shirt, cupping her breasts, massaging them through the thin material that supported them.

His erection pressed against the curve of her buttocks, insistent and demanding. Her panties were wet, and her nipples throbbed, aching for his mouth on them.

Quinn lifted his head, his eyes dark, his face flushed with passion. "Let's take this inside."

They tore at their clothes impatiently, flinging them haphazardly at the chair and tumbling onto the bed.

"I wanted to go slow this time," Quinn panted. "Seduce you. This morning I could barely control myself. But if I'm not inside you in the next five seconds, I might lose my mind."

"I'm ready," she whispered.

When he touched her heated center, the moisture gathered there told him she was right.

"I want you." Her voice was hoarse with passion. "Now. Please."

With no foreplay or delicate touches, Quinn positioned himself, and in one stroke seated his cock completely inside her. He remained motionless, catching his weight on his forearms and looking directly into her eyes.

"I never thought I'd have this again," he rasped. "I never thought I'd *allow* myself to have it. Funny, I knew Lisa a long time before we married, but in some ways, in just a few days, I feel a deeper connection to you. Am I crazy?"

"If you are, so am I. I feel it, too."

Then the time for talking was done. Quinn lifted her legs to his shoulder to give him a deeper angle of penetration and began the slow glide in and out of her slick, wet core. He rocked against her, hitting that sweet spot that made her catch her breath.

As aroused as they were, an orgasm rolled over them with speed and intensity that shook them both, every muscle in their bodies quivering as hips thrust and liquid heat bathed them both.

They lay there afterward joined together, hearts thudding against each other, hers racing just a bit faster.

"Kate?"

"Mmmhmm?"

He raised his head and kissed her with such tenderness she wanted to cry. "I'm glad I stopped on the road the other night."

She couldn't catch her breath to speak. It was new for her, this powerful linking. He had poured himself into her in a coupling as emotional as it was physical. Against all odds, at the very worst moment of her life, a man had walked into it and in the blink of an eye captured her heart.

Suddenly, she was able to think about the future.

Chapter Ten

"We're through waiting."

Less than four hours had passed and Miguel Osuna was once again in Peter's office, his ugly bodyguard in his usual position behind him. Miguel leaned back in his chair and pulled out a cigar, his thick fingers caressing it as if it were a woman's body. He never smoked them anymore, but holding them and stroking them seemed to give him enormous satisfaction.

"You were just here." Peter wanted to throttle the man, but he knew what that would cause. "You've barely had time to leave and come back. Don't you think I'd have called you if something showed up? Why don't you just stay in Sarasota and I'll keep you updated?"

"Because so far you haven't had anything to update us with. Perhaps you need more incentive. *El jefe* is getting very perturbed and impatient."

Peter's stomach knotted at the threat implied in the statement.

"She's dumb," Peter insisted. "I keep telling you that. And far from resourceful. She's just been lucky, is all."

Miguel's mouth twisted in a sly smile. "You know Esai, and I wonder, Pedro, if she's really missing at all."

"What do you mean?" He stared at the man. "Of

course she's missing. We saw her leave."

"Maybe you and she have a little plot going behind our backs. She pretends to steal the flash drive, you give her the codes, she empties the bank accounts, and the two of you fly off somewhere with the cartel funds."

Peter felt himself turn pale, and sweat beaded on his forehead. "Surely, no one really thinks that. It would be suicide on my part."

Osuna nodded. "More than that. You'd certainly never live to spend any of it. Neither of you would live long enough." He uncrossed his thick legs and leaned across the desk.

"That's ridiculous." Peter placed his hands flat on the desk to conceal their trembling. Screwing the cartel was a quick trip to hell. "You have nothing to fear on that count. I assure you."

"In any event, we're making some more changes. I've just finished a long telephone conversation with my brother, and we've made some decisions. That's why I'm here again today. To tell you in person."

"What decisions?" *Oh, God, now what?*

"It's time for you to get your ass out of the office. Take that magic computer of yours and start backtracking every place she's been. Spread some of that money around the way you're always bragging you do and see who talks. If money doesn't work, a little muscle might."

"But—"

"And check all the people already on our payroll. You have a copy of that list, right? In one of your *special* files?"

"Of course."

Another reason to get that flash drive back before anyone could crack the codes.

"Someone somewhere has gotten a hint of her. I feel it. Go back to the beginning. Do whatever it takes to get that information."

"You want me to leave here?" Peter stared at him. "And go where? And what about the law firm?"

"*Stupido.* Until we get that flash drive back, the law firm can't afford to operate as usual and put ourselves under possible scrutiny. We have to close the doors. Which makes the head of operations very unhappy."

"Close the firm?" Peter still couldn't get his mind around it. "What the hell for?"

"Aren't you listening to me? So we don't draw unwanted attention to ourselves. We can't do anything for fear we've somehow been compromised. Everything is at risk."

"But—"

"Call it a paid vacation for everyone and send them home. We'll have someone taking calls in case a stranger dials in by accident. Do it today. Then get on a plane for Los Angeles and start your hunt from there."

Peter had to swallow the urge to scream. "I'm not sure that's such a good idea."

"Esai is sending you a list of all our contacts from Texas to California," Miguel went on, as if Peter hadn't spoken at all. "Once you get to L.A., get with the locals on one of your special secure phones, have them meet you at the terminal and start asking questions. Find out what the hell is going on. Get me that *puta.*"

He stopped as he reached the door and turned around.

"Oh, and by the way. Since you don't seem to take *me* too seriously, from now on you'll be reporting to Esai. And *el jefe*. So don't make any mistakes." He pushed himself from the chair and nodded to his bodyguard. "I want that bitch. You hear me? That's your number one priority."

The door closed softly behind him.

****

Peter wondered if it wouldn't just be easier to cut his throat now and get it over with. He was getting sick of it the whole thing. Being yanked out of his comfortable position in Florida. Flying across the country on a wild goose chase. Having Esai Osuna calling him on his cell every half hour.

And whose stupid idea was it to start at the Los Angeles bus terminal and try to pick up leads? The woman was gone from there for four days. There wouldn't be a soul who even remembered her. The ticket clerks barely knew each other. Esai and Miguel thought there might still be a way to trace her there, a starting point, but they'd never set foot in this place filled with masses of teeming humanity.

For two men who ran a billion-dollar, complex drug cartel, they didn't seem to have a lot of brains.

But they really aren't the ones who run it. And that person isn't someone you want to argue with.

Not many people knew that the Osuna brothers weren't the real heads of the cartel. The true identity would shock a lot of people. And it wasn't a person Peter was eager to get on the bad side of.

Shit, shit, shit.

"Show her picture around," Esai said when Peter got hold of him, trying to point out the uselessness of the whole exercise. "The boss has ordered it. Then check all the buses that left within an hour of the time our idiots took the wrong female. See where they went. Call your contacts in those places. This is a direct order from the boss."

Trying to get a little ahead of things, he'd called everyone, all the people who sucked money out of the Osunas, anyone who might be able to tell him anything. Calculating how far or fast she might travel in a day, he'd hit their people in ten states. A fucking pain in the ass, he grumbled to himself. Complaining to anyone else did no good. They'd simply point out it was his mess he was cleaning up. Whatever, no one knew anything or no one was talking, an unhappy state of affairs either way.

So here he was, in the L.A. bus terminal with two more idiots that Esai had sent to help him, on an impossible task.

He bought a cold drink from a vending machine and rolled the icy can across his forehead, trying to stave off the familiar headache. So far they'd wasted two hours here, no one knew anything, and he was sure he'd caught at least ten different diseases from the people gathered in the big waiting area. Rubbing elbows with the great unwashed wasn't his idea of the best way to spend an afternoon.

And then, against all odds, they caught a slight break.

"Pedro?" Diego Salazar moved up beside him. Thin and swarthy, he had the ability to blend in anyplace and possessed a skill with a knife second to none. Too bad he couldn't think.

"Find out anything?" Peter asked.

He pointed to the man with him. "Mickey did."

Mickey Salado was Salazar's physical opposite, big and with his mother's fair coloring. And an intimidating presence that loosened a lot of tongues.

"I finally got a ticket clerk to admit he thinks he remembers her. Maybe. He thought. Said he only noticed her because she was acting so weird."

"Weird how?"

"Nervous," Mickey explained. "Edgy."

"Maybe?" Peter let his sarcasm show. He hated working with these men. "He *thought*?"

"It's more than we had before," Diego pointed out. "At least we know she was definitely here."

"*Maybe,*" Peter repeated. "And we already figured that since she cashed the second check at the bank across the street. Just like in North Carolina. It still tells us nothing. For all we know she flushed herself down the toilet."

"But—"

"Never mind. Anything else?"

Mickey looked at the tiny notebook in his big hand. "Four busses left about the time the men took the wrong woman that day," he reported. "Albuquerque, Denver, Seattle and Jackson Hole."

Peter pressed the can harder against his throbbing head. How to decide which bus the bitch had taken? This was a fool's errand, and he'd tried to tell Esai.

"What if she's not taking buses anymore?" Diego suggested.

Peter's eyes popped open. "What do you mean?"

"I mean, what if two close calls at bus stations were enough for her. You said she got all that cash. Maybe she bought a car with some of that money she pulled out of her account."

Peter was about to curse him for the idiocy of his idea when he realized the man might actually be onto something. Kathryn might be dumb, but she wasn't entirely stupid. If she'd figured out buses no longer gave her the anonymity she wanted, she might make other choices.

"Okay. She wouldn't buy from a regular dealership," he mused, trying to make his aching head function. "Too much paperwork and she might not have the ID they'd require. Also, she'd probably be stingy with her money. So, a junk shop. And one pretty close to here." He closed his eyes for a moment, then opened them and gestured toward Mickey. "Get the car and bring it around to the front. We'll start a canvass in a tight circle. This isn't the best neighborhood in the world. There have to be plenty of used car places who don't care about anything but cash."

And please let us find it soon. I want a motel room, a thick steak, and a bottle of bourbon. And maybe not even in that order.

Traffic was heavy, as it always was in L.A., and the constant stop and start and honking of horns did little to soothe Peter's nerves. Nor did the fact his cell rang five minutes after they got into the car. When he saw the number, he cursed under his breath.

"Yes, Esai." *Can't the asshole leave me alone for an hour?*

"So. Any results?"

"We're working on it. We have an idea." He looked at the two men with him. "Actually, it was Diego's."

He explained to Esai what they were doing and

waited through a long silence.

"Not bad," the man said at last. "Call Nobo and have him pick up the bus station canvass. You keep on this track. You may just be onto something."

Please, Lord, let it happen.

"Fine. I'll call him right now." His disconnected the call before Esai could spew forth any other orders. The call to Nobo Ortega was brief and unpleasant. The man thought the bus station idea just as stupid as Peter did, but he also liked breathing through his nose instead of a slit in his throat.

"All right. I'll get my people, and we'll check those locations. Also up and down the line to each location." He sighed. "What a fucking pain in the ass. By the time we find this bitch we'll be fighting over who gets to have at her first."

An hour later Peter was sure L.A. had more cheap car lots than any place else on the planet, and none of them would give him the information he was looking for.

And then they stopped at Highway Harry's.

Harry took a tad bit of convincing, but like Miguel had said, a little muscle or a little money and you got results. Peter left there with the license number of the car Harry had sold to a woman on the day they mentioned, a woman who "looks something like that. But she used a different name."

Which eventually he was only too happy to provide them with.

"I need to go back to the motel," he told Mickey, who was driving. "I need a wireless connection so I can boot up my laptop."

Get ready, Kathryn. I'm coming after you.

Chapter Eleven

Kate woke slowly, her body in the softness of a languorous feeling, Quinn wrapped around her like a cocoon. She had no idea how much time had passed since she and Quinn had gone at each other like sex-starved teenagers. She only knew she had never felt so sexually satisfied or worshiped in her life.

"I wore you out." She could hear the smile in Quinn's deep voice.

"You can wear me out any time." She nestled closer to him.

"Keep doing that, and you'll be in trouble again," he warned.

"That's the kind of trouble I like."

His big hand cupped her breast, tweaking the nipple, while he nipped lightly at her ear. Just like that her body responded, and she wanted him again. He teased the nipple, tugging lightly then pinching it, each movement of his fingers sending heat directly to her core. She squeezed her legs together, trying to control the throbbing in her already wet sex, the pulsing in her inner walls.

His cock thickened and hardened against the cheeks of her ass, the feel of it arousing her even more. A soft moan drifted from her mouth as he drifted the flat of his hand over her belly, pausing to trace the swirl of her navel. Then he covered her mound, his palm resting on the rounded flesh as his middle finger slipped between her labia and stroked through the slickness.

"I love how wet you get for me," he murmured. "How hot you are. How responsive."

Kate tried to tighten her thighs around his hand. "More," she whispered. "Please."

"Like this?" He pressed his finger against her clit, brushing the pad of it back and forth.

Instant heat streaked through her, ramping up her need. When she opened her legs to give him better access, he lifted the top one and pulled it over his thigh, exposing her completely to his touch.

He tweaked her clit, tugged on the sensitive nub, stroked then pinched it again. Each movement of his finger sent another jolt of electricity through her.

"Feel good?" His mouth was at her ear, his hot breath fanning her skin.

"Yes." She could barely answer him as aroused as she was. Her entire focus was centered between her legs, on her slick channel just waiting for him. She wanted him inside her, his cock filling every inch. She tried to urge him with her body.

His laugh was low and rough.

"In a hurry, darlin'? We have plenty of time."

"Tease." She puffed the word out on a breath.

"Absolutely."

Then he stopped talking and concentrated on what he was doing. He slid one thigh between hers, keeping her leg upper leg on his hip, and thrust two fingers deep inside her. With the pad of his thumb on her clit, he moved his fingers in and out in a slow, steady rhythm that had every pulse in her body beating in response. He kept up a steady rhythm, his strokes never slowing, and all the while, he murmured in her ear the incredibly erotic things he wanted to do to her. With her.

Kate had never experienced anything like this in her life. What she'd thought was sex wasn't even in the same ball park as this. Quinn held her firm, pinning her in place as his fingers glided in and out and his thumb played a wicked dance on her clit. He eased a third finger into her and with one stroke triggered a climax. She shook with the spasms, her sex clutching his fingers again and again.

"That's it, darlin'. Just like that. Let it happen, I've got you. Love feeling that sweet little pussy. That's it."

When the spasms died, he eased his fingers from her. "Look at me, Kate."

She looked over her shoulder, and he raised his hand to his mouth and carefully licked each finger clean of her juices. It was one of the most erotic things she had ever seen.

Sliding his leg from between hers, he eased her onto her back and rolled on top of her, cradling her head between his palms. Heat flared in his dark eyes with a hunger she was sure reflected in her own.

"Incredible," he murmured.

It certainly was.

He kissed her, tasting her lips with the tip of his tongue, probing her mouth with kisses that stole her breath, his tongue wild, tasting everywhere. Their tongues met in a choreographed ballet.

He drew back and nibbled on her lips before lowering his head to take one of her nipples into his mouth. The pull and suction ignited the flame inside her again, fanned by the scraping of his teeth against the sensitive bud. He moved from one breast to the other, one nipple to the other until the tips were so sensitive she was sure she'd come from just one more touch.

He shifted slightly and traced a line between her breasts with the tip of his tongue. He took a moment to swirl the indentation of her navel before moving down to the top of her slit. Opening her labia, he licked the sensitive flesh up and down and then up again, then tugged on her clit with his teeth.

And just like that she was ready for him again.

"Please," she begged. "Oh, please."

"Right now."

Rising to his knees, Quinn lifted her legs and placed them on his shoulders. Positioning his cock at her opening, he eased himself inside her with a slow, steady stroke. Her inner walls clenched around him, adding to the erotic thrust and scrape of his erection.

"Look at me, Kate." His voice was thick with need.

When she did, she was sure she could see into his soul and he could see into hers. It was an incredibly emotional moment in a maelstrom of emotions.

Quinn pulled her to him with his big hands, stroking her back, the swell of her hips. He coasted his hands beneath her buttocks to stroke the cleft between her buttocks, the tip of one finger pressing against the opening there.

He began the slow rhythmic slide of his cock in and out with measured strokes, the angle of her body allowing him deep penetration. In and out, back and forth. Thrust, retreat, drive. The slow glide and drag of his swollen shaft drove her up to that peak of arousal.

Kate locked her ankles behind his neck to pull her into him even more tightly. He held her at the edge, not giving her the release she sought while she silently pleaded with her eyes and her body.

Please, please, please.

Ready to explode himself, he increased the pace until he thrust hard into her one last time. They climaxed together, bodies shaking and clenching as they fell into a pool of intense, erotic sensation.

Finally the spasms slowed, the shudders abated, and their breathing returned to something close to normal. In the aftermath, she felt a joyfulness in their coupling she'd never experienced before in her life. She felt him not just in her body but her heart. She felt as if she were home.

Quinn eased her legs down slowly and slid from her body. Propping himself on one elbow and caressed her face with the tips of his fingers, tracing the line of her jaw, her eyelids, the shape of her lips.

"You are…incredible."

She smiled. "I can say the same."

They lay in comfortable silence, neither finding the need to speak, for a long time. Finally, Kate spoke.

"Quinn?" Was this the right time to ask him?

"What is it, darlin'?"

"You said you've been alone for four years. That you hadn't been with a woman for a long time. You know everything about me now. Can you tell me what happened to you?"

"I never talk about it with anyone." His voice was sharp with pain.

She cuddled against his hard body, her hand resting on his chest. "Aren't you the one who told me that some things are better if you share them?"

"Throwing my own words back at me?" His fingers drifted up and down her arm.

"Absolutely."

Silence covered them like a suffocating blanket, but Kate made herself wait. When he spoke it was in a low voice she almost didn't recognize.

"Four years ago my wife and child were murdered."

Shock ran through her like a bolt of electricity. Whatever she'd expected, that wasn't it.

"Oh, god." She couldn't figure out what to say. "I'm sorry. I never would have asked if I'd known. I'm so, so sorry."

His body was so rigid it almost vibrated. "It's okay. I haven't talked about it in so long it might actually do me some good."

"If it's too painful for you…God, am I stupid. Of course it's painful for you."

"I can do this, Kate. Just stay curled up against me like this and listen, okay?"

"All right." She sifted her fingers through the curls of hair on his chest, rubbing them lightly over the sweat-slickened skin.

When he spoke again, the voice might have belonged to a stranger. "Four years ago, I had a great job, a wonderful wife I loved more than life and an amazing two-year-old daughter. My folks were retiring and getting ready to enjoy the rest of their life." He paused, and his swallow was audible. "Then, in an instant, it was wiped out. Gone."

"What do you mean gone?"

Quinn tightened his hand on her arm. "Like I told you earlier, I was a federal prosecutor in San Antonio, part of the South Texas district. I had just finished the trial of some real badass scumbags. They made millions smuggling people and drugs across the border. A very rough group. Killing meant nothing to them."

Kate stroked her hand over his chest in circles, feeling the heavy thudding of his heart beneath her touch, the tension in his body. "Go on," she urged.

"It was a long trial, but we got the convictions and stiff sentences we wanted. Then I heard from my sources that the guys I convicted put out a contract on me. I foolishly ignored what they said because those kinds of people make threats all the time. I was just so glad to see them locked away and be done with the whole case."

He tightened his arm around her almost reflexively. "I was in the mood to celebrate once the sentences were handed down. I called my wife, Lisa, and told her to bring our daughter Nicole and meet me in front of the courthouse at noon. We were standing there on the sidewalk, chatting with some of the other attorneys in the office, when a car came by, slowed down, and someone began firing."

"Oh my god." Kate could imagine the horror of the scene. She wanted to tell Quinn to stop, to leave it alone, but she had a feeling that once he'd started he needed to get it all out.

"It happened so fast," he went on. "No one could react in time. I was only wounded in the arm, but Lisa and Nikki were killed instantly. God, there was so much blood. So much blood. And there was nothing anyone could do for them."

Kate just kept moving her hand in slow circles on his chest and pressing her body against him, not knowing what else to do.

"Well," he continued, "I was hell bent on

vengeance. I shifted my case load to other prosecutors and spent all my time looking not only for the shooters but also for who gave the order. And I was close." He paused for a heartbeat. "Too close for them, I guess."

"Something else happened?" Kate knew even as she asked that one more horrendous fact was going to come to light.

"It seems they weren't finished sending me messages. My parents were driving home from Austin on the back roads one night in the rain. Someone ran them off the road and over an incline, then shot out the gas tank. It exploded. A passing car saw it happen, but there was nothing they could do to help. And the shooter's car took off too fast to even get a license number."

He finally turned toward her again. In the fading light slanting in through the windows, she saw the stark lines of his face, like a stone mask, but his voice held so much heartbreak that Kate could hardly bear to listen to any more.

"Oh, god, Quinn."

"Anyway, there I was. I had nothing left to lose, did I? I was determined to get those bastards, so I sold my house, quit my job, and spent every waking minute digging in the sewers finding them. And finally, I did." He raised his other arm and covered his eyes with it, shutting out images best forgotten. "Finally, I did."

"You found all these people and brought them in?"

"In a manner of speaking."

"I don't understand."

"I delivered them all to the prosecutor's office in San Antonio. The living and the dead."

The tone of his voice, like cold death, let Kate

know that was the end of it. All that he could dredge up and spit out.

"No wonder you hide away up here, shutting everything else out. So…you don't work anymore?"

"Everyone in our family believed in lots of insurance." He gave a short, bitter laugh. "My parents had listed me as the beneficiary on their policies. And Lisa and I had large policies on each other. If anything happened to one of us, the other would be able to provide for Nikki. Well, that didn't exactly work out, did it? So I took all the money and invested it. Maybe I'd be better off if I did have to work. Less time to think about things."

"Did you ever think about going back to your job?" She held her breath waiting for his answer.

Please, no.

"I lost my taste for it. For everything. These days, I'm more comfortable being by myself up here in the hills. People around here know me, and they respect me enough not to intrude."

"Oh, Quinn."

"So," he said, cutting off further questions, "now you know it all."

She wet her lips with the tip of her tongue, her mouth feeling dry as dust. In that moment, she thought being dead was not nearly as bad as being the one who survived. "I can't begin to imagine the pain you still feel," she said at last. "But I know that resolving the situation was the right thing to do."

He lifted one of her hands and played with the fingers. "So here we are, you and I, each dragging our baggage with us. I know this sounds weird, but something pulled me over to the side of the road. Made me stop. Made me feel…connected to you." He leaned over and kissed her, then fell back again. "I never believed in Fate before this, but I don't know what else to call it."

"I feel it, too. Don't you see? As if we're too halves of the same whole suddenly fitting together. How weird is that?"

"You've made me feel alive again, darlin'." He smoothed her hair back from her forehead, watching her, still trying to absorb the speed with which it had all happened. "I want you. I need you. I don't know what I have left to give to anyone anymore, but whatever there is, I want to give it to you."

"Then that's the answer. Whatever happens, happens. No more second guessing. I'll take whatever you can give me." She climbed on top of him, pressing full length against his hard nakedness, and kissed him until they were both breathless.

They slept little that night, unable to get enough of each other, feasting, reveling, touching everywhere. The discovery and acceptance of their feelings was high octane fuel that stoked their need.

Quinn explored every inch of her body, learning how to make her respond in ways she didn't know she could. She in turn aroused him with her hands, her tongue, her lips. She loved the sounds he made when she took him into her mouth, his groans as the tension built in his body.

It was raw, impassioned sex, earthy and unrestrained. He took her every way possible, prolonging her orgasms, watching with those glittering eyes as she shuddered in a blazing, earth-shattering response. Yet no matter how many times they made love, their hunger refused to be sated. A door had been opened, and they couldn't rush through it fast enough.

By morning they were finally spent.

Kate felt ravaged. She was sure walking would be a problem, but she didn't care. They had not just made love, they had mated, each to the other. She was his, and he would take care of her. She closed her eyes, secure in the circle of his arms. Physically and emotionally drained, she was asleep in seconds.

****

Quinn watched her lying next to him, her body replete, her breath a soft whisper. This powerful connection forged between them was full of promise. She had touched his soul, this scared, desperate woman, and he had poured himself into her.

Kate.

His heart was so full he thought it would burst. Kate had shown him how to love again. Now Lisa and Nikki might finally rest in peace, and that came with the redemption of his soul. At last, he might be able to live with himself. To find peace. Again, he felt Lisa's approving presence, and tears gathered behind his eyelids.

He'd failed last time when he should have been alert. This time would be different. He knew it. This time he'd be prepared.

At sunrise, he finally fell asleep. For the first time in four years, he could close his eyes without pain searing his heart and the bloody after-image of Lisa and Nikki, lying dead at his feet, burned onto his eyes. Unexpected peace stole over him.

He felt whole again.

Chapter Twelve

Quinn was in his kitchen making coffee, putting off the call to Jake as long as possible. His cell was on vibrate so as not to wake Kate. He swallowed a smile as he thought of all the reasons she was sleeping so late. When the phone buzzed against his hip, he grabbed it and flipped it open.

Shit!

"Quinn?" Jake's voice thundered across the connection.

"Yup. Right here."

"I thought you were going to call me this morning."

"Sorry, *compadre*. My fault. Time just got away from me."

"Any other time I'd be overjoyed. Are you alone?"

Quinn frowned. "Why? Do I have to be?"

"You might want to have this conversation in private."

"Listen, Jake. What's going on? I talked to...the person you're interested in last night, and she's willing to meet with you. But just you." He quietly let himself out onto the front porch and settled on the bench at the far end. "Even though you shot your mouth off yesterday when I asked you not to. So what's up?"

"Please try to understand this isn't just any old case here, okay?" Jake's voice held a pleading note.

"There's a hell of a lot at stake."

Quinn's grip on the phone tightened. "No kidding. Tell me something I don't know."

Silence hummed along the connection, then Jake cleared his throat. "I have someone here who wants to talk to you."

Quinn felt anger rise within him, tinged with the edge of fear for Kate. *Thanks, Jake.*

"Long time, Quinn." Dean Morgan's deep voice resonated across the connection. "And Jake really didn't have much choice in this. He knew what he had to do."

"Hello, Dean." *God damn it.* Quinn's body tensed. "What can I do for you today?"

"Jake tells me you might have someone staying at your place that we'd all like to talk to." He paused. "A woman every gun in the Osuna cartel is hunting."

"Jake has a very active imagination."

"If he's right, I want to know how you met her and where she is right at this moment."

"You don't want much, do you?" Kate would freak out six different ways if she knew anyone but Jake had this information. Damn, damn, damn.

"Don't play games here, Quinn. You can't just waltz into town out of nowhere after four years, ask about a case the whole DOJ is focused on and not expect people to react. You have no idea what's at stake."

"Is that a fact?" Now the anger was surging through him and his good intentions were rapidly disappearing. "It seems to me I might know better than anyone else on your staff what's at stake in situations like this."

Silence hummed across the air. "I'm sorry. You're right, of course. Forgive my insensitivity. But you're going to have to bring the Burke woman into this office."

"Damn it, Dean. That woman's life is at stake."

"No one knows that more than we do. But you can't just keep her hidden up there in the hills, Quinn. You need to bring her in."

"Like hell," Quinn exploded. "The office didn't do a very good job of keeping Lisa and Nikki safe, and they were only bystanders."

"Be reasonable." Dean kept his voice steady and calm. "We had no way of anticipating what happened."

"You should have and *I* should have. We didn't, so this time I'm taking precautions. Besides, what makes you think she can tell you anything?"

"She can at least give us an idea why the hell the whole Osuna cartel is looking for her."

Oh, that she can.

"If she does know, maybe she's not too anxious to put herself out there at risk."

Dean was silent for a moment. "Surely, she can at least tell us what she knows about Peter Fleming. Besides, if the Osunas want her this badly, I want her, too. And before they find her."

Frustration raged through Quinn knowing Dean wasn't going to be put off for very long.

"Listen," his ex-boss went on. "I know Jake told you this is a very volatile, high profile case. We've been banging our heads against stone walls ever since the DEA agent bought it, and we aren't getting anything except a headache. We *need* something, Quinn. I shouldn't have to tell you how that goes."

"Okay, okay, I get your point. Do you get mine?" He swallowed some coffee, now turning cold. "She's scared out of her mind, and she doesn't trust anyone. I came to Jake for information only because I needed to find out exactly who was after her that had her so badly frightened. That's it. He ran to you with his speculations, which doesn't sit too well with me. I could easily put her someplace where you'll never find her. And you know I can do it."

"Kane Barton will fry your ass if he finds out and gets hold of you," Dean told him.

Kane was the senior U.S. Attorney for the district and everyone's boss in the division.

"Then I'll have to make sure that doesn't happen. And you might point out to him my ass isn't his to fry anymore."

The silence thrumming across the connection was like a living thing.

"All right." Dean broke the stalemate. "I don't like this, but I guess I don't have much choice, short of storming your house. What do you suggest? What's your offer?"

"I already told Jake I'd call him this morning. He just jumped the gun. Here's what we'll do. Let Jake come out here and talk to her. She's very skittish and with good reason. Then, if we have to, we can work into a meeting with you and Kane. But Jake first. Alone."

The heavy sigh was audible. "All right. I'm willing to cut you a break here. But only for a limited time. Let Jake come out and talk to her. Then we'll see."

"Put Jake back on the phone."

"Yo." Jake's voice rumbled across the connection.

"Dinner at seven tonight. Don't be late. And I run the meeting."

Quinn broke the connection and slid his cell phone into his pocket. Professionally and intellectually he knew Dean was right. Kate was the first person in a direct link with the Osunas available to them. And of course, there was that flash drive, which belonged in the hands of the Justice Department.

Personally he wanted to keep her as far from the action as he could. Away from any situation where her presence could be compromised, even though he knew to protect her she had to tell what she knew. Had to help bring down the cartel or they'd never stop hunting her. He'd told her he'd keep her safe, and he didn't want to break that promise.

Damn, damn, damn.

****

When Kate opened her eyes the next morning, she was pleasantly sore and very well satisfied. Even though a fresh challenge awaited her, she felt stronger, more able to face it. Because of Quinn.

She smiled to herself. Time was now divided into two segments—before Quinn and after Quinn. She'd lived a lifetime with him in a very small amount of time.

The nights were incredible. Making slow delicious love followed by blissful sleep, surrounded by Quinn's body, safe in his arms.

Yawning, she stretched and pushed out of bed. Finding his shirt on the chair next to the bed, she held it to her face for a moment, inhaling the now familiar scent that was purely Quinn, a woodsy male scent that sent warmth flooding through her.

Then reality slapped her, and she remembered that this morning he'd be calling Jake again, and neither of them knew what would happen after that. With a weighted sigh, she slipped the shirt on and went in search of the man himself.

The kitchen was empty when she walked into it, but the aroma of fresh coffee teased at her nostrils. Through the tall windows she could see Quinn on the porch, pacing, cell phone glued to his ear.

She hoped he was right, that his friend, Jake, could help her find a way for this all to be over. Then maybe her life could get back to something approaching normal.

Normal. That was a laugh. She wasn't even sure she knew what normal was any more. She was just reaching for a mug when Quinn let himself back in, a grim look on his face. Her stomach lurched.

Oh, God, now what?

****

Kate was standing in the kitchen wearing one of his shirts when Quinn walked back into the house. The sight of her made him hard as a rock. She looked so damned sexy, stretching to reach a mug, the shirt riding up on those wonderful legs, the fabric sliding off one shoulder. He had to restrain himself from grabbing her and hauling her to the bedroom.

Maybe afterwards. After he told her dinner was on.

He was still astounded by his need for her. It had grown until it clawed at him and filled every corner of his body and soul. Somehow, she had the key to unlock the part of him he'd kept locked up behind bars for four very long years. He guessed there was a lot to be said for chemistry, but it was more than that. She was one with him now, and he knew he'd never be the same again.

Nor did he want to be.

When he closed the door, she turned and her smile went straight through to the core of his soul. Okay. He would get them past this nightmare. Then they could look at building a future together. A future that, two days ago, he would have sworn didn't matter or even exist.

He wanted to smile back at her, but the conversation with Jake was too fresh in his mind. He knew what was coming, and he had to prepare her for it. Dinner might wear a friendly face, but with a case as hot as the one against the Osunas, Jake would only cut them so much slack.

Kate caught the look on Quinn's face, then poured her coffee with hands that shook slightly. He came up behind her, his sudden touch almost causing her to slosh her coffee. She turned in his arms and searched his eyes, trying to read him, but he'd lived with a closed expression for so long...

"Refill?" She held out the pot, nodding at the empty mug on the counter.

He nodded. "Then we'll sit down and talk about what Jake had to say."

They sat at the bar, her shaking hands wrapped firmly around the coffee mug. She took a slow sip, then set the mug back down. Her stomach was turning somersaults, and a cold feeling crept up her spine.

"Just spit it out," she burst out. "Whatever it is can't be worse than sitting here making myself sick with worry. I assume that was Jake you were talking to on the phone. He wants to do something you're against, right?"

"Right. He called me before I could get back to him."

"Did you tell him about dinner? What did he say?"

He took her hands in his, closing his fingers around them. "I told you last night I was sure Jake had talked to Dean Morgan, my former boss, about this."

She nodded. "And?"

"He put Dean on the phone. Kate, this thing is so much bigger than either you or I realize."

Her face turned so pale Quinn was afraid she might faint. He held the coffee mug up to her lips.

"Drink. It's okay. No one's coming out here to drag you away."

"Are you sure?" Her heart was racing.

"Positive. I made a deal with him. I told him we'd let Jake come out here and talk to you and assess your situation and take it from there. I didn't say a word about the flash drive. That's our ace in the hole, to help us call the shots."

She started to protest, but he held a finger to her lips. "It's the best thing we can do, Kate. We talked about this, remember? He needs to hear what you have to say, and then you have to give him that flash drive. They'll open it, get their information and move forward with their case. Keep in mind, as long as you have it, you'll still be a target for the cartel."

"I'm not giving that drive to just anyone, Quinn."

We pay people everywhere. Cops, prosecutors...

She couldn't get the words out of her brain. Fear of the drive falling into the wrong hands and leading back to her consumed her.

"And that's why you're going to give it to Jake,"

he reminded her. "Because we can trust him. I swear it on my life."

"I'm sorry." She bit her lip. Trust, even with Quinn, was hard for her to give. "I know I'm just being paranoid because of what Peter said."

He sighed. "All right. I can talk until I'm blue in the face, so let's do this. Tonight you can meet Jake and judge for yourself. Fair enough? But keep in mind that stopping the cartel is the only way to keep you alive. And that flash drive is the key."

"I guess that's okay." *No, it's not,* she wanted to scream, but they didn't have too many choices here. If only her father hadn't been caught in a trap. If only Peter hadn't walked into his office. If only…

Quinn brushed his knuckles along her cheek, a light caress. "Remember, I'm with you all the way here."

He pulled her against his body and took her mouth in a kiss that began as a gentle caress then took on a life of its own. He pressed his lips hard against hers, holding her face between warm hands. She grabbed his wrists but in a moment relaxed, and he lifted his head.

Kate tried to put everything she was feeling into that kiss, but then, like a dash of cold water, something struck her and she pulled back. "Wait, wait, wait. What about Jake's boss? And his boss? They know about me now, so who else does? Are they trustworthy? How do I know they aren't…"

Quinn cupped her chin, holding her head steady, his gaze locking with hers.

"They were also my bosses until I quit the office four years ago," he told her in a calm voice. "I trusted them, and you have my word that you can, too."

Desiree Holt

"I have to believe in you," she said, almost in desperation. "You're all I have."

"I won't let you down. That's a promise." He slid off his stool, taking her with him and leaning down for another kiss.

Kate knew he meant it to be tender and reassuring, just the briefest of contacts, but as soon as his mouth touched hers, she opened for him, hungry for more than the light contact.

Gripped by a desperate need to crawl into him where it was safe and warm and secure, she tasted him greedily. She shuddered as his tongue, now provoked, dueled with hers, and just like that, fire erupted between them. She was drowning, a whirlpool of sensation closing over her, drawing her deeper, pulling her in.

Lifting her in his arms, he carried her into the bedroom. In seconds he had them both stripped naked. Covering her with his body, he plunged them into a mating so ravenous, so savage, it left them breathless.

It was a long time before they thought about anything else.

****

They were lying naked on his bed, the ceiling fan cooling their sweat-slicked bodies, neither of them anxious to move.

Kate threw an arm over his chest, leaning her head against the hard wall of muscle, rubbing her cheek against the soft fur of his curls. "I'm so sorry about your family, Quinn. I can't imagine the pain you've had to live with."

His fingers trailed idly up and down her arm. "I think maybe some mystic force was ready to give me a swift kick in the ass and put you out on the highway for

154

me to find. I never thought it possible, but when I hold you, the pain isn't nearly as bad."

"Too bad I had to come with such a truckload of trouble. I don't want you to get hurt because of me."

"I'm a big boy, Kate. I could walk away at any time. But I'm not. I'm here for the long haul, so hang onto that thought, okay?" He rubbed his lips over hers, his tongue just barely probing.

"Okay." The panic was still hiding deep inside, waiting to be released again, but she was sure deep in her bones there wasn't anything Quinn couldn't handle.

"Tonight, you'll tell your story to Jake," he reminded her. "Everything. Including the flash drive. He'll help us figure out what to do next to get you out of the cartel's line of fire."

"What time did you tell him to be here?"

"About seven. Meanwhile, there's something I want to do. A little extra precaution I want to take."

"Precaution?"

"Uh huh. Now that I know exactly what kind of people are hunting you, I want you to be able to protect yourself. Just in case. So we're going to buy you a gun and do a little target practice."

"A gun?" Her voice squeaked. She'd never held a gun in her life.

"Yes. So let's get dressed and get moving

Chapter Thirteen

Peter adjusted himself on his motel bed, pillows against his back, computer on his lap, and cell head set in place. He'd just come back from dinner, booted up his laptop and finally, finally had something to report. The messages in his tracking folder gave him the first hope he'd had since that godawful night. And eased slightly the headache that had been pounding at him for days.

He speed-dialed an all too familiar number, then put the phone on speaker so he could work while he talked. The call was picked up after only one ring.

"Esai?"

"Well, well. Pedro. Is that a positive note I hear in your voice? How nice for a change."

Esai Osuna's voice always grated on Peter's nerves. And he hated it when he and Miguel called him Pedro. That was a part of his life he'd long ago buried and had no wish to resurrect, regardless of circumstances.

"Isn't it, though." *Hold the sarcasm. He has no sense of humor.*

"Have you found the car?"

"No, not yet. But it's just a matter of time. We have eyes on every kind of road in five states. We're covered no matter which way she went. Besides, it's only been a few days. She can't have gotten far. But—"

"Dios! Are you crazy? She could be anywhere."

"Not in the junker she bought," Peter told him.

"How many men does it take for a simple job?" Esai demanded. "Do we not have enough cops on our payroll in enough states to make sure she doesn't slip through?"

Peter was clicking keys on the keyboard. "That may not matter. I've found something else."

"What do you mean, not matter? Exactly what is going on? Answers. I want answers. Right now."

Peter ground his teeth. He *had* to get out of this whole situation. Somehow. But not before he killed these two arrogant assholes. Slowly and painfully.

"Remember those web sites I set up that you and Miguel blew off as a waste of time? Sites that would bounce back to me and identify anyone who logged onto them?"

"Yes, yes, yes." Esai's impatience bounced through the connection.

"You both were so sure that nobody who mattered would be stupid enough to Google us, right?" Peter was working hard to keep the smugness from his voice. But didn't he deserve at least one Gotcha?

There was a short pause. "Are you telling me you actually got results from them? Can you tell from where?"

"Yes. Despite a surprisingly sophisticated attempt to camouflage the source, I tracked it back. You'll never believe to where?"

"Spit it out."

"The library in San Antonio."

"Here?" The man couldn't hide his surprise and excitement. "In my town? So good fortune is smiling on us for a change."

"I'd say it's at least patting us on the head."

"But can you be sure it's her? We don't need any more false starts here, Pedro."

Damn you, Esai.

"I think it's an unbelievable coincidence that Kathryn has ended up in San Antonio."

"If indeed it's her." Esai's voice was cautious.

"But who else would suddenly decide to search for information on me and the law firm?" Peter protested. "The feds certainly don't use public computers, and no one else has a reason to be interested."

"We'd better hope so," the man warned.

"I'd say she's stopped running, at least for a while. She obviously feels pretty confident she won't be found out for her to risk something like this."

"Do you think she'll stay put? She's been a step ahead of us every time we've had a lead. Why won't she take off now?"

"It's a chance we have to take. This is the closest we've come to her since our...miscalculations." And God, how he hated remembering those. "You should have someone check it out."

"If she's in the area, finding her car should be that much easier. I'll put men on it right away, looking for the car and anyone who resembles the bitch. And you had better get yourself on the next plane here."

"Me?" Peter sat up straighter, pain shooting through his head. "Come to San Antonio? What the hell for?"

"Listen to me, Peter." Esai's voice was deceptively soft. And calling him Peter rather than Pedro was not a good sign. "This is your mess. You need to be here to clean it up. And I'll be watching while you do it. Send Mickey home and have Diego come back here with you. Let me know your flight details, and I'll send a car for you."

Peter felt a trickle of sweat work its way down his spine. He'd hoped to see the last of Esai's pet. Diego Salazar was a stone cold killer. The two men had been together since they were teenagers in Mexico, scrabbling out any kind of living they could. When the cartel was established, Esai had made a place for him and Salazar was fiercely loyal to him. Peter knew that Miguel would get rid of the man in a heartbeat, but he had a cold-blooded, vicious streak that made him valuable in his own way.

"I don't think we need to involve him in this just yet," Peter protested. "He can—"

"He can get on the plane with you and make sure you get where you're supposed to be going." The threat was boldly implied. *Don't think of running, or else.*

"Listen," he began again.

But he was listening to a dead line. He disconnected the call.

Shit, shit, shit.

How much worse could things get?

When his phone rang fifteen minutes later, Peter had just finished confirming the plane reservations, telling Salazar to get a move on and packing his stuff. He looked at the number on the Caller ID and his stomach clenched.

"I understand you aren't too excited about coming to the city," the ice cold voice said. "Consider it an order from me."

"No problem. I'm all set." Peter did his best not to

shout. He didn't need this particular call. He was capable of taking care of things. More than capable. "I just don't understand what I'll be doing there."

"When you get here, I want you to get in touch with Pendera at once. He's *your* contact. See him in person. That always works best."

"Has something more happened?" Peter massaged his temple with the fingers of one hand.

"We don't know yet. That's why we need information from him right away. If Kathryn's in this area, we need to find out if somehow she's made contact with anyone in his office. He should know about it if she has. And if he doesn't, he needs to get busy and find out."

So far they'd paid a lot of money to Efron Pendera, an assistant prosecutor on the U.S. District Attorney's staff for South Texas. They expected him to pass information on the Strike Force progress but so far had received little in exchange.

"Fine. I'd planned to get with him anyway. What about her car? Any word yet?"

"We have people out searching for the car," the voice answered. "We've drawn a hundred mile perimeter, and we've got people working within that circle. You are to call everyone on our payroll in the area that you recruited personally and enlist their assistance. If she's passed along that data storage unit already…"

"If she had," Peter pointed out in a tight voice, "you'd be talking to the U.S. Attorney instead of me."

"You're so damn sure of that, are you?"

"Yes, I am. She's still got it."

"Then find her. I want her, I want the drive, and

then I want her dead."

"Fine." He fought to keep a controlled tone in his voice. "I gave Esai my flight information. And you'll be happy to know he has Salazar sticking to me like glue."

"I'll be happy when this thing is resolved. Not before."

The flight to San Antonio was bumpy, and sitting with Salazar next to him didn't help. The only thing that made it bearable for Peter was flying First Class. He managed to consume enough scotch to smooth out the rough edges, then closed his eyes and pretended to sleep.

One of Esai's henchmen waited at the airport to fetch them. His orders were to bring the two men to Esai's home in Northwest San Antonio immediately. When the man walked into the house, Peter took one look and thought, *Oh, shit.*

Like Osuna, this was a man who would kill people like flies just for annoying him. He was well over six feet, his lean but muscular body clothed in an expensive-looking silk shirt and trousers. He was dark skinned with thick black hair, bushy eyebrows, and eyes blacker than coal. His heart was probably just as black.

Thin lips twisted in a cruel smile as he greeted Peter. "So. We have problems."

"Which I'm working on," Peter hastened to assure him.

"We'll see. Now. Your quarters here are just temporary. You'll be moving to the condo after tomorrow."

Peter's stomach clenched. Being at the condo

would be like being in prison or worse. They'd watch his every move, breathe down his neck, ask a flood of questions that he might not be able to answer. "Why? What's the problem? What's wrong with me just staying right here?"

Esai shrugged. "I'd say nothing, but it's not my decision. Meanwhile, I want to have the downtown library checked again in case she returns."

"I don't think she will," Peter argued. "She got what she wanted. Or didn't get it."

It's a stupid idea and will only cause another screw-up.

"I still think we can't ignore the possibility," Esai insisted.

"Well, I certainly can't go. Send Salazar if you want to." Peter tried to put a tone of authority into his voice. The worst thing he could do was to show fear. "On the remote chance she does come back, she'll recognize me and run like hell. Besides, I need to keep in touch with the people who are looking for her car. She's here. Somewhere in this area. We'll find her."

"Fine." Esai gave him a hard look. "I'll have your suitcase put in your room. You can set up shop in my den for the moment. Martha will bring you coffee. You smell like you could use it. Dinner is at eight."

Peter dropped his jacket on a chair next to the desk, set up the laptop, and logged onto the Internet. Esai's entire house was a wireless hot spot, so he was connected in just seconds. Then he opened his cell phone.

From the hallway, he heard the voices of Esai and Salazar drifting back to him. Then the door to the garage opened and a moment later a car pulled away.

And good luck on that.

He began his routine, calling everyone on the list who might have a lead on the car while searching his databases for a hit on the license plate. He had just finished a long and frustrating phone call with a state policeman on their payroll when his cell rang.

"This is Alfredo Morales," a voice said.

Peter recognized him at once. A county sheriff's deputy who'd been taking their money for years.

"You called because…"

"I found your car for you."

Peter's pulse picked up speed as his adrenaline level rose. "And the woman? Did you find her, too?"

"Not yet, but she can't be far away. Not with the condition of the vehicle."

Peter frowned. "What do you mean? Where did you find it?"

"In a repair garage in a little town just outside of San Antonio."

"And?" Peter prodded impatiently.

"It's been dismantled and the parts sold. The guy who owns the garage said it was abandoned on the highway, wouldn't run, and he towed it in. No papers. No indication of ownership. He waited a day and claimed it as salvage."

Peter thought a minute. "Any chance the guy that owns the garage knows more than he's telling?"

"Nah. He's an old guy who's lived here all his life. He doesn't need the money, just does this to keep himself busy."

"Shit. So we're no further ahead than we were before."

"At least it pinpoints more closely the area where

you might locate your female. If she had to ditch the car, she can't be far away. There's no bus service out of this town, for one thing."

That meant Kathryn would have had to find more transportation, although Peter was learning, unpleasantly, how resourceful she could be.

"Look around everyplace. Tell everyone to do this as quietly as possible, but be thorough." He rubbed his forehead. "Do your job. Keep your eyes open. Ask the right questions. I have an extra bonus for the person who locates her."

"I'll pass it along. These little towns aren't any bigger than a flyspeck. A stranger's sure to stand out."

"Keep in touch."

At least they had something concrete, for a change. Thank God for that. It might get the brothers off his back for a while. He held out little hope for Salazar's trip to the library. A useless waste of time and in the end sure to cost them more than it was worth.

Anyway, Salazar wasn't his call. People who thought they were so much smarter than he was had stopped listening to him. He had become a pariah in the organization, a situation he was damned determined to remedy.

He decided to hold onto the information about the car until he had something more concrete—like Kathryn herself. A rabbit he could pull out of his hat. No sense putting himself through the wringer for nothing.

He was doing a little experimenting on the computer, playing around with the best way to set up the financials and flow charts again, when Esai stormed into the den. Rage hung around him like a solid cloud.

He jabbed the remnants of his cigar into a crystal ash tray with a vicious gesture.

Peter raised an eyebrow. He knew he was baiting the bear, but he couldn't help himself. "Something else go wrong?"

"That fucking Salazar." He began pacing the confined space. "He's given us a little problem. Again."

"Oh?" Peter swallowed a smile of satisfaction. He was sure his instincts had been correct.

Esai stopped pacing and planted himself in front of the desk. "We gave that idiot pictures to work with. Pictures that showed the woman with different looks. He probably threw them away."

"What happened?" Peter down-sized his document and leaned back in his chair.

Esai pulled out another cigar and rolled it between two fingers. "He gave the people at the library the story we put together. Nothing complicated, so he couldn't screw it up. He was supposed to be looking for his missing sister. His family had gotten an email from her and traced it back to one of the library computers. They're worried about her. You know. All that shit."

"And?"

"The people there were very nice. Not suspicious at all, he said."

"So what went wrong?"

"The woman he spoke to became very excited. Told him how fortunate he was, because his sister was back again this very day. Even pointed out her out." He made a rude noise. "Salazar swears she looked just like one of the pictures of our little bitch."

Peter was sure what was coming and his stomach knotted. Not again. "Let me guess. It wasn't her."

"Not even close." Esai flung his hands in the air.

Peter felt the bitter taste of bile in his mouth. "So when she turned out to be the wrong person, he...disposed of her."

Esai nodded. "We have to hope that he got rid of the body successfully enough that she won't be found for a long time. Miguel was right. The man is losing his touch. I should have listened to him and gotten rid of Salazar long ago."

Peter raked his hands through his hair. "Christ, now what?" He turned back to his keyboard and closed the document he'd been working on. "We have another dead body to get rid of."

"That's the fucking truth." Esai took down a bottle of brandy from the bar on one wall and poured himself a generous amount. "He damn well better make sure he doesn't leave any traces when he does it." He slugged down the brandy in one gulp. "Now more than ever we have to make sure she hasn't hooked up with the feds. Call Pendera. Tell him it's time to pay up."

****

"Pendera here."

"It's Fleming."

Peter leaned back in his chair, visualizing the swarthy Efron Pendera in his prosecutor outfit—well-fitting suit, crisp pale blue shirt, and conservative tie. He always thought the man had a handbook on how prosecutors should dress. From the background noises, Peter assumed he'd caught the man out on the street.

"What do you want?" The hostility and resentment in his voice were as sharp as a knife.

Too bad. The man doesn't mind taking our money. Now he needs to work for it.

"It turns out our target has very nicely stumbled into the San Antonio area. We need to know if she's contacted anyone in your office. Tell me exactly what's going on there right now."

"*Cristo!* I'm out here on the street, for God's sake. Let me get to a more private place, and I'll call you back."

"Five minutes," Fleming warned.

"I'll do my best."

Peter leaned back in the chair, his feet propped on the desk, and thought about Efron Pendera. The man had a gambling addiction for which there was apparently no cure. The Osunas had bought up his markers and very carefully explained that now he belonged to them. They'd had him on a short leash ever since. The problem was, he'd provided them with precious little in all this time, especially now when they really needed it.

Ten minutes later, Peter's cell rang. "That's a lot more than five minutes," he accused.

"I had to get to a place where I could talk." The strain in the man's voice vibrated across the connection. "The street is too open for this kind of conversation, and there was no convenient place safe to duck into."

"All right. It's time to earn your money. God knows you've taken enough of it without giving much in return."

"I keep telling you," Pendera whined. "They don't tell me a lot of things."

"Then find a way to get them," Peter growled. "Now listen. We want to know if they've mentioned any woman who might be connected to the Osunas. Or me, God forbid. Someone who might have…something

167

to give them."

"What kind of something?"

"Something that could send us all to prison. Does that shove that stick up your ass a little farther?"

"*Madre Mia!*" The man's voice cracked. "What the hell does she have?"

"First, I want to know if anyone's been talking about her. A witness. Whatever."

"I haven't heard anything." There was a pause. "I meant to tell you this, but I knew you'd be pissed off. They've taken me off the major group for the Strike Force and given me other cases to handle."

Peter wanted to hit something. "Did you manage to fuck up in some way? Are they suspicious of you?"

"No, no, no, no. Please, Pedro. I'm doing the best I can. They just decided to pare it back to the core team."

"Your best at this point is going to get you a nice place at the cemetery if you don't end up in prison first. I don't care how you do it, but I need that information. Now. This woman disappeared from Tampa less than two weeks ago. Her car has finally been found in this area, which puts her far too close for comfort."

Silence hummed over the connection.

"Efron? Did you hear me?"

"Okay. Here's something. I haven't heard a word about finding a female or anything like that. But something did happen this morning. I swear I was going to call you about it, but I was waiting to see if I could find out more information."

"What are you talking about? Damn it, Efron. You know better than to hold back."

"All right, all right. There was a meeting this morning between Jake Garza, Dean Morgan and Kane

Barton. Since then, the three of them have been quieter than a church, talking only to each other. And everything behind closed doors."

"And you didn't see fit to call us and tell us at once? Are you nuts? I specifically told you *anything* out of the ordinary you were to report."

"Pedro, I'm sorry." The man was whining, a pathetic sound from a grown man. "I was waiting to see if it had to do with the cartel. They didn't bring the Strike Force in on it so it could have been one of the other cases in play."

"Damn it. I told you to call me Peter." He blew out a breath and fought to control his impatience. Listen, *pendejo*. When we tell you to let us know about anything—*anything*—that's exactly what we mean. You'd better do some digging. If this involves the woman, that would be very dangerous for all of us. I want to know everything they know. Do you understand?"

"I'll do my best. Honest to God, you can believe me when I tell you that."

Peter thought for a moment. He hadn't intended to mention the flash drive, but Pendera was so stupid he needed a road map to know what to look for. "Has anyone mentioned a flash drive? A memory stick? Anything like that?"

"Flash drive? No. I swear to you. Why?"

"Never mind why. Just keep your eyes and ears open. Wide open. If you hear anything at all, no matter how insignificant you might think it is, I want to know at once."

There was a long pause. An unsettling feeling came over Peter, a feeling that Pendera had been holding back.

"What else? I sense something rattling around in your brain."

"Okay. I didn't want to say anything, but…"

"But what, *pendejo?* I told you to keep nothing back." Peter could almost smell the fear over the connection, and he didn't like it.

"Since yesterday morning, I've been getting a feeling I don't like at all."

"What do you mean?" Peter was instantly at attention. "What kind of feeling?"

He heard Pendera muttering to himself, a prayer or incantation, and ground his teeth. What the hell?

"I-I heard Quinn's name mentioned last night."

"Quinn? Christ and all the angels." The words exploded from Peter's mouth.

Everyone in the drug business knew about Quinn's vendetta against the Ramirez cartel and the ruthless way he'd destroyed it. Those who didn't end up stuck in prison forever were dead. Even after four years, the story of the blood bath was a legend still whispered in the business.

"That's all we need." Peter's head throbbed and pinpricks of pain stabbed behind his right eye. "I thought, after that disaster, he quit his job and went off to hide in the hills or something."

"He did. But now it seems he and Garza have hooked up again."

"Jesus. If by some vicious twist of fate Kathryn's involved with him, we're all screwed."

"Absolutamente. You are right on that score."

"How the hell would she even meet someone like him?" Peter shifted the phone to his other ear and reached in his pocket for antacid tablets. He was about to burn a hole in his gut. If the Osuna Brothers didn't kill him, his body would probably self-destruct anyway. "You'd better find out. And pretty damn fast." As he was about to disconnect the call, an unpleasant thought smacked Peter in the gut. "Efron, do you happen to know where Quinn lives?"

"No. No one does."

"Bullshit. Someone has to. His friend Garza? Someone else in the office?"

"I swear to you…"

"Don't swear. Just find out. Make it happen. You know what your options are."

He snapped his phone shut with a vicious *click*. If Kathryn had somehow found her way to that devil, Quinn, they were all royally fucked and he might as well plan his funeral now.

Chapter Fourteen

The shooting range was like a foreign country to Kate. The small Kahr 9mm Quinn purchased for her in his name was like a puzzle she couldn't solve.

"What if I shoot myself instead?" She tried to grin.

Quinn wasn't having any excuses. "Trust me, when I get through teaching you, that won't even be a possibility."

His own guns were a .38 Smith and Wesson and a Sig Sauer 9 mm, powerful looking weapons.

Kate eyed them hesitantly. "They look so big."

"That's why we got you something you can handle. Come on. Let's get started."

She hoped she could stop shaking before she actually had to shoot the damn thing. The big lunch Quinn had insisted they stop and eat was bouncing around in her stomach like golf balls. How embarrassing if she threw up all over her brand new gun.

But Quinn spent a long time getting her used to the heft and feel of the little weapon and teaching her how to load it. Finally, he set up the paper targets he'd purchased from the range manager.

"Here we go," he told her. "Don't be nervous. This will be a piece of cake."

"Easy for you to say." She concentrated on breathing in and out and not heaving her guts.

He grinned and kissed her cheek. "Hold the gun like I showed you, just like we practiced, and you'll be fine. Now. Raise both arms, sight along the line to the target. Take a deep breath, let it part way out, and pull the trigger."

He reached around her, supporting her arms but not touching her hands. Sighting along the gun barrel, she drew in a breath, let it out part way, and squeezed.

"Damn!"

She tensed, looking at Quinn anxiously. "Did I do something wrong?"

"Oh, hell, no. You got him right through the heart. Okay, let's do this again and see if that was a lucky accident or if you're a sharpshooter in the making."

She emptied the clip, going through the same routine each time. When she was finished, she looked at him for approval. He was grinning.

"What?"

"Are you sure you never held a gun before? You're not pulling my leg?"

"Absolutely. Why? What's wrong?"

"Nothing. Come take a look." He walked her up to the target and pointed. "See that? We call that burning a hole. All six shots in a tight little circle, right in the middle of his heart."

"Is that good?" she asked.

"Good? Are you kidding? You have no idea how hard that is to do. You can't get more perfect than that. I'd have been happy if you got him anywhere in the chest, which is the best place to aim for. The stopping zone. But"—he took the gun from her hand—"let's reload and see if you can do this again."

They worked at it until mid-afternoon. By the time

they'd gone through nearly all the target ammunition they bought, Kate's arms were trembling from the strain and her shots were beginning to stray. Nevertheless, a wild exhilaration gripped her.

All right, Peter, bring it on. I'm ready.

Quinn spent the next half hour on his own practice. He was totally focused on what he was doing and unbelievably accurate. Kate watched, mesmerized. She could see what he meant about a gun becoming part of your body.

But of course, it wasn't just his marksmanship that had her attention. With his black T-shirt and well-worn jeans molding his body, he looked like a sculpture standing in the gravel. The muscles in his arms and back rippled as he fired each shot. If her body had reacted before, now it tingled all over.

Finally, Quinn was done, and came back to the table. "We'll do this again soon," he told her. "I want to keep at it until I'm satisfied you can do it in your sleep. If nothing else, it will give me peace of mind."

As soon as they were back at the house, Quinn pulled three steaks from the freezer. "Jake is big on red meat. I'll defrost these and get the grill started."

Kate found the dishes and silverware while he took down two bottles from his wine rack. She looked up and saw him watching her as she set everything out, arranging the table. The expression on his face gave her a sudden feeling of warmth. Of rightness.

When she had the last item in place, he put his arms around her and rested his chin on her head.

"You fill this house, Kate. And my life. It's the last thing I expected to happen, but I guess the man upstairs had plans for me. For us."

"Oh, Quinn." She blinked hard at the tears that suddenly wet her lashes.

"I haven't felt like this for a long time. You look so right in this house."

When he bent his head to kiss her, she lifted her face to him, sliding her hands up through the silk of his hair.

Like an alarm clock intruding on a dream, the telephone rang, its tone harsh and strident. For a moment, neither of them registered what the sound was. Then Quinn swore, relaxed his hold on Kate, and reached for the offending instrument.

"Just wanted to let you know I'm on the way," Jake told him. "I should be there pretty soon."

"Yeah, great." Quinn was still trying to steady his breathing. "See you in a few."

"Jake?" Kate asked, her face still flushed. She was busy rearranging her clothing and working on her own breathing.

"Yes. With his usual impeccable timing." He pulled Kate against him, tenderly this time. "It's all right, darlin.' It's just as well he called. I don't think the kitchen table would be too comfortable for what I have in mind. Let's get some iced tea to cool down." He dropped a light kiss on her mouth. "But watch out later on."

With potatoes baking in the oven and the coals heating in the grill, and needing to distract themselves, they took the last of the iced tea out to the front porch and sat in the rockers to wait for Jake. The sun was draping its evening colors over the far hills when a Ford Explorer came down the road and turned into the driveway.

Quinn rose from his chair. "There's the man himself. Are you ready for introductions?"

"I guess I'd better be," she said, standing up and smoothing her hands against her thighs.

Okay. Here we go.

Seeing Jake the day before had brought back memories Quinn kept shut up and locked for a long time. As he waited for his friend to pull up the driveway, the painful, horrific images came tumbling back, like a movie unwinding in slow motion.

Jake standing next to Quinn the day his wife and daughter were shot down. Jake beside him like a rock as he'd watched them buried on one of the coldest days South Texas had ever seen. The ice on the ground must have found its way into Quinn's heart, because it had been stone cold since then. The killing of his parents had tipped him over the edge.

The day Quinn walked out of Kane Barton's office was the last time anyone saw him until months later, when he arrived with five members of the Ramirez cartel, bound and restrained and slightly the worse for the wear. He'd simply called for Jake to meet him at the front of the building and bring a couple of agents with him.

At the curb, Quinn opened his door and indicated the waiting men should remove the prisoners in his vehicle. Then he'd handed Jake an athletic gym bag and a thick file folder, bound with rubber bands. The gym bag contained a collection of guns. The folder held fingerprint cards, Polaroid pictures of the men, and about three inches of paperwork on the cartel.

"Everything you need is in there," he said, got in his truck, and drove away.

****

When Kate shook Jake's hand, his grip was warm and firm, friendly yet somehow reserved.

"Thank you for agreeing to meet with me" The smile he gave her didn't quite reach his eyes, and Kate couldn't miss the trace of suspicion lurking there. The way he was handling this was solely out of friendship for Quinn, and he was expecting her not to jeopardize that.

He's making up his mind about me. Reserving judgment. I guess I don't blame him. If it were my friend involved I'd probably feel the same way.

She arranged her face into what she hoped was a welcoming expression, praying her quaking stomach would settle down. "Thank you for coming out here. I appreciate the fact you're in a difficult situation."

Jake's eyes took in every bit of her. Assessing. "I owe Quinn a lot, as does my boss. We agreed to bend the rules a little for him. Once."

Message delivered.

"Thank you again. For that."

"Well, then." The surface smile was back.

Quinn's smile didn't reach his eyes, either. "Anything to make things easier here. I hope maybe we can catch a little break."

"You know I'll do my best," Jake told him. "But I've got my orders. We all know that, right, folks?" He looked from one to the other. "I'm ready for a good steak and some fine wine. And after we eat we'll get down to business."

"After we eat," Quinn agreed.

Jake followed them into the house and dropped his jacket and briefcase on an arm chair while Quinn went to see about the steaks.

Despite the fact the men, especially Quinn, made an obvious effort to keep the conversation light, everyone knew what the evening's agenda was. Kate did her best to enjoy her meal, but tension coiled in her stomach like a snake ready to strike at any moment. She had no idea what would happen after she told Jake her story or whether he'd believe how she came to have the flash drive. That wasn't something she'd discussed with Quinn, but it had gnawed away at her.

What if he thought she was lying? That she was actually part of the cartel and had fled over a disagreement, taking the flash drive as a bargaining chip.

No. She pushed the thought away. She'd make him believe her. And Quinn would help.

Finally, when the dishes were cleared and the second bottle of wine opened, Jake leaned back in his chair and looked hard at Kate.

Quinn took one of her hands in his. "Jake's on our side, darlin'. Keep that in mind."

Is he? Or am I making a mistake here?

Jake cleared his throat. "All right, Kate, why don't you clue me in on how you and my friend, Quinn, here just happened to get together."

Kate tensed at the barely concealed sarcasm. "What do you mean, *happened* to get together?" She looked at Quinn. "Is that some kind of slam?"

"He certainly doesn't sound like it."

Jake looked directly at her. "Kate. Don't take this the wrong way, but I don't know anything about you and neither does my boss. Either of my bosses. One of my assignments tonight is to make sure you aren't just yanking Quinn's chain. Okay? Can you understand that?"

Her dinner threatened to heave itself back up in her throat. She should have expected this. She started to get up, but Quinn put a hand on her shoulder, steadying her. "That's uncalled for, Jake, and less than I would have expected of you."

"Hey, Ace," he protested. "You'd feel the same way in my place, and don't deny it."

"I appreciate the fact that you're all so concerned about Quinn," Kate told him, her voice very formal and cold. "But if you really are Quinn's good friend, then you know no one could possibly yank his chain, as you so delicately put it. I would be a fool to try. What you see tonight is what you get. Period."

"Kate, it's okay." Quinn squeezed her hand. "I know it's Jake's job to be suspicious, despite what I say. Don't let it throw you. All right? I can deal with it." He looked at Jake. "But that's the end of that kind of thinking, buddy. Old friend. Old pal. Or you'll be back on the road to the city with nothing to show for it but a good steak dinner."

All the good humor from dinnertime disappeared with the snap of a finger. Jake narrowed his eyes at Quinn's words, studying him for what seemed an eternity. Then he dipped his head once. "If you say so." Looking back at Kate, he said, "Shall we get started, then?"

Kate took a large swallow of her wine and glanced at Quinn.

He gave her a reassuring nod. "From the beginning, darlin'. Just like you told me. We're past time to hold anything back."

He linked his fingers through hers, giving them a gentle squeeze. The gesture was as much a signal to Jake as it was to her.

She's mine. Be careful here.

Doing her best to ignore Jake's barely concealed skepticism, Kate laid out her story one more time. She gave him everything. The death of her parents. Her suspicions about the fire. Peter. The pills. The conversation she overheard. Her crazy bus odyssey, changing her appearance, pulling money out of her accounts, and what happened when she did. And finally, about meeting Quinn on the side of the road.

Jake listened attentively, watching her face the entire time. When she finished, he leaned back in his chair. "You know, when we started looking into Burke-Fleming, and you came across our radar, we tried to figure out if you fit into this puzzle anyplace. But it just didn't make sense. You didn't seem to have a clue what was going on or a role to play."

"That's because I don't." She tried to keep the hostility out of her voice. "If I know anything at all, it's by sheer accident. As far as my mother and I were concerned, this was just a regular corporate law firm. That's the God's honest truth. Trans Global was a major client, and their people took up a lot of my father's time. And Peter's when he came on board. Quinn's the one who clued me in on reality after he met with you."

Jake's lips thinned. "Then you know your father's law firm was created solely to create a legitimate structure for the Osuna cartel, a way to manage its business. The Osunas are about the worst I've seen in a long time. They're into drugs, weapons, money laundering. Probably even smuggling people and dabbling in prostitution. Selling guns to terrorists. It would take a team of very good forensic accountants years to dig through it all. If we even had a place to start."

Kate folded her hands together so tightly her knuckles were white. "I just have a hard time believing my father was part of this. And my uncle, until he died in a small plane crash."

"Kate, here's the plain truth." Jake leaned forward and pinned her with his gaze. "Someone financed that law firm so it could open its doors. It just appeared one day out of whole cloth, fully operational. We traced your father's finances and your uncle's all the way back to when they opened their offices. They didn't have any money of their own to speak of. Then suddenly they did. Do you think the money fairy just left an envelope on their doorstep?"

Kate felt hot and cold at the same time, and the snake inside her stomach was coiling and writhing. She squeezed Quinn's hand harder. "And Peter? How did they find him? My father said he was the son of an old friend."

"I'm sure he is." Jake's mouth twisted in a cynical grin. "Or something like that. We know about Peter Fleming. The man is dangerous and too smart for his own good."

"Don't I know it." Her tone was bitter.

Jake took a minute to fetch a pen and yellow pad from his briefcase, then took his seat across from her again. "If you don't mind, can we go through this one more time? Just to make sure there isn't something you might know that you didn't think was important. This time I'd like to take notes."

"Believe me, Jake. You've got it all. What little there is." She took another sip of her wine. "But if you want it again, let's get it out there."

Wearily, she gave it to him one more time, all of it, watching as he made notes in his sprawling style of writing. Her uncle's death. Peter's appearance. The propane tank that exploded, killing her parents.

"And by the way," she interjected. "They had that tank checked regularly. My father was a fanatic about it."

And finally, in even greater detail, the conversation she walked in on that night that sent her fleeing for her life.

Jake was thorough with his questions, taking Kate back and forth for what seemed an eternity, prodding, poking, making her repeat things three and four times. She tried to remember everything she knew about Burke-Fleming, dredging up any tiny thing, trying to visualize people she'd met or remember anything she'd heard.

"And you've been running ever since," Jake said matter-of-factly.

"Yes. I have. And believe me, it wasn't any picnic."

"I'll say this for you," Jake commented. "Not too many people could have done what you did, evading them so successfully. You've got a lot of guts."

"They almost got me twice," she reminded him.

"Yes, but they didn't, and that's what counts." He might be suspicious, but his eyes showed a new respect for her. "Well, Kate. Or Kathryn. What should I call you, anyway?"

"Kate, definitely." She tried to smile. "I'm happy to be rid of Kathryn."

"Something else bugs me." He looked at Quinn and back to Kate. "Why do you think they wanted to get rid of you in the first place? What was the point in killing you? As far as Fleming was concerned, you were no danger to him." He narrowed his eyes. "Were you?"

"I've been thinking about this." Quinn leaned forward. "From what she heard Miguel say, I'd have to guess it was just too big a risk having her around. Not knowing what she might stumble over, ask questions about. She was the last survivor, and you know the Osunas don't leave survivors."

A shiver rippled over Kate, and her blood seemed to freeze in her veins. "It's hard to believe they wanted to kill me just *in case* I might learn something."

Jake shrugged. "Not unheard of in this business."

She leaned closer to Quinn. She knew he was waiting for her to bring up the flash drive herself, but giving it up meant leaving her with no bargaining chip. "So now what, Jake? Where do we go from here? I don't seem to have given you anything you can use."

He studied her as he spoke. "We've had a very interesting conversation here, Kate, but I hate to be the bearer of bad news." He looked back at Quinn. "You know she's gonna have to come in and talk to the bosses." He gestured at his yellow pad. "This won't be nearly enough to satisfy them."

"No. No way." She shook her head. "I thought that's why you came out here, so I wouldn't have to do that."

"When I give this information to Dean Morgan and Kane Barton, they'll want to question you in person to satisfy themselves. You're the only link we've been able to get our hands on. As a matter of fact, I think they were hoping you'd show up with me first thing tomorrow morning."

Kate turned in her chair, trembling. "Quinn? You promised me. You said we could trust Jake. That it would be okay." She looked at Jake, still watching her with hooded eyes. "I'm not putting myself out there like that. I'm sorry, but I'll say it again. I heard Peter himself say they've got people paid off everywhere. *Even prosecutors and federal agents.* All over the country. Remember?"

"Jesus." Jake ran his fingers through his hair. "Are you telling me you actually heard him say those words? Because it's damn near next to impossible to get to anyone in our office."

"Do I have a reason to lie to you?" she demanded. "Why do you think I didn't run to you or the police first thing? Shouldn't I have done that right away?"

His hand tightened on his pen. "If there's any possibility of truth in that, Noah and Clay will be royally pissed off, too."

"Who?" Quinn frowned at him.

"Special Agent-in-Charge Noah Delaney is the FBI's point man in the investigation. Clay Rogers is the DEA's chief representative. They'll be kicking butt when I tell them their houses might not be so clean."

"So you see," Kate cried, "how can I be sure he hasn't already gotten to someone in your office? That they won't find out about this? And me?"

"Nothing is ever foolproof, but our office is as tight as it can get. Kane Barton, the U.S. Attorney for this district, is the most honest man you'll ever meet. He's not a man to mess around with. If the Osunas got to someone on our staff, we'll squeeze him out in a hurry. And life won't be very pleasant for him when that happens."

"But not until after they've found me and k-killed me." She clenched her teeth to keep them from chattering.

"Honey," Quinn began.

"No." She stared at Jake defiantly. "I'm not doing this. Or anything else. You don't trust me. Why should I trust you?"

Quinn leaned his mouth close to her ear. "You can trust him because I do. Because I made a promise to you. And you know you have to give him your little treasure. If you're afraid to just hand it over, isn't the smart thing to do for you to give it to his boss yourself? I swear to God, Kate, I can vouch for those guys. No reservations. We have to get the cartel off your back and this is probably the only way."

"Can I possibly ask what you're talking about?" Jake broke in?

"In a minute," Quinn told him. He lowered his voice again. "You have the means to see these people put away. But let's do it on our terms, okay?"

She looked at him a long time, then nodded. "Okay. I guess it makes sense. But our way, right?"

He nodded. "Or we don't do it. We pack up and get the hell out of here. Find someone else we can work with."

"Okay." Jake threw his pen down. "Enough. What the hell's going on?"

"Maybe we can do each other some good." Quinn looked at Jake. "You up for a little horse trading?"

Jake scowled. "What kind of horse? And how much trading?"

Quinn turned back to Kate. "I think it's time to bring out your little surprise."

Jake shifted his eyes from one to the other. "What little surprise? What aren't you guys telling me?"

"If we show you something very important, will you get Kate off the hot seat with the brass? You can tell them she'll come into town but on our terms."

"I can't say until I know what you've got." Any trace of a smile had disappeared from Jake's mouth and his eyes. He was serious as a heart attack now.

"Let's just say it's something the Osunas and Peter Fleming would kill to get their hands on," Quinn told him.

"Are you by any chance talking about the reason for the big dragnet the cartel has out for you, Kate? The reason there's such a big target on your back?"

"Do we have a deal?" Quinn asked again. "Yes or no, or we're done here."

"I could take her in as a government witness."

"Not unless you plan to arrest her." Kate had never heard Quinn's voice so cold. "And don't even *think* about trying to get a subpoena. You know how fast I can disappear."

Jake threw up his hands. "All right, all right. If it's as good as you say, I'll cut you some slack. But not much. This is too damned important. And you know it's not entirely my call."

"But you can *make* it your call. You can convince them."

"Fine." He shook his head. "If I get fired, you'll have to make room for me out here."

Quinn turned to Kate. "Tell him."

Kate took another sip of wine and set her glass down carefully in front of her. "I left one little thing out of my story. The night I left, I took a flash drive Peter had left in his computer. According to what I overheard, it has all kind of records on it. Transfers and things like that."

Jake looked as if he was about to strangle on his own tongue. He took a careful sip of his wine, his eyes shifting from Kate to Quinn and back again. "Let me get this straight. You've been running around the country with a little gizmo that has all the records for the Osuna cartel on it? And you have it in your possession now?"

Kate nodded and moved closer to Quinn.

Jake glared at Quinn. "You knew this when you came to me? And didn't think it was important enough to mention? To ask for my help then?"

"He gave me his word," Kate interrupted. "He knew how afraid I was. Especially about prosecutors being bribed."

Jake looked as if he wanted to throttle her. "Kate, you have to give it to me. This could be the very thing we need to break the case open. The information we've been killing ourselves to get. And you have to come to our offices to be interviewed. Face it. You can't hide in Quinn's house forever. I promise you, if this is what you say it is we'll give Quinn all the backup he needs to keep you safe. You have my word on that."

She took a deep breath and let it out. "The cartel reaches out everywhere. There's no one but Quinn I can trust. But I'll make a deal with you, because I want this over, too."

"What kind of deal?" Jake's voice was skeptical.

"Like Quinn said, we want to do this on our own terms. You have to guarantee a situation where I'll be safe and assure me your boss is not on the cartel payroll. Agree to what we want, and I'll hand it over to *him*."

"Listen, we'll have armed guards if that's what you want," Jake told her, his face tight with anger. "And they won't be cartel employees. But we need that drive and any other information you might have."

Other information? Oh, damn! How could I forget this?

"Wait." Kate looked at both men again. "Before I get the flash drive, there's something else I almost forgot."

Because I've been so scared my brain doesn't work quite right.

But sitting here, talking about this with Quinn and Jake, the library visit came popping back.

"Jesus, Kate," Jake said. "Now what?"

She looked at Quinn. "My trip to the library."

"Library?" Jake asked.

She swallowed and let out a slow breath. How could she not have remembered this? "I, um, wanted to do a little research on the law firm. Apparently, everything I knew was a lie so I wanted to see what I could find out. You know, get some background." She shrugged. "But it was a useless attempt."

"Kate." Jake's voice was very quiet. "Are you telling me you actually Googled these people on the Internet?"

"Yes, but it was a waste of time."

"And did you get anything?" Jake asked.

She wrinkled her forehead. "Not very much. And nothing on the law firm." She looked at Quinn. "And I'm so sorry, but I did something you told me not to do."

To his credit, he didn't jump up and throttle her. "You did a search on Peter. After I specifically told you that was a bad idea. Is that what you're saying?"

Her heart did a swan dive. "I'm sorry. I know how to cover my tracks, and I just thought…"

"Never mind. We'll discuss this later," Quinn told her in a flat voice. "Just tell us what you found?"

"Nothing. It was so strange, but I couldn't find anything at all on him."

"What happened when you hit the sites?" Jake asked.

"Not much." She shrugged. "Most of them came up with the message *Server Offline* or *Error, Page not found*. Please tell me what's wrong."

The silence in the room became so thick Kate thought she could touch it. Both men stared at her.

Quinn looked at his friend, and they said with one voice, "Traps."

Chapter Fifteen

"Traps? What traps?" Kate stared at both men. "What are you talking about?"

Jake looked as if he had a bad taste in his mouth. "Peter would certainly want to know if anyone's trying to dig for information on him. We know he's a computer genius, so it's a given he had electronic traps on the links you accessed. They alert him when anyone taps into them and sends the IPS address of the computer doing the search."

Now her heart was doing cartwheels, but she did her best to conceal it, although her fingers du

"I don't think I tripped anything," she assured them, praying it was so. "I know how to build layers of anonymous servers to hide the original source before actually doing a search. I've done this before. I was very careful. So even if he got an alert, I'm pretty sure he couldn't back trace to me. Anyway, I used a library computer. I could be anyone."

"Oh, yeah?" Jake shook his head. "Exactly how many people do you think would be going to a library to look up Peter Fleming? Or that law firm, which has *only one client?* Think, Kate. It gives them a geographic location on you."

"Jake's right," Quinn put in. "Damn it, I should have thought of that, but I just let myself get rusty. Out of the blue, in the midst of all this craziness, someone decides to do an Internet search on Peter and Burke-Fleming. You don't think that would set off alarms somewhere?"

"And remember," Jake added, "this is Esai's town. Knowing this, no one would be foolhardy enough to do a search on any computer, let alone a public one."

"Maybe they'd think it was your office," she said almost desperately. Hopefully.

Jake shook his head. "They'd know better than that. For one thing, we wouldn't use public computers. And it wouldn't be anyone trying to cut into their business. They'd have other sources." He pounded his fist on the table. "Damn it. Let's hope they aren't focusing they're search on this area now."

Kate paled. "I'm sorry. You're right." She looked at Quinn. "You didn't want me to do it, and I should have listened. It was a stupid thing for me to do. I just never thought about traps or anything like that. I thought I could cover myself."

Quinn slapped his palm on the table. "No, I'm the stupid one. I never should have let you do it. But I've been out of this for so long, I didn't think about electronic traps."

The ringing of his cell phone interrupted the tension in the air. He spoke briefly and when he hung up his face was grim. "Time to stop fooling around, Kate. That was Mike at the garage."

"W-What about? We already junked the car."

"Some guy came in today looking for a vehicle with your license plate number. Said he was looking for his sister, checking any place she might have had her car fixed. His family was worried about her."

"How the hell did they find her?" Jake wanted to

know. "How in the fucking *hell* did they figure out where she was?"

"Oh, my God." Kate thought she would faint. She was shaking so hard Quinn had to hold onto her. "Yes, Jake. How did they get those plates? I bought it…I just…" She had to clench her teeth together to keep them from chattering.

"I'd say when they lost the trail they went back to square one in L.A. and started from there. Then someone probably had the bright idea they might have scared her enough at the bus terminal that she decided to buy another car. They know she has to hoard her money, they don't know if she has proper identification and she needs to find someplace close. So they start looking for junk car places around the terminal, doing a block to block. And Bingo! Up pops wherever you bought the car.

"Highway Harry," she whispered.

"Who may be riding the highway in the sky by now," Jake pointed out. "After some physical exercise, I'm sure he was more than happy to tell his new friends anything they wanted."

"Including the make of car he sold Kate and the license tag," Quinn put in. "They get the cops they bought and paid for to search for it in their computers and keep an eye on the roads."

Jake nodded. "Put that together with your trip to the library and the alerts that dinged back to Peter and there you go. They have an area to focus on."

"But how did they get to Mike's specifically?" She was hanging onto her control by a very thin thread. "This is a huge area to search."

"I'm sure good old Peter called the Osuna brothers,

told them he's got a hot location on their target and everyone should get their asses out and start canvassing the San Antonio area. My guess again is by sheer dumb luck they found someone who saw your car being picked up by the tow truck. Maybe asked around in a diner or a coffee shop. Whatever. Who the hell knows? The crooks catch all the breaks."

"W-What did Mike tell them?" she asked Quinn.

"That he found it on the highway and claimed it for salvage. But you can bet they'll start pinpointing this area, getting everyone on their payroll to track you down. And that means we've got a huge problem." He pulled Kate tight against him.

"A no brainer," Jake agreed. "They want Kate, and they want that flash drive. So now, boys and girls, we're done playing games. And Kate? If you're frightened, you've got a right to be."

She gripped his fingers until hers almost lost their feeling, her body trying to push itself inside his.

"What do you think?" Her voice was barely audible.

Killing her will be easy. I'll call you when it's done.

"I think we have to do what Jake says," he told her, his voice low and soothing. "But we aren't going to run around like some idiots. We'll make preparations so we can keep you safe." He looked at Jake. "Right?"

"Right." He raked his fingers through his hair, a good sign of his frustration at the turn things had taken. "Listen, Kate. You say you're willing to give that drive to Kane Barton? Now is the time to do it. We've got to get these guys and put them away before they really *do* kill you. Stopping them is the only chance you've got."

He got up and went to the cupboards, took down a glass and filled it from the tap. He stood at the sink chugging it, then refilled it before he sat down again.

"Tell me what you want. Then let me talk to Dean and Kane in the morning and see what we can set up. Dean may want to call you and talk to you again himself."

"To make sure we're still here?" Quinn's voice was heavy with sarcasm.

"No. Listen, Ace. I know you. You're smart enough, now that we've got this information, to know this is one thing you can't outrun. Right?"

Quinn gave him a grudging acknowledgement. "All right. And I do have a suggestion about how to do this. We obviously can't just march her down there in broad daylight with the entire work force present and watching."

"So what's your idea?"

"Try this. What if we do it at night when almost everyone's gone?" Quinn suggested. "You can sneak us in through the underground garage, like we've done with other people before. That way we have a contained situation, and it all but eliminates the risk."

"But there is still some risk involved, isn't there?" Kate asked. "Nothing is one hundred percent."

Jake leaned across the table toward Kate, his face grim. "I can tell you one thing that's a hundred percent. If you don't help us tie a knot around the Osunas, these assholes will kill you deader than yesterday's news. Look how close they are to you already."

She felt the blood drain from her face. Even the warmth from Quinn's body couldn't shake the cold invading her.

"Okay." Her voice was small and tremulous. "I'll trust you two to take care of me. But I'm not handing over the flash drive until we get there. That's my insurance that you'll take care of things properly."

"I'll probably get my ass handed to me when I report on that, but I'd say this is the best way to play it." He pulled out a tired smile. "You're doing the right thing, Kate. My office could go about this a lot differently, but we'd be putting you at greater risk, and I don't want that. I'll call you guys first thing in the morning after we've got everything set up."

He picked up his briefcase, getting ready to leave.

Quinn kissed the top of Kate's head as he, too, rose from his chair. "I'll just walk Jake out to his car and be right back, darlin'."

Kate watched the two men walk out to the driveway, then began to clear away the glasses from the table. The fear she'd been able to control the past few days had erupted full blown with this latest piece of news. If she could have bolted, she would, but she had to trust Quinn on this. And Jake was right. Where could she run to now?

****

Out in the driveway the two men spoke in quiet tones.

"You know I don't have a choice," Jake said as they stood by his SUV. "She has to come downtown and bring that gizmo with her."

"But her safety comes first. Just keep that in mind. Anything looks suspicious, and we're out of there."

"She seems to have a lot of guts. She'll get through this, especially with you to help her. But you and she had better understand something else. When this goes to trial, she'll probably have to testify."

"We'll cross that bridge when we come to it. Right now, let's get through tomorrow."

Jake studied his friend. "She seems like a special lady, but this is a very dicey situation. And you've already been through one fucking tragedy."

"I'm fine, Jake. Really. But thanks for the concern."

"You've come a long way with her in a very, very short time. You sure you know what you're doing?"

"Absolutely. And this time I don't intend to lose what I've got. Once in my life is enough."

"Okay, then. I've said my piece. I hope this works out."

The men shook hands, and Quinn went back inside.

Kate was standing on the back porch, watching the moon. He moved up behind her and laid his hands gently on her shoulders.

She leaned into him. "I'm frightened, Quinn. They found my car. They traced back my Internet searches. And I'm about to walk into strange territory with men I know nothing about."

"I'm right here with you, darlin', and we're going to keep it under control. *I'm* going to make sure of that. We'll take all the precautions we need to. And I'll be right beside you." He slid his arms around her, pulling her tight against him.

I'm not going to lose another woman. I'll do whatever it takes to prevent that.

She turned and locked her hands behind his back, pressing her cheek to his chest. "Do you realize last week we hadn't even met? Now I feel as if we've known each other forever."

"Me, too," he answered softly. He kissed the top of her head, inhaling her scent. "We've lived a lifetime in a few days." His mouth moved to the side of her neck. "I know it's late, and we've got a big day tomorrow, but God, Kate. I just have to be inside you. I need to feel you around me."

"I need that, too," she told him.

He swept her up in his arms. "Don't forget what I promised you for tonight."

"Oh, yes. I remember all right. I'm not letting you forget."

Quinn lifted her in his arms and carried her to the bedroom. He set her on her feet by the bed and began removing her clothing with as much control as he could muster. There was an urgency between them tonight that was different. More intense. More emotional. Tonight, they needed…everything.

The sight of her naked body made his cock thicken even more and his balls ache. He had never craved a woman this way, not even Lisa. Tonight, he would not allow himself to feel guilty over that. Tonight, it was all about the two of them, Kate and Quinn.

He ran his hands over her body, memorizing each curve and dip and swell. She was delicate yet strong, her breasts more than filling his palms, the curve of her ass so tempting he pulled her to him and ran his hands over them, tracing them. He swept the tips of his fingers the length of her spine, then down into that hot cleft between the cheeks of her ass.

"One of these nights I'm going to take you here," he breathed, pressing his fingertips to her opening. "If you let me."

She shivered beneath his touch but nodded mutely.

"But tonight you still have too many clothes on," she pointed out. "I want to see every inch of you, too."

He stripped and tossed his clothes to the side, her gaze on him the entire time. When he was stark naked, he reached for her, but she surprised him. Taking a step back, she dropped to her knees and wrapped the fingers of one hand around his cock. He sucked in his breath at her touch, his blood pounding in his veins.

He watched her as she slid her fingers up and down his thick shaft, hoping he had enough control to let her do what she wanted. He sensed this was not a common thing for her. Something she'd done rarely, if ever, and the emotion of it smacked him right in his heart. He called on every bit of his discipline to stand there while she stroked him.

Tightening her fingers on him, she slid the other hand between his thighs, cupping his balls and giving them a gentle squeeze.

Jesus!

She continued to glide her hand up and down his shaft, playing with his balls and driving him so crazy he was afraid he'd explode. Then she did the unexpected and took him into her mouth. He nearly detonated.

"Uh, Kate." His brain was so fogged he didn't know where he found words to speak. "You, uh, might want to be careful there."

She jerked her head back, scraping her teeth on his cock, and looked up at him with a worried expression on her face.

"Am I doing it wrong? I didn't know—I've never—"

Damn. He was right. She'd never done this before, and that only made him hotter.

"You're doing it just fine, darlin'." He swallowed. Hard. "But you're taking me close to the edge here, and I want to be inside you when I come."

"Oh." She licked her lips, the sight almost putting him over the edge right then and there. "Should I stop?"

"Not yet." He'd hold on as long as he could.

She closed her fingers around him again and swiped her tongue over the dark head, once, twice, again. She was sliding her hand up and down again when she dipped the tip of her tongue into the slit to lick the drop of fluid there, and that was it for him.

"I'd love to let you keep on, but I need to be inside you right now." Would he ever get to a point with her where he didn't have this acute need to sheath himself in the warmth of her sex?

In seconds, he had her on the bed on her back, legs spread and knees bent. He moved over her, positioning his hips between her widespread thighs and bending her knees to give himself greater access. His breath caught at the glisten of moisture on the lips of her sex, and he couldn't help himself. He had to take one taste.

"Ohhhhh." The sound whispered from her as he ran his tongue the length of her slit and back again. He wanted to spend hours just licking her and tasting her, playing with her clit and sliding his fingers in and out of her waiting channel. Maybe one of these nights he'd have enough control to do it.

But not tonight. No, not tonight. Tonight he was again like a man possessed. He placed the head of his cock at her opening, and with one swift stroke, he plunged inside her.

"Okay?" He breathed, watching her face.

Kate nodded.

"Here we go." He moved his hips, setting up the familiar rhythm. He wanted—demanded—the steady strokes that would tip them past the flashpoint.

And then it was there, an orgasm of such gigantic proportions he wasn't sure he'd live through it. Every muscle convulsed, her inner walls clenched and unclenched around him. Liquid poured from her, bathing him. On and on, he drove her, his thick shaft stretching her.

She reached one plane, gasping, and with a roll of his hips, he carried her with him to the next level. They were both struggling for air, his heart threatening to pound itself out of his chest. And finally, when he'd taken her over the edge twice, he carried her with him one more time as he allowed his own release.

Quinn collapsed forward, catching himself on his forearms, struggling for breath, sweat gluing their skin together. It could have been minutes, an hour, a week. He had no idea how much time had passed until he roused himself and slid carefully from her body. He rolled to the side, taking her with him, watching her closely.

"You okay?" He brushed her damp chestnut curls back from her cheeks. Her hazel eyes had tiny flecks of gold in them as she studied his face. "Everything okay?"

She huffed a little laugh, "Are you kidding? More than."

He stroked her cheek, and his rough silk lips pressed kisses to her ear.

"You're mine now," he rasped. "Mine. Do not forget it."

"Yours," she agreed.

"I will protect you and take care of you. Count on it." He drew in a lungful of air. "We'll get past this and then take a look at the rest of our lives. Okay, darlin'?"

She nodded, nestling into his strength and was asleep almost before she closed her eyes.

Chapter Sixteen

Quinn's phone rang at seven-thirty in the morning, but it wasn't Jake's voice on the other end.

"All right, we'll do it your way, Quinn, but don't fuck with me and pull some last minute stunt." Kane Barton's voice boomed across the connection. "I'll come out and arrest both of you myself."

"Nice to hear from you, too, Kane." Quinn worked to keep the anger from his voice. That big man himself had made the call was an indication of the seriousness of the situation.

"Jake was in my office first thing this morning pleading your case, with Dean assuring me this is the right way to go."

"If you don't want a dead woman on your hands, it is." Quinn bit off his words. "I expect Jake explained everything to you?"

"Yes. And you can be sure it's only our personal relationship that's got me to agree with this. Otherwise, I'd have Jake out there with a warrant and two armed guards."

"I'm glad to hear we still have a personal relationship." Quinn's voice was tinged with irony, remembering the last time they'd seen each other. When he'd delivered the cartel members—dumped them at his feet—their parting had been anything but cordial

There was a brief pause. "I have a lot of respect for you, Quinn, and I'd like to think, even after all this time, we're still friends. I understand your concerns, and I certainly don't want to endanger anyone's life. But I have to have that flash drive, and Jake says she'll only give it up to me."

"If you do it the way we asked," Quinn agreed.

"I see nothing wrong with that, although I'm losing a day when our techs could already be working on it." His heavy sigh was audible. "And what the hell is this about people in my office being paid off?"

"I'm just telling you what Kate heard," he said, repeating Peter's words, "but it's definitely the kind of thing they do. And very carefully, so there's no trace back to them."

"Now, wait a minute," Kane began.

"I'm not pointing fingers, just passing along information. But as delicate as this whole thing is, it wouldn't hurt for everyone to take a look at their staff and see if someone seems a little hinky."

"I'd hate to think I've got a virus on my staff, but you're right. I can't afford not to check. All right then. Let's go over the details of your little road trip."

"We'll do it tonight, like I said, when almost everyone's gone. We can drive directly into the garage and take your private elevator up to your floor. Kate's scared to death about coming into town, but she agrees that this gives her the maximum safety possible."

Kane was silent for a moment. "Fine. And I'll be sure to pick my own security people. What time?"

"Seven o'clock. And Kane? If we get anything off that flash drive, it would be nice to tell her. After all, without her, we wouldn't even have it."

"I'll see what we can do after I look at it myself. I'll expect you and the woman and that nice little piece of equipment at seven."

Quinn disconnected the call and turned to Kate. "We're on." He explained to her exactly what they would be doing and how.

"And you're sure I'll be safe this way?" she asked.

"As safe as we can make it. I spoke to Kane Barton himself."

Her fingers twisted the terry cloth of the towel she'd wrapped around her body. "Quinn, I know I keep saying this, but I'm really scared. The more I learn, the more terrified I am. With a cartel this powerful, anything could happen tonight."

"Yes, it could. I won't lie to you. There's always the possibility something will go wrong no matter what. But there's no guarantee we'd be safe just hiding up here, either. Or trying to find another rabbit hole to crawl into. Especially now they've zeroed in on your car. The only thing to do is get this over with and put the bad guys out of business."

"I know," she sighed, still playing with the towel.

He cupped her cheeks and feathered kisses on her eyelids. "I'll be right beside you every step of the way. I won't leave your side."

She stared out the oversized dining room window, watching the sun's rays dancing on the wild grasses. "You know, for a little while, I pretended none of it was real. That this—" She waved her hand at him and the house. "—was the only reality. Telling you and Jake brought it all back into focus again."

Quinn pulled her into his arms, pressing her against his chest.

"It will be better after tonight," he soothed. "When we leave for town, we won't go through Windswept. There are plenty of back country roads to take without going directly to the Interstate. Roads where I can spot a tail and lose it if I have to." He smiled into her eyes. "Once we get past tonight, we can come back up here and hide forever."

"And Peter?" she asked, biting her lip. Every time she thought of him she felt sick.

"He'll be too busy saving his own ass to worry about yours. You can bet on that."

"God, I hope so." She shivered. "I want my life back."

He pressed his lips to her hair. "I love you, Kate. I'm going to do my best to keep you safe." *Mine,* he thought savagely. Then he swatted her lightly on her ass. "Come on. Let's get dressed, and I'll fix us some lunch."

When the sun began to set and they got ready to leave the house, she watched Quinn take out both of his handguns, load them, and carry them to the truck.

"Do you expect to have to defend me in the prosecutor's office?" she teased, although in her mind it wasn't so farfetched. "I didn't think they were that tough."

"Just a precaution, darlin'. Just a precaution."

****

"Peter."

Not much penetrated his control, but Peter Fleming chilled at the sound of the voice on the other end of the call. "What do you want?" He'd been dreading this call, tried his best to avoid it.

"Is that any way to open this conversation? I

should think that someone in your position would want to curry as much favor as possible."

"And what position is that?" But he knew. This call only confirmed it. A sour taste rose from his stomach.

"You know what position. Any further word on the location of the girl?"

"Maybe." It was time to buy himself a little breathing room. Briefly he reported on what he'd learned about the car and the library.

"So we can be sure she's in the area."

"I'd say so."

"Then find her. Now. Misjudging that girl and letting her slip through your fingers was bad enough, but to let her steal that storage unit with so much information on it…"

"It isn't as if I *let* her." His tone was acid sharp.

"Never mind. It happened. That's all that's important. Just get more men on it if you have to. By the way, as soon as I'm back in town, I'll want you to move to the condo."

Damn!

"Why? I'm doing just fine here at Esai's."

"Because I can keep a closer eye on you there. And if we have to rebuild the entire corporate structure, I want you doing it under my eyes."

I'll bet you do. Bitch.

"I'm going to call Pendera again shortly," he said. "He tells me there's some activity in his office. He didn't know what so I told him to find out or I'll cut off his balls. We don't pay for ignorance."

"How delicately you put it. But whatever works, I suppose." The voice became even colder. "Meanwhile, in our inefficient bumbling, we've killed people who have nothing to do with us. You know how I feel about that. It's the kind of thing that draws unwanted attention."

Peter always wondered why it even raised an eyebrow, the killing of insignificant people. The collateral damage. Blood was sprinkled liberally on everyone's hands in the organization a hundred times over.

"It isn't the killing I mind so much," the voice went on, as if reading Peter's mind. "It's the loose ends it leaves. Threads that might lead back to us."

And that's the heart of the matter.

"The men were very good with the cleanup," Peter protested.

"Three bodies with no reason to be murdered create a lot of questions," the person argued. "We can't afford that. The next dead body I see must be hers."

"I've got it, okay?"

"Something for you to keep in mind as you proceed here. If you think you're immune from the same retribution as everyone else, let me assure that's not the case. Your protection is only as good as your performance, despite what you might think."

A click indicated the call had been terminated.

Peter sat with the dead receiver in his hand. The caller was perhaps the only person that gave Miguel and Esai a sense of unease. What chance did *he* stand? For the first time in his life, fear spread its icy fingers through his body.

He was on his fourth cup of coffee and his second helping of antacid tablets when his cell phone rang.

"I need to see you at once." Efron Pendera sounded as if the hounds of hell were after him.

"You have something for us?"

"Not on the phone. Meet me in that little diner on Navarro. It'll take me about fifteen minutes to walk there." He disconnected without waiting for an answer.

Cursing in two languages, Peter went in search of a set of car keys for one of Esai's fleet of cars.

His phone rang again while he was driving.

"It's Alfredo," the voice said. "I showed her picture around using the same sob story. Most people just shrugged me off, but a couple of people recognized her. Said she's gone off with some guy who lives up in the hills." He cleared his throat. "Someone they seemed reluctant to talk about. Want me to pursue it?"

A sick feeling rocketed through Peter's stomach. "His name wouldn't happen to be Quinn, would it?"

"Yeah? How'd you know?"

"Never mind." *Shit, shit, shit.* "Did you find out where he lives, by any chance?"

Alfredo snorted. "I could find the Lost Dutchman Mine a lot easier. And no amount of muscle or money is going to pry it loose from anyone, I can tell you that. Who is this guy, anyway?"

Peter popped another antacid tablet. "Someone you wouldn't want to know. Keep trying and call me back in an hour."

Fifteen minutes later, he slid into the diner booth opposite Pendera, waving away the hovering waitress. "What's so urgent I had to drop everything?"

"I managed to overhear a conversation this morning that everyone needs to know about."

"Yeah? How did that happen when you haven't been able to find out squat up until now?"

Pendera took out his handkerchief and mopped his

forehead. "Fortune smiled on me. By some circumstance, I happened to be outside Kane Barton's door when he was having a phone call with someone. A man named Quinn."

"God damn it," Peter muttered, barely restraining himself from banging his fist on the table. "I'd like to kill that fucker myself. Go on."

"Thank God the walls in the building are paper thin." Nervously, he repeated the subsequent conversation he'd heard Barton have with Jake Garza and Dean Morgan. "I left as quickly as I could, without raising suspicion, and called you. So what do you think? Is this what you're looking for?"

"Yes." Peter wished he'd agreed to meet in a bar. He wanted a drink in the worst way. "If we don't grab the woman before she steps into their office, they'll have the goddamn flash drive and we'll be in deep shit. And it doesn't look like we'll have any luck locating the man she's with beforehand. Damn it all to hell anyway."

Peter drew in a long breath. He was losing it, and he couldn't afford to do that. Not now. He was silent for a moment, turning everything over in his mind. He punched a number into his cell.

"Salazar? I have a job for you. Meet me at Esai's in half an hour." He snapped his phone shut, sighed, and pinched the bridge of his nose. "Efron. You're sure Quinn is bringing the girl in at seven tonight? Your information is correct?"

"Yes. Right into the garage and up in Barton's private elevator."

"All right. I don't like it, but I'll have to take her there. It will be the only time she's exposed. We can't let her get to that meeting." He opened a paper napkin. "Draw me a diagram of the garage."

Pendera shook his head. "Pedro, that won't work. It's impossible to get someone in there. There are guards everywhere. And cameras."

"Not everywhere, *pendejo*. How do the janitors dump the trash?"

Efron stared into his coffee cup. It was obvious he didn't want to do this.

"Efron?" Peter's voice was soft, but the tone lethal. "Don't fuck with me on this."

"There's a side door by the dumpster. It's also used as an emergency exit."

"No guard? Easy access?"

"You need a key card to open it. A guard opens it for the cleaning crew."

"And you have such a card, don't you, amigo?"

Pendera squirmed under the steady gaze. "Yes."

"Hand it over." He stretched out he his hand.

"Peter, I can't…"

Peter snapped his fingers. "The card. Now."

Sweating profusely, Pendera pulled the key card from his wallet and dropped it into Peter's hand. He had to make two tries, he was shaking so badly.

"Now the keys to your car."

"What?"

"I'll get them back to you. Don't worry." *Because you aren't ever going to need them again.* "Be sure you're inside that door at six-thirty just in case. You hear me?"

Pendera stared. "Yes. I hear you." He looked as if he also heard the bells of doom clanging in his head.

"Go back to work. Act natural. Don't screw this

up."

He dropped dollar bills on the table to pay for the coffee and walked away.

****

Quinn left the house early enough to take several detours before actually heading downtown. They were well east of Windswept before he picked up the Interstate. One or two times he thought he spotted a tail, but then the car veered in another direction.

"Probably someone going home," he told Kate. "I'm just making sure."

If the Hill Country was a pioneer woman draped in earth tones, San Antonio was a laughing senorita in a riotous explosion of color—vivid reds and yellows and blues that tantalized the senses. The city was full of life and rich in history, from the winding San Antonio River to the Mexican Marketplace to the Alamo, the famous Cradle of Liberty. It was a blend of cultures, of personalities, a throbbing life force, that wrapped you in its flowing cape and challenged you to embrace it.

The streets were crowded with people in colorful attire, tourists and residents alike out for an evening's festivities. The faint sounds of a mariachi band drifted up from the Riverwalk below, punctuated by the laughter of the pedestrians. Horns honked as cars negotiated turns, and bells dinged as the bicycle police pedaled their routes.

"I'd love to be able to really see the city sometime," Kate said wistfully, as they wound their way through the streets. "It all looks so exciting."

"San Antonio is a wonderful place," Quinn told her. "I used to spend a lot of time down here. The restaurants are great, and there's always something going on." His face tightened. "Lisa and Nikki used to love eating right by the water, then riding on one of the sightseeing barges."

Kate reached over and touched his arm. "I'm so very sorry about what happened." What else could she say?

"It's all right." He moved her hand from his arm and curled his big one around it. "At least now you've freed me to talk about them."

Kate studied his beautiful face, the angular planes, the square jaw, the eyes like onyx framed with thick lashes, all capped with that silky midnight hair. She wanted to memorize it in case something happened. When she reached up and touched his cheek, tracing the line of his cheekbone, he took her hand again and kissed her palm.

"I'll say it again, Kate. Everything will be fine. We're on the right track here."

"God, I'll be glad when this is over." She leaned her head back against the seat.

"Just a little while longer. Then at least tonight will be out of the way."

The guard at the garage entrance called upstairs for Kane's okay, then waved them through.

"Mr. Barton says Mr. Garza will meet you at the elevator," he told them. "He said you know where it is."

"Thanks." Quinn drove on into the concrete cavern.

They parked in a slot right next to the elevator just as the doors opened and Jake emerged. Quinn jumped down from the truck cab as Kate released the catch on her seatbelt and gathered her purse. The men shook hands.

"We're all set upstairs," Jake said. "Everyone's

waiting." Then, noting Quinn's sport shirt worn loose rather than tucked in, added, "Is that shirt hiding what I think it is? You can't take your guns upstairs, Quinn. You know better than that. Besides—" He opened his jacket. "—I'm carrying and so is Dean."

"I know. I just feel naked without them. And I want to make sure we give Kate all the protection possible." He grinned. "It was worth a shot."

"Well, stash them away, and let's move. I don't want to stand here any longer than possible."

Quinn pulled the gun out of his waistband at the small of his back. Kate opened her door and turned to exit the truck, and Jake headed toward the truck to help her as Quinn bent down to put his gun in the box under his seat. A soft *thunk!* sounded, and the driver's side window shattered.

Chapter Seventeen

As soon as he heard it, Quinn recognized it for what it was. A shot from a weapon with a silencer. He whirled in a crouching stance, gun still gripped in his hand.

"Down!" he shouted. "Kate, get down."

He looked only long enough to see that Kate wasn't visible and Jake had pressed himself against the alcove wall, gun in hand. Eyes swiveling, Quinn searched for the source of the shot.

"Won't need a gun?" he hollered to Jake.

He started to rise from his crouch when he heard another soft *thunk* and something pinged on the metal of the truck right next to him.

"A silencer," he yelled. "Shots coming from the cars behind the elevator."

Jake, still using the alcove for cover, had his cell phone out. "I'm calling upstairs. Don't take any chances."

Using the parked cars as shields, Quinn moved to the other side of the elevator housing. Two more bullets zinged over his head, and he fired in their direction. Then he heard a motor turn over and a door slam. Tires squealed as a car backed out of a space just up ahead and burned rubber toward the exit. Quinn stood up and fired three more shots at the retreating vehicle. He had the satisfaction of seeing glass shatter, but then the car was gone.

Shoving his gun back into the waistband of his pants, he ran back to his truck.

"Are you okay?" he asked Jake.

Garza, holding his cell phone to his ear, nodded.

"Kate?" he called as he came around the truck. "You can stand up now, darlin'. It's okay."

No one answered him. When he reached the passenger side of the truck, his heart stopped beating. Kate lay crumpled on the floor, one arm outstretched, a pool of blood widening beneath her.

"Call for paramedics," Quinn shouted to Jake as he knelt beside her, hands searching for the wound. "Tell them to get their asses here right now."

The hours after that were a kaleidoscope of activities for Quinn, time shrinking and expanding. The shooting had barely stopped before the elevator doors opened and several men pounded out into the garage. Two of them were security guards with guns drawn, but Jake shook his head at them. Whoever had done this was long gone. Kane Barton and Dean Morgan crouched beside Quinn as he tried to assess Kate's condition and find the source of the bleeding.

"EMTs are on the way," Kane said. "Where's she hit?"

"I don't know."

He was afraid to turn her over, afraid not to. Gingerly, he rolled her toward him, saw the blood flowing from her arm and her side. He yanked his handkerchief from his pocket, bunched up her blouse and pressed it against her side, the source of the greatest bleeding. Holding it tightly, he blinked at the tears clouding his eyes. Everything in the garage receded except for him and Kate, lying there so small and white, covered in blood.

"Kate? Darlin'? Can you hear me?"

I promised to protect her. If she dies, it's my fault. Shit, shit, shit. Not again. Please God, not again. Don't let me fail twice.

Tires screeched as vehicles roared into the garage. Heavy footsteps sounded next to him. He felt a hand on his arm and shook it off.

"Quinn." Jake's voice, solid and steady. "The paramedics are here."

Quinn didn't move or make any sign of acknowledgment.

"Quinn. Damn it, let them get to her."

More hands, pulling him away as two strangers in blue coveralls took his place beside Kate.

Voices, floating around him.

"Get a tourniquet and pressure packs on her."

"She's shocky. Start an IV drip now. Get the high-flow oxygen going."

"Call the hospital. I've got the patches on for the EKG. Tell them to stand by for her vitals."

Quinn loomed over them. "What is it? What's going on? Damn it, someone tell me something."

"She's bleeding a lot," one of the EMTs said. "She's lucky, it's not arterial blood. But the bullet's still in her, and we don't know what damage it did. We need to get her to the hospital right away."

"Kate." Oh, god. The pain he felt was like a knife to his heart.

"They're taking care of her." Jake's voice. Soft. Kind. Reassuring.

More people arriving. Men in suits, in casual

clothes, in police uniforms. Kane Barton, looking like a thunderhead, issuing orders in a harsh voice.

Quinn shook his head to clear it, then barged his way into the ambulance. "I'm riding with her."

No one was about to argue with him.

Images piled on each other in his brain. The wild ride to the hospital, sirens screaming. Jogging beside the stretcher as they wheeled Kate into emergency. Protesting violently when they insisted he wait outside the treatment area.

The normal activities of the hospital swirled and eddied around him, but he might have been in an isolation room for all the attention he paid to it. Jake, Dean, and Kane found him pacing the corridor in the trauma area, muttering curses under his breath.

"How is she?" Dean asked.

"I don't know. They won't tell me a damn thing. God." He raked his fingers through his hair. "How in hell did this happen? How did I *let* it happen?"

"No one *let* anything happen," Jake stated. "What I'd like to know is how someone knew you guys were coming and when? We didn't discuss it with anyone."

"There's a leak somewhere," Quinn said and turned to Kane. "This is exactly what Kate tried to tell you. What she was afraid of. None of you took it seriously. Well, it's serious now. You'd better fix it quick, damn it."

A doctor emerged from the treatment room, searching for someone, and Quinn stepped forward.

"What's happening?" he demanded.

"I'm Dr. Halsey. Are you with the young woman just brought in?"

"Yes. I want to know what her condition is."

"Are you family?"

"I'm her fiancé." Quinn gritted his teeth, ignoring the shocked faces around him.

"All right. We've got her stabilized, but the bullet's still inside her, and we've got to get it out. I've called for a surgeon."

"But she'll be all right." A statement. A question would bring answers he wasn't ready to hear.

"I think so, but we can't tell any more than that until we get her in surgery. Can you sign the consent forms for her?"

"Yes. Give them to me." He grabbed the clipboard and scrawled his signature.

A man in green scrubs jogged down the hall and joined them. "I'm Dr. DeWitt, the surgeon." He nodded at Halsey. "We're all set upstairs. Let's go."

Quinn saw that two uniformed officers had arrived and were now stationed on either side of the treatment room entrance.

"They'll be on guard outside the operating area and Recovery," Kane told him, "and then outside her room. I cleared it with the hospital, then called SAPD, and they were only too happy to help. I could have put agents on the door, but I figured the uniforms look scarier if someone gets ideas."

"Did anyone see anything? Hear anything? Did you check the guard logs at the garage entrance?" Quinn asked, raking his hands through his hair.

Trust me, I told her. I'll take care of you. Damn, damn, damn.

Dean nodded. "Nothing. No one who shouldn't be there."

"Then how the hell did he get in?" Images of Lisa

and Nikki on the sidewalk flashed through his mind, then the picture of Kate lying bloody on the concrete. *Not again. God, please don't let it happen again.*

"You can bet I'll find out." Kane Barton loomed over them, his voice tight with rage.

"This is my fault," Quinn raged, sick with guilt. "I talked her into doing this. I told her I'd protect her, and now she's nearly dead because of me."

"Hey." Jake was beside him, one hand gripping his shoulder. "This is nobody's fault. We knew they were narrowing their search. We just didn't expect it in our own garage. Don't beat yourself up over it. And she's going to be fine. Believe it."

The doors to the treatment room opened and scrub-clad figures wheeled a gurney out. Quinn homed in on it, ignoring people who tried to brush him aside, taking Kate's small, cold hand in his own, trotting along as they moved rapidly down the hall. He felt sick as his eyes raked over her white face, the IVs running into her system, the various instruments attached to monitor her.

"I think she'll be okay," Dr. DeWitt said as they jogged along beside the gurney. "But we need to get her in the OR right now. Don't hold us up, okay?"

They let Quinn ride up with them in the elevator, but when huge double doors swung open, they wheeled Kate through, and he was left alone again. He turned as a second elevator opened, the two cops from downstairs taking up their places outside the operating suite. Kane, Jake, and Dean were right behind them.

"Let's go sit over there," Dean said, gesturing toward a cluster of molded plastic chairs at the end of the hall. "Come on."

"I can't sit." Quinn shook off the man's arm.

"You can't do her any good pacing the floor, either," Kane said. "Let's at least put our time to good use and see if we can make sense out of this."

Reluctantly, Quinn nodded and followed them to the waiting area.

"I didn't even get to tell you it's nice to see you again, Quinn," Kane began. "We've missed you. Sorry for the hardass attitude about this, but you have no idea the magnitude of this case. Or the reach of this organization."

"This is why I didn't want to bring her into town," he reminded his former boss, his gut twisted in agony.

"I think, on this one, it wouldn't have mattered where you were. If they wanted her, they were going to do their damnedest to get her."

Exactly what Jake had said, last night and today.

Before Kane could say more, another crowd of men tramped off the elevator, some in suits and ties, others in jeans and polo shirts. Quinn recognized a few of them from the garage. Kane and Dean went to meet them.

"The guys on the Strike Force," Jake told him in a low voice. "Some of them were at the office. The others were contacted at home. Kane's going to meet with Noah and Clay, and they'll be making assignments ASAP." He looked at his friend. "We need to get you a change of clothes."

Quinn glanced down at himself. His shirt and T-shirt were soaked with blood. Kate's blood. Her life, seeping onto him as he'd held her in his arms. Terror gripped him all over again. Could she lose this much blood and still be all right?

He shook his head. "I'm not leaving here."

"I know. I know." Jake sighed. "All right. Let me see what I can do."

He got up and walked down the hall.

The group of men was just dispersing. Those who knew Quinn from before stopped to express concern. Then they were gone, back to their offices or out on the streets to piece together the night's fiasco.

Jake was back in less than ten minutes carrying the top half of a set of hospital scrubs which he handed to Quinn. "Put this on. At least when Kate opens her eyes you'll look semi-presentable."

Kane Barton waited until Quinn had exchanged his bloody clothes for the cotton garment, then looked at him and said, "Give."

Quinn forced himself to focus, dredging up every detail, every scrap of information, he could remember. How he'd met Kate, everything she'd told him, all the information he and Jake had pulled from her. Jake added details that Quinn forgot. And then everything he could remember about the shooting. They went back and forth until Kane was satisfied there was nothing more to be had.

"You realize that first bullet was meant for you," Jake pointed out. "If you hadn't bent over to put your gun back in the truck, you'd be in the morgue right now."

"A gun?" Dean, leaning against the wall, raised an eyebrow. "You were bringing a gun to the federal prosecutor's office?"

"Yeah, and it looks like I needed it, doesn't it." Quinn dry washed his face with his hands. "I don't understand, though. I thought Kate was already out of the truck when he fired."

"She was just getting out," Jake told him. "Another two seconds and she would have been safe."

"They weren't aiming that first shot at her, anyway," Dean added.

Quinn's face was set in angry lines. "They needed to take me out to get to her. If the shooter had gotten me, the next bullet would have been for you, Jake, and Kate would be history. They want her alive, so they can find out what she's told to who. And retrieve their flash drive."

Jake's face when he turned to his two bosses was grim. "I told you she was worried about a leak in our office. Looks like she wasn't wrong after all."

"Yeah, Quinn's mentioned that once or twice." Dean Morgan's expression was dour.

"Speaking of that little item," Kane, said, "do you happen to know where it is now?"

Quinn reached into his pocket and pulled out the little silver rectangle. He'd retrieved it from Kate's purse while the paramedics were attending to her. "You'd better take damn good care of this thing. She may have given her life to protect it."

Kane's face was dark with fury but not at Quinn. "You can be sure as hell I'll be asking a lot of questions in the morning. We also have to figure out where to stash Kate when the hospital releases her. A safe house. At least until we've got the Osunas locked up nice and tight."

"Forget it," Quinn said, in a voice that said don't interfere. "I'll be taking care of that. This is not up for discussion."

"We'll get back to that as soon as I find out how tonight happened." Kane rose from the bench where he'd been sitting. "Dean and I need to get back to the office. We have a lot to do right now to figure out this mess." He shook hands again with Quinn. "I want to make some other security arrangements here at the hospital, too. Jake, you want to walk to the elevator with me?"

Quinn watched the men speaking quietly in the hallway. He'd take whatever help he could get here, but then Kate was all his. He'd let her down once by listening to other people. It wouldn't happen again. Next time, he'd make the choices.

In a moment, Jake was back, carrying two cups of vending machine coffee. Quinn drank without even tasting it. He paced. He sat. He paced again. Jake brought more coffee, which he barely remembered drinking. Each time the doors to the operating suites opened, he held himself erect, rigid, preparing himself for the expected blow. Each time, when only strangers emerged, he looked away.

At last, when he was sure he'd lose his mind, Dr. DeWitt came through the double doors, scraping his surgical cap from his head. He looked tired but not solemn.

"She'll be all right," he said before Quinn could get the question out of his mouth. "The bullet caught her arm because of the angle as it entered her side. It hit a rib and splintered, scattering fragments and nicking a lot of internal organs." He wiped a thin sheen of sweat from his forehead. "We had to do a lot of repair work, and she'll be in quite a lot of pain at first, but she's going to be fine. She just won't be running any relays for a while."

"Can I see her?"

"Just for a second. She's on her way to Recovery. We'll notify you as soon as we move her to a room. I wanted to put her in ICU, but Kane Barton killed that idea. He wants her isolated."

Quinn nodded. "I agree."

"We'll set her up in a private room with whatever she needs. And Kane's sending over his own nurses once she's settled." He turned his head as the doors opened behind him. "Here she comes now."

If Kate's appearance had scared Quinn before, the way she looked now terrified him. She was even paler, if that was possible, blending into the whiteness of the sheets. One arm was in the hospital gown, the other uncovered and swathed with bandages. More bulky bandages peeked out the side of the gown. But it was her utter stillness that made his heart stop.

"Are you sure she's okay?" Quinn persisted, gripped by anxiety. "She doesn't look it."

"She's just had some very extensive surgery," the doctor reminded him. "She lost a lot of blood, and she's still not out from under the anesthetic. Give her a couple of hours. Even then, I wouldn't expect too much for a day or two."

"All right." He reached for Kate's limp hand and squeezed it to assure himself there was still some warmth in her body.

They reached the far end of the hall where another set of doors opened, the gurney was rolled through it and once again Quinn was left behind in the antiseptic-smelling corridor. He didn't even hear Jake come up behind him until he spoke.

"I called my office and gave them an update on Kate's situation. The cops have moved to Recovery, although I don't think the nurses are too excited about it. Kane also called the hospital administrator who should be in his office by now. Let's go hunt him up."

"I want to wait until they move Kate to a room."

"That will be at least two hours, Ace. They'll let us know when it happens. Come on, buddy. You can't do her any good standing here."

Quinn stared at the doors through which Kate had disappeared, unwilling to move and be somehow disconnected from her. Then, reluctantly, he turned and followed Jake to the elevator.

Chapter Eighteen

When the phone at Esai Osuna's house rang shortly after midnight, the message cryptic and urgent, he and Peter raced to a condo on the far north side of San Antonio, knowing all hell was about to break loose.

Everything had turned to shit. Salazar had dropped Pendera's lifeless body in the dumpster and positioned himself in the garage. But then he'd shot Kathryn by mistake. Pendera's body was likely to be found any moment and Salazar was somewhere on the loose. Kathryn was either dead or dying, and in any event, surrounded by so much protection a fly couldn't get through.

And it was a certainty the feds had the all-important flash drive. The one thing that could sink them if they didn't work fast.

The cartel operations had literally ground to a standstill. The key players were gathered for a council of war at the home of the leader who had returned to San Antonio filled with wrath. Miguel had flown in on his jet from Florida and was staying in one of the guest suites at *el jefe's* condo. Peter and Esai had been summoned to join the happy group.

Peter wondered if he closed his eyes and wished very hard as he'd done when he was a young child, would he be transported to another place where none of what was happening was real.

A tall, striking woman, jet black hair swept back in a French twist, lips a bright slash of scarlet, smoked furiously as she paced the thick carpet in the lavish living room. The air was thick with rage and frustration. She stared viciously at Peter.

He stared back, said simply, "Hello, Mother."

"I can't imagine what possible explanation there can be for this fiasco." Eva Osuna Fleming Gallagher Burke's voice was cold and hard, her eyes filled with rage as she looked around the room, first at one person, then another.

"There is none." Esai Osuna looked as if he had a bad taste in his mouth. "Your son lost the girl, and the feds have the flash drive, also thanks to Peter. I don't imagine things could be any worse."

"You know this isn't all my fault," Peter protested. "I tracked the car and pinpointed the area she was in. Can I help it if the incompetents you people sent out there couldn't find her in such a small area?"

"That does not change the fact that the government now has that flash drive," Esai reminded him, "with all the details of our operation. All of them."

"The drive is encrypted," Peter reminded them. He was sure he'd repeated the same words a thousand times over the past few days. "I wrote the code myself. It won't be one they can break."

"Don't delude yourself," Eva told him. "Today the government has cryptologists who can break any code ever written. We just have to hope it takes them long enough that we can restructure ourselves first. The physical process is already underway. When they start looking for money and merchandise, they'll find nothing but empty warehouses and bank accounts with zero balances."

"I think we all need to step back a bit and take a deep breath," Peter told her. "Stop pointing fingers at each other. That doesn't do a damn bit of good." God, anything to shut her up. He was getting tired of being the evening's whipping boy.

"Peter, in case the degree of your stupidity has escaped you, let me spell it out for you." She lit a cigarette and blew out a thin stream of smoke. "You of all people know the lengths we went to in creating a dummy corporate structure that mimics a multi-national operation. It allows us to move goods and supplies and exchange money all under the guise of corporate business. People might suspect, but there was no way to prove anything."

"Yes," he interrupted, "but—"

"I'm not finished." She inhaled another lungful of smoke. "Now, in a blink, all of that has changed, putting us at an extreme disadvantage. I wouldn't think you'd need me to point this out to you. Every bank account we set up so painstakingly. Every supplier and distributor. Everything is on that little piece of technology you so stupidly left out in plain sight. Now we have to recreate everything from scratch."

"And that doesn't include what could be our biggest problem," Miguel interjected.

Eva whipped around. "And what would that be?"

"The people on the payoff list. When they discover they've been exposed, they might turn on us to save their own necks."

"*Cristo!*" She stubbed out her cigarette with vicious strokes. "Too bad we can't kill them all. We're exposed in a way I never thought we would be. Well, let's start with the most important names and figure out how to handle them"

"I'll take on that responsibility," Miguel said. "I think we can safeguard most of them. The others will just have to be smart enough to keep their mouths shut."

"If you'll just let me explain something," Peter tried again.

"There is nothing for you to explain. I am ashamed to think that a son of mine is so brainless he's put us in this position." She paced, her skirt swishing around her legs as she moved from one side of the room to another. "And the bodies that keep piling up in plain sight. Can no one carry out a simple assignment anymore? The fiascos in Charlotte and Los Angeles were bad enough, not to mention the library debacle. But what happened at the federal building is a disaster. We should have gotten rid of Salazar long ago."

The Osuna brothers sat quietly, listening. Esai shifted in his chair, watching his sister. What would the reaction be, Peter wondered, if the world knew that this woman was the true brains and power behind their cartel? That it was her money that seeded it, her brilliant idea to create a phony law firm to cover all their activities? Her idea to educate the brightest sons and daughters of their distributors as lawyers to do the grunt work?

He often wondered where the loyalties of their people would lie in the event of a power struggle. Whose side would they be on? His? Miguel's? Eva's?

"At least he also took care of Pendera," Peter pointed out. "You can bet there'll be a full scale rout in the prosecutor's office tomorrow. We won't have to worry about him cracking under the pressure."

"Pah!" She waved a hand in the air. "Pendera was a flea. But now any chance at the female is lost. The data transporter is gone. All we have to show for our poor efforts is a string of dead bodies and a Herculean task ahead of us."

"Regardless, we need to get busy regrouping," Esai said. "We still have an operation to run. We can't just stand still."

Miguel turned to Eva. "How long do you think it will take before they are at our door with warrants in hand?"

"I won't even speculate. But I'm preparing for anything. Remember, they still have no idea I even exist, so this condo is our safest place." She blew another stream of smoke. "Peter, you'll be setting up shop in the den for the foreseeable future."

"Here?" Please, no. He had to get out of here. He dug two antacid tablets from his pocket and tossed them in his mouth.

"Meanwhile," Eva said, ignoring him, "we'll go about our business quietly. As long as the basic system still functions we're in business, and no one will be the wiser.

"How will we keep track of things?" Miguel asked.

"Peter can set up an encrypted file just to keep a running list. As he gets the new structure in place he can plug in the information."

"And the people on the payoff list?"

"I leave that in your hands, Miguel. Handle it however you see fit. Warn them. Eliminate them. Whatever works best and fastest. Peter, you'd better get started on this immediately. The new bank accounts are critical."

"Of course, Mother." He made no effort to hide the sarcasm. "Whatever you say."

"This is your mess," she spat at him. "Clean it up."

Peter said nothing, just poured himself a drink from the bar against the mirrored wall. What shocked him most was the news that Kathryn had somehow hooked up with the legendary Quinn. How the hell had that happened? What an incredible piece of bad luck.

How in God's name had everything fallen apart like this? He'd had such a sweet deal. Now he saw his cherished lifestyle disappearing like a wisp of smoke. But he had an ace in the hole, which was why he was here rather than exiled to some godforsaken mud hole. He was the only one who could rebuild the corporate structure and encrypt everything.

Taking his drink with him, he quietly slipped out of the room into the den. Once he was finished with his work, he absolutely had to find a way out of this.

Chapter Nineteen

"Thank you for coming down here," Quinn told the man standing in front of him.

Roused from his home, hospital administrator David Nolan was only too happy to help the U.S. Attorney any way he could. Now he was in his office, explaining the situation to Jake and Quinn.

"Kane Barton outlined the security measures the DOJ has in place," he told them. "He's asked me to personally supervise everything in this situation. Miss Griffin's room is now effectively sealed off from normal activity. Kane told me he's sending over special private nurses, but I believe you already know that. They'll be the only ones who'll have access to whatever she needs. Usually every chart is electronic and the nurses and doctors can access them when they need to. For this situation we're going back to paper only. We'll keep her chart in the room and DeWitt will be the only doctor to see her. Eliminates a lot of hospital traffic that might be a problem."

"Thanks" Jake shook administrator's hand. "We can't afford to take any chances with her. I want no information at the nurse's station, nobody but our people in and out of this room."

"Understood. I'll take care of it."

Quinn stood silently listening, making his own plans in his head.

It was nearly two in the morning when Kate was ready to be transferred to a private room and was moved from Recovery under heavy guard. Jake walked to her room with Quinn, satisfying himself that everything was in order. Two SAPD policemen stood guard grimly outside the door. Inside, a woman in blue and white hospital scrubs was waiting for them.

"I'm Nancy Quayle," she introduced herself. "I'll be taking care of Miss Griffin. I do this a lot for the DOJ. Which one of you is Quinn?"

"I am," he said. "Why?"

"I was told to let you know that I'm also a licensed federal agent." She lifted her top slightly to show them a badge and a gun clipped to the waistband of her pants. "Your girl will be well guarded."

"That's fine," he said, his voice flat, "but I won't be leaving this room and I have my own hardware." Kane had arranged the okay on that.

Nancy looked at Jake.

"He used to be with our office" Jake told her. "It's all right. Whatever he says, don't argue with him. Maybe Kane forgot to mention that."

Her eyes widened just a fraction in surprise, then she turned to back to Quinn. "Fine. Just don't get in the way of my taking care of my patient."

"No problem."

"There's one more of us coming," she informed him as she busied herself with Kate. "She's also an agent. We'll be taking twelve-hour shifts. Keeps the traffic down and limits access to Miss Griffin."

Jake touched Quinn's arm. "All right, Ace, I'm going back to the office. There's nothing more I can do here. I'll come by in the morning to check on things."

"I want to know whatever you find out."

"Will do."

"I mean it, Jake," he warned. "No keeping things from me."

"You have my word. See you in the morning." Then he was gone.

Nancy Quayle moved away from the bed. "You can come sit by her now if you wantn. I'll be checking her vitals and her IV regularly and giving her meds, but I don't think you'll be in my way. Just move when I need you to."

"Thanks."

Quinn pulled a chair close to the bed, listening to the beep and whir of the monitors, his eyes following the drip of the life-giving fluids being pumped into Kate's body. She seemed to be breathing a little easier. Her color hadn't returned yet, but he knew that was as much from the surgery as the blood loss.

He reached over to the hand that didn't have anything attached to it and enfolded it in his. Her skin felt icy cold, and he wished he could transfer some of his body heat to her.

Quinn hadn't felt such murderous rage consuming him for a long time. His first impulse had been to rush out, dig up his old contacts, and run to ground the people who had done this. But he couldn't tear himself away from Kate. He had some crazy idea that just by holding onto her hand he could infuse life into her, speed the healing process.

The pain that grabbed his heart when he'd seen her on the floor of the garage had not eased. He'd never forget the sight of her, small and crumpled with her blood oozing out of her body. At that moment, he thought he'd died himself. It reminded him too much of another scene four years ago.

But unlike Lisa, Kate was alive, even though she lay broken and bandaged. He couldn't shake the feeling it was his fault, that bringing her into town had been a big mistake. He should have insisted Jake come out to the house with Dean and Kane and taken care of business there. Then he could have swept Kate off somewhere to a hidey hole until the whole mess blew over.

Some protector he was. He'd told her to trust him, given her his word that he'd take care of her, but so far he was doing a lousy job. If everyone had just taken her story about payoffs in the prosecutor's office—and elsewhere—a little more seriously.

Damn it to hell anyway.

No more gambling with her life, he promised himself. When he got her out of here he'd tuck her away up in the hills until this was all over, no matter how long that took. He didn't give a rat's ass what the Department of Justice wanted. Trading off her life to make their case wasn't an option.

As he sat and watched her, it shocked him to realize what an intricate part of his life she'd become in just a few short days. Was it love? It was different than what he'd felt for Lisa. But just as good. Maybe because they'd both seen so much tragedy and disaster. He *wanted* Kate Griffin in his life. Forever. So he'd better take damn good care of her.

Quinn dozed in the chair off and on as activity in the room ebbed and flowed around him. Kate roused once, but only to moan, and Nancy injected more pain medication into the IV.

But as the blackness of night faded to predawn grey, her weak and raspy voice brought him awake at once.

"Quinn?"

He reached for her hand. "I'm here, darlin'. Right beside you."

"Hurts," she whimpered.

"I know. I'm so sorry." He lifted her hand to his lips. "I'm not doing such a hot job taking care of you."

"Not…you're fault." She was struggling to get the words out.

He leaned over and touched his lips to hers. "We can argue about that when you're back to your old feisty self."

"Bullet…meant for you."

He'd hoped she wouldn't realize that. "I'm too tough to kill."

"My fault. Brought…danger to you. That's…why…didn't want…tell you."

"Hush. I don't want to hear that kind of talk."

She touched his hospital scrub with one finger. "Nice…outfit."

"I wore it just for you." His heart turned over that her sense of humor could poke its way through her pain and trauma. "Can I get you something?"

"Water. Mouth…so dry."

Nancy heard her and was there at once, holding a cup with ice chips and a small plastic spoon. "Feed her little spoonfuls of this, a tiny bit on her tongue so it can wet her mouth. We don't want to give her actual liquids yet until we're sure all the anesthesia's out of her system. Vomiting won't help her pain. Or the surgeon's fancy stitch work."

"Okay." He took the cup from her.

"The doctor's going to keep her heavily sedated for a day or two. Apparently they had to do a lot of digging around inside, and she'll really feel it."

"Do whatever you have to. I don't want her in any more pain than necessary."

Each time she roused, Quinn fed her more ice chips, wiped her forehead, brushed her hair away from her face. Her breathing still seemed labored, but Nancy assured him it was nothing unusual. Despite the heavy medication she was being given, her subconscious was registering the intense level of pain.

At seven, Nancy introduced him to Sharon Langford, the day shift nurse, and the new guards on the door made themselves known as well. Except for Dr. DeWitt, that was the only traffic in and out of the room. David Nolan had been as good as his word.

At eight Jake arrived, freshly groomed, suit and shirt immaculate. But nothing could disguise the heavy circles under his eyes that bespoke a sleepless night. His face was almost as haggard as Quinn's.

"Breakfast," he said, holding up a box from Krispy Kreme. In his other hand, he carried a shopping bag, which he handed to Quinn, and a newspaper. "Thought you might like to feel human."

"What's this?"

"Razor, soap, change of clothes, stuff like that. Wal-Mart's finest. Nobody else is open all night. I figured you wouldn't leave here to go home and change." He pointed to the patient bathroom in the corner. "You can shower in there. The hospital won't object. They're good to go about whatever we want."

"Thanks." Quinn ran a hand over the stubble on his

jaw. "I didn't even think about it. Just let me know what I owe you."

"We'll worry about that later. Go change. I'll sit with Kate, then fill you in on where we are." His face sobered. "And show you a little item in the newspaper that will make you as sick as it did us. It was on the late news last night."

Quinn froze. "About Kate?"

"Yes and no. Go shower, then we'll talk."

Kate was still asleep when Quinn came back into the room, the result of the continuous pain medication, but she seemed to be resting a little easier. He had to admit he felt somewhat better clean-shaven, showered, and dressed in fresh jeans and shirt. But it did nothing for the knot of dread in his stomach anticipating what Jake had to say.

Jake had produced two cups of coffee from somewhere. They carried them with the doughnuts over to the window, away from the bed.

"Okay, give," Quinn said when they were settled with their food and drink. "What's in the paper?"

"First of all check the front page of the Metro section," he said. "Big news when someone shoots at people in a federal building. Especially these days."

Quinn scanned the article, then threw the paper on the table. "I notice you told them the victim's condition was unknown. Good move. Maybe they'll think she's dying and leave her alone. But your face tells me there's more."

Jake turned to page three and handed the section back to Quinn, folded to show an item on the bottom of the page.

"Woman missing," the headline stated. The article

went on to ask if anyone had seen this woman who'd disappeared from the library two days ago and not been seen since then. Her car was still in the city parking lot next door, and no one had heard from her.

"Shit." Quinn felt sick to his stomach. "Look at her picture. Add the longer hair and the tailored clothes and she could pass for Kate."

Jake nodded. "That means it didn't take them long to trace her back to the computer she used. Whoever they sent to check it out must have still been using an old picture of her."

Quinn dragged his fingers through his damp hair. "Jesus, Jake. This is getting out of control."

"It's unusual for them to do anything that gets this kind of publicity," Jake pointed out.

"Yeah, but they couldn't know we'd put it all together. This means we need to take extra precautions where Kate is concerned, because they're getting more desperate." He swallowed some of the coffee. "All right. Tell me something good."

"You should know Kane is seriously pissed that what happened to Kate was because his office apparently sprung a leak. I think he dragged everyone including the secretaries down to the office last night."

"Yeah, yeah, yeah. But did you find out anything?"

Jake popped a bite of doughnut into his mouth. "A couple of people remembered Efron Pendera hanging around outside Kane's office while we were in there on the phone with you. Trying to look casual, they said."

"Could he hear you talking with the door closed?"

"We weren't shouting, but those walls aren't the thickest. If someone listened hard enough he could catch what was being said." He snorted. "You don't expect you'll have to hide from your own staff. From now on we talk in the conference room with white noise in place."

"So what did this Pendera have to say for himself?"

Jake didn't answer right away. He put his coffee down on the window sill and stuffed a last bite of doughnut into his mouth.

"Come on," Quinn prompted. "He's gotta be the mole. What did he say?"

"Pendera's dead."

"What?" Quinn stood up, almost knocking over his coffee. "The hell he is."

"The cleaning crew found his body in the dumpster behind the justice building when they went to take out the trash early this morning."

"Shit."

"Exactly." Jake tossed back the rest of his coffee, then crumpled the cup and dropped it in the wastebasket.

"Was he shot? DeWitt gave Kane's messenger the fragments of the bullet he took out of Kate. I don't think you can tell much about it, but maybe you can get one intact from Pendera's body and try for a match."

Jake shook his head. "No such luck. His throat was cut. Nearly severed his head, as a matter of fact."

"Damn and damn again. What else?"

"It was Pendera's car the shooter made off in last night. The arrangements had to be made ahead of time. That about seals it that he was on the Osuna payroll."

"Damn it to hell anyway. Kate was right. Wonder what else he's fed them?"

"We'll find out. We've pulled his cell phone, office phone, and home phone records. We also got a warrant to search his house. His wife totally collapsed, and her family came to take her away, fortunately, so she didn't have to deal with that, too. There's a team out there now."

"How many people know about Kate?"

Jake looked as if he had a bad taste in his mouth. "It was kind of hard to keep her a secret after last night."

"That just increases the risk factor where she's concerned. Hell." Quinn jammed his hands in his pockets and stared out the window.

"We're keeping her bottled up tight here, and I know you won't be more than two inches away from her. We just have to figure out what to do when she can leave."

"Forget that. I told Kane I'm taking care of that, so you all can just drop it from your minds."

"I hear you. But Kane insists he wants to take charge. You'll have to fight it out with him."

"No fighting. My decision. It's my fault she got shot to begin with, agreeing to bring her into town. I'm not trusting her safety to anyone else." He shifted his gaze to a corner of the room. "Not that I'm doing such a fucking good job."

Jake frowned. "You can't run with her, Quinn. You know we need to have her available. Kane hasn't even had a chance to talk to her yet."

Quinn turned to him so filled with fury that Jake took a step back. "*I'm* the one who called *you*, remember? *I'm* the one who played by the rules here, told her she didn't have any choice. *I'm* the one who insisted she come into the city. Look what happened. I'm not risking her life again, so just back off."

"Don't be stupid. You'll never get her out past Kane's guards."

"Fine. Then I won't." He turned away.

"Ace, don't get yourself in a jackpot here. I know how you feel—"

Quinn jerked his head up. "No. You don't. You can't possibly. So just get the hell out of my face." He clenched his jaw so hard his bones ached. "I want you to forget we ever had this conversation, okay?"

"You're kidding, right?"

"Don't fight...in sick...room." Kate's voice, weak as it was, stopped them cold.

In a flash, Quinn was at her side, touching his lips to her forehead. "Sorry we woke you, darlin'. Just two jerks letting off steam. How do you feel?"

"Like a truck ran over me." Her voice was still halting but a tiny bit stronger.

"Glad to see you're back with us, Miss Griffin." Dr. DeWitt had come into the room unnoticed. He glanced at Jake and Quinn. "Can I have a minute to take a look at my patient?"

Quinn stepped away from the bed while DeWitt and Sharon checked Kate's wounds and Sharon changed dressings. The doctor pulled her file from the nightstand drawer where it was being kept out of sight, read it, entered some notations, then gave Quinn a tired smile.

"She's doing quite well, considering all the probing we had to do for the bullet fragments. We'll get her up for a few minutes later today. That won't be much fun for her, but I don't want to leave her lying in bed and risk pneumonia. I'll check back this afternoon."

"I'm going to bathe her and change her sheets,"

Sharon said after DeWitt left. "How about stepping outside for just a few minutes?"

Quinn was ready to dig in his heels. Jake, obviously deciding to head off an argument, took his friend by the arm.

"Come on. She's not going anywhere, and she's safe in here. We can talk out in the hall. Besides, I have some news for you. Maybe it'll help change your mind about what happens when Kate's discharged."

As soon as they were out of the room, Jake walked him to the end of the hall. A ghost of a grin drifted over his mouth as he looked at Quinn. "We cracked the files. I waited to tell you when no one could overhear us."

"Hot damn." Quinn smacked a fist into his palm. "So give. What did you find?"

"Only the mother lode—the whole Trans Global corporate structure, just like we hoped. Jesus, you'd think they were a real company the way they did it."

"This means Kane can proceed to get search warrants against the brothers, right?" Quinn asked.

"Yes, but we're moving very carefully on this." Jake's face looked grim, his lips thin and the hollows deepening in his cheeks. "First. There are three files with a totally different encryption code, so we're still working on those. Second, if the Osunas could pay off a federal prosecutor, it's not too big a leap for them to pay off a federal judge. We're not applying for warrants until we're sure the judge we go to is one hundred percent clean. Kane's conferencing with the Attorney General and the FBI Special Agent in Charge before he does anything else."

"Jake, listen to me." Quinn felt the note of desperation creeping into his voice. They had to get these people so they couldn't get to Kate. "As long as we don't take steps against the Osunas and their people, Kate is still in danger. They can still come after her."

Jake took a long time answering. "You might as well face the fact that Kate's going to be in some danger until everything is done and finished. Trial and all, especially if we need her to testify. But we'll take precautions. That's why Kane wants to find a safe house. After he talks to her and makes sure he's not missing something."

Quinn ground his teeth in frustration. "With all due respect, not all safe houses are safe. Tell Kane whatever you want, but no one will know Kate's whereabouts. He'll get to talk to her when the doctor okays it. Testifying is still up for discussion."

Kate was still awake when Sharon called them back into the room, propped up on pillows, pain cutting deep lines in her face.

Quinn looked at Sharon. "I thought she was getting some pretty heavy medication."

"She is, but I had to move her around a lot to bathe her, and changing the dressings wasn't much fun for her. I just gave her the next dose. It should start to work in a minute or two."

"I'll catch you later," Jake told Quinn and kissed Kate on the cheek. "Get better, pretty lady."

Quinn moved the chair back up to the bed, took Kate's hand again, and began talking to her in low, soothing tones. In seconds, her eyes fluttered closed and she was asleep. The medication kicked in and she was breathing more easily than before. Her color had improved slightly, too.

Sitting for hours in the room, watching the daylight

fade to a rosy afternoon glow, then to the gray-to-black of night, Quinn used the time to think about what to do next. He'd been very blunt with Jake. The hell with what the DOJ wanted. Kate's safety was priority number one, and he would take care of it himself.

He needed to do this. To make up for what had already happened, something he continued to blame himself for. In retrospect, going to Jake had been a mistake. He should have figured out a different way to go after what he needed and maybe Kate wouldn't be lying in a hospital bed. To keep her safe he'd have to get everyone out of the loop as fast as he could.

By late afternoon he had a glimmer of an idea. First, he needed to make sure Kate was a lot stronger. Then he'd make a telephone call and see if he could set things up.

****

Five days had passed since the surgery. All the monitors had been disconnected and removed and DeWitt had switched her from intravenous to oral medications.

That first day, when they'd gotten her out of bed, she gritted her teeth and broke out in a sweat. The second time was easier. Now, she could actually walk without looking like she was going to pass out.

But Quinn was still frightened every time he looked at her, and said as much to Nancy.

"She's showing a lot of improvement," the nurse assured Quinn. "Her color's good, she's moving around a lot better, and she seems to be sleeping easier."

"She still looks like death on a holiday to me," he commented sourly.

"Honey, give her time. She's had some major hurts

put on her. DeWitt's finally put her on solid food so that's a definite good sign."

For the first couple of days, as he sat by Kate's bed, he was constantly feeding her water and juice through a straw, wiping her face with a cold cloth, holding her hand. Whenever she surfaced from the narcotics and the pain grabbed her, he murmured to her in the same soothing voice until the medication took hold again.

As she improved and stayed awake for longer period of time, they actually carried on conversations, mostly learning little things about each other. Quinn told her what they'd found on the flash drive and brought her up to speed on where the DOJ was actually moving against the cartel. Neither of them said it out loud, but they were both on edge waiting for that shoe to drop.

Each day her walks in the corridor grew longer as her strength returned. Quinn was amazed at how quickly she was recovering, remembering the terror of those first couple of days after the shooting.

She'd just finished making a complete circuit of the floor, Quinn beside her giving her his strength, when Jake stopped in, bringing the newspaper.

"Anything else from that flash drive?" Kate, propped up again in bed, focused her gaze on Jake. "Come on, 'fess up. I want to know everything."

"I wish. But our guys are on it nonstop." Then he grinned. "You're sure looking better every day. How do you feel?"

"Just like I could run a marathon," she joked. But even as she spoke, the exhaustion of the morning took hold and her eyelids fluttered closed.

Jake looked at Quinn. "I'm getting pushed big time by the chief for him to come and interview her. So far DeWitt's stonewalled them, but time's running out, Ace."

"Just give me one more day, okay? I'll check with DeWitt when he comes in this afternoon. If he gives it the go ahead, I'll call you and set something up for tomorrow morning."

"Don't let me down," Jake warned. "My ass is on the line here, too, you know."

"One more day," Quinn assured him.

After Jake left, Quinn folded himself back into the large chair and rubbed his eyes. The overpowering hospital odor of antiseptic and illness was doing nothing to help his growing headache.

Damn Jake and everyone anyway. This was not about them, it was about her. He'd lost one woman he loved because of this business. He wouldn't risk it with another.

He wanted a life with her. A future. The more he sat in the hospital room, the more certain he was of that. But to get there, he had his work cut out for him. He'd put Jake off for twenty-four hours. That meant putting his plan in operation today.

"She'll be sleeping for a while," Nancy told him. "Why don't you go get some coffee or something to eat."

"Okay. Thanks. I won't be gone long."

But it wasn't food he wanted. Much as he hated being away from the room, he had a phone call to make, in a place where he couldn't be overheard.

Jogging down the stairs, rather than waiting for the slow as molasses elevator, he came out on the ground floor in a small enclosed green space, surrounded by a brick wall. Leaning into one corner, he dialed a number he hadn't used for far too long.

"Vanetta."

Quinn and Nick Vanetta had met when Quinn was still a prosecutor and a very high profile, very wealthy CEO needed the very best in sophisticated protection. More than familiar with the reputation of Guardian Security, the company Nick owned with his partner, Reno Sullivan, Quinn had recommended them for the job. The two had been close friends since then.

Nick, like Jake, had been doing his damnedest since the Ramirez fiasco to get Quinn to pick up the pieces of his life again. Maybe even come to work for them. Quinn had yet to return his calls.

He chuckled to himself now. He didn't think this call was exactly what Nick had in mind when he'd tried to shake him out of his isolation.

"It's Quinn"

"Well." Silence stretched between them. "How nice to know you're not dead after all."

"I know. I'm sorry. I… It's been a bad time."

"A bad few years, I'd say. I'd ask how you're doing, but I'm assuming since you called me at work and not at home that this isn't a social chat."

"You're right. I know I haven't done very well keeping in touch, and I'm sorry. But I need a really big favor."

As briefly as he could, he described the situation and told Nick what he needed from him.

"I'll say this for you," his friend said when he'd finished. "When you decide to rejoin the world you don't mess around."

"Can you do it?"

"Yeah. I'm not too excited about getting crosswise with the U.S. Attorney's office. However, if our places were switched, I'd be asking you the same thing."

"So it's a go?"

"How could I say no? Give me until six to get it set up."

"You can do it that fast?"

"Hey. Fast is my middle name."

Quinn let out the breath he'd been holding. This was a lesson in exactly how deep friendship went, and he thanked God his friends hadn't given up on him during the past four years.

"Nick?"

"Yeah?"

"Thanks."

"No thanks necessary. Talk to you in a few."

Quinn disconnected, then took a moment to gather his thoughts. Getting Kate out of here was the only smart thing to do. He needed to move her to a place where she wouldn't be at risk, then put Part B of his plan into motion.

He looked at his watch. Okay. Time to get moving.

Chapter Twenty

Peter Fleming was hot, tired, and irritated. The den where he was doing his work was beginning to feel claustrophobic.

His first order of business was moving the money to new temporary offshore accounts, where it would sit until he recreated the structure. That required a lot of work. It was the same as starting over. And this time, unfortunately, he'd be doing it with three pairs of eyes watching over his shoulder.

When Esai gave the order to close the law office, he'd printed out everything on the computers, locking the files securely in his briefcase and taking the duplicate flash drive from his safe. He learned that after leaving Tampa men had gone in and yanked the hard drives from all the computers, destroying them and dropping them in the middle of the Gulf of Mexico. So all he had was what he'd brought in the locked briefcase that never left his side.

Sitting at the desk in Eva's den, working his magic from the keyboard, he fantasized about taking the briefcase, slipping away and living the rest of his life on what he had in Argentina or Brazil. Then reality would set in, and he knew even Easter Island wouldn't be far enough away to hide from the Osunas. Relative or not, they'd skin him alive, literally, then cut his body into very small pieces.

"Have you finished setting up the new permanent accounts yet and the procedures for moving the money?"

Peter's fingers jumped on the keyboard at the sound of Miguel's voice. The man moved as silently as a mouse.

"And have you already written the new code?" the man went on. "We have to be two steps ahead of the *federales.* If they manage to decode the files on that damn data storage unit, they could be moving in any minute now."

"I'm on top of it," Peter answered, grinding his teeth in irritation. "But I've been at it less than a day. This takes time. I told you. I can't just call a bank and say, could I please open a new secure, anonymous account? Oh, and by the way, I'm moving money into it and I want you to wipe out the trace."

"But isn't that exactly what you're doing?" Miguel persisted.

"Yes, but I don't want to leave electronic fingerprints *anywhere.* Not even with the bankers. And it has to look legitimate. Just as the new 'corporate' structure does. So please. Just let me do my work."

Yes. Go away and leave me alone. Quit breathing down my neck.

"How are things coming?" Esai now stood beside his brother, the smoke from one of his favorite thin cigars curling in the air.

Peter shoved his chair back from the desk. "Is everyone going to stand over my shoulder while I do this?"

"Time is running out, Peter." Eva's imperious voice cut through the air as she joined her two brothers.

"I don't dispute the fact that your encryption is the best, but sooner or later they'll break it. We're already on their radar, so I've come to a decision. I believe we still have a few days, but then we need to leave here and set up our headquarters someplace else. We're going back to Mexico, where the climate is currently more favorable to us." She turned to her son. "You, too, Peter."

"Fine." *Over my dead body.* He swallowed the last of his coffee, wishing for something stronger.

Miguel's jaw dropped. "Leave everything behind? Are you serious?"

"She's right," Esai put in. "Every day they get closer to cracking the codes and reading the files, they're that much closer to having what they need to come after us officially.

"Our one piece of good fortune," Eva said, "is that no one knows about me yet or this place. We're all safe from prying eyes as long as we stay within this compound. That may delay them long enough for us to put our plan into place."

"How long do you think that will last?" Miguel asked, clipping the tip off a cigar.

"I don't know. Peter seems to have more confidence in the safety of his encryption that I do."

"Listen, I wrote every one of those codes myself and inserted codes *within* codes," Peter pointed out. "They don't have the electronic pass keys to open them. It will take them forever."

Eva gave her son an icy smile. "Don't be so arrogant. They'll do it sooner or later. Most likely sooner."

Esai and Miguel looked at each other, sick

expressions on their faces.

"That stupid girl and your even stupider son have completely destroyed the life we've built up," Esai said.

"This is just a…temporary setback," Eva said in a cold voice. "Once Peter finishes his work, we'll be back in business. I have helicopters ready to move the moment we're ready."

"If you're right and we have to leave, why haven't we done it already?" Miguel protested. "Why couldn't Peter do his thing from Mexico?"

"Two reasons," she snapped. "I want some insurance that the *federales* won't get in our way. That girl is our best bet, the best kind of leverage we can have."

Esai raised an eyebrow. "What good is she now? Especially since we can't even get near her."

"Idiot. She's a bargaining chip. Something to make them back off. Yes, Kathryn Burke is just the ticket. We'll offer to trade her for a clean getaway, returning her unharmed as soon as we're safe across the border." Evil gleamed in her eyes. "Or at least that's what we'll promise them."

"But…" Miguel began.

Peter stared at her. "Surely, you can't believe they'd go for something like that."

"Surely, I can. She seems to mean a great deal to the key people in this case. We'll see just how valuable her life is to them."

"And exactly how do you plan to get hold of her?" Peter persisted. "She's not exactly accessible.

A humorless smile twisted her lips. "I just received a very interesting telephone call with information that will help us with that. I think your Kathryn will be in our hands sooner than any of you think."

"What do you want me to do with everything when I finish?" Peter asked, anxious for them to be out of the room.

"Store it all on an Iron Key encrypted flash drive," Eva told him. "More than one if you need it. I picked some up while you were at Esai's. And back everything up to an external hard drive. Lock everything in the briefcase and give it to me. So how much longer?"

He shrugged. "A lot quicker if everyone would get the hell out of my hair." He deliberately turned his back on them, knowing he was pushing it. But they needed him for this. That was his ace in the hole.

"Then we'd better leave you to your work and get busy with what we all have to do."

As he settled back at the computer in his affluent prison, he was unhappier than he'd been for a very long time.

Chapter Twenty-One

The afternoon marched along slowly, Kate dozing off and on, Quinn busy with his own thoughts. Precisely at six, he excused himself, telling Kate he was just going to get a cup of coffee. Back in the courtyard again, he speed-dialed the same number, and Nick Vanetta answered at once.

"Quinn?"

"Yup."

"All right. Go back to the room. In a few minutes two men will show up pushing a gurney. They'll have a request to transport Kate for tests signed by DeWitt."

"How the hell did you do that?"

Nick snorted. "I've got a good forger. Don't worry. You just get Kate ready."

"Done."

He took the flights of stairs two steps at a time. Kate was struggling to sit up when he entered the room.

"Lie down, darlin'," he told her. "You need your rest."

Sharon Langford was pretending to leaf through a magazine in the corner chair, but Quinn knew her hearing was tuned to full volume. He bent close to Kate, putting his lips next to her ear. "In a few minutes some things are going to be happening," he whispered. "Do you trust me, Kate?"

She nodded.

"Then just do whatever I tell you and don't say anything. If you're okay with that, just squeeze my hand."

She curled her fingers around his as tightly as she could, and he smiled.

"Good girl." He pulled the chair closer and settled down to wait.

The breaks the nurses took were the only time Quinn was completely alone with Kate. He was sure Kane had convinced himself nothing could happen during a thirty-minute period. Besides, they were only worried about someone breaking in, not out, and there were still two cops on the door. He'd timed this precisely with Nick.

Sure enough, right on schedule, Sharon put down her magazine and said, "I'm going to run down to the cafeteria, but I won't be gone long."

"Take your time," Quinn told her. "We're fine."

The next few minutes felt like an hour. Then a light knock sounded at the door. One of the cops on guard duty stuck his head in.

"Say, Quinn, there are two men in hospital scrubs who say they're here to take Miss Griffin for some tests. They've got orders from the doc. Do you know anything about that? We were told they weren't moving her from the room for anything."

Quinn nodded. "DeWitt called me directly a few minutes ago so I'd know these guys were legit. I was just about to tell you they were on their way." He shrugged. "They decided to do an MRI."

"All right, then. If you say it's okay. Here they are."

Kate opened her eyes, and Quinn kissed her cheek,

then took her hand. "All right, darlin'. It's show time. Don't say a word, and just do whatever I tell you, okay?"

Fright glittered in her eyes, but she just nodded, squeezing his hand as hard as she could.

A minute later, the door opened and two men in hospital scrubs came in, pushing a gurney. One of them came over to shake Quinn's hand.

"We'll have small talk later," Nick Vanetta said. "Right now, we need to move. One of your sentries out there might just decide to double check on this."

They moved with quiet efficiency, and in seconds, Kate was shifted from the bed to the gurney. Quinn saw her bite her lip against the pain of movement, but she never made a sound. Nick opened the door, nodded to the two cops, and then they were rolling the gurney down the corridor, Quinn jogging along beside it.

People gave them curious but casual glances while they waited for the elevator at the far end of the corridor, the one that opened into the ambulance bay. Nobody asked questions, however, and no feet thundered down the hall to stop them. From somewhere, Nick had procured an elevator key, so the ride to the ground floor, while tense, was nonstop. The car bumped to a stop, and the doors slid open to a waiting ambulance and a man in EMT coveralls leaning against the open rear doors.

"Any sightseers?" Nick asked him.

"No. I just blended in with the scenery. But we'd better get moving before someone wonders why I've been here so long."

He handed a bottle of water to Quinn, who shook two of Kate's pain pills into his hand.

"Take these, darlin'. We've got kind of a rough ride ahead of us, and I want you to sleep."

She obediently opened her mouth for the pills, then drank from the bottle of water, and they loaded her into the waiting vehicle.

Quinn turned to his friend. "I can't thank you enough for this."

The tall, dark, lean good-looking man grinned. "I always liked to play cops and robbers. I just never thought I'd be one of the robbers."

Nick introduced the other man in scrubs. "Quinn, this is Nolan Hanks. He's been with us a couple of years and is great for stuff like this. I'd trust my own sisters with him. He'll follow you in that black Explorer over there. If you see it on your tail, it's him. You're ambulance driver's got directions." He checked his watch. "You'd better get going."

He reached in his pocket for a key and handed it to Quinn along with a small knapsack. "Prepaid cell phones. You don't want to take a chance using yours. There's six of them in here with my number preprogrammed, so you should be okay. And the cabin's fully stocked."

"Thanks. I owe you big time."

Nick looked at Quinn with worried eyes. "Take care of yourself, okay? And your lady here. Next time I see you, I hope it's over a beer on your porch or mine."

Quinn climbed into the back of the ambulance to sit on the bench beside Kate. Nick slammed the doors shut and banged on them twice, and the ambulance pulled out onto the street.

****

Kate had no idea how long they drove. Once, they

stopped and Quinn transferred her gently from the ambulance to a Ford Expedition.

"Not much longer, darlin'," He kissed her cheek.

She heard the faint sounds of him exchanging words with the ambulance driver, then someone else. Finally, he climbed into the driver's seat of the Explorer, and they were moving again. She dozed, the pills doing their job as Quinn had promised, and roused only when they stopped moving again.

"We're here," Quinn said softly.

She opened her eyes and stared through the window. They were parked in a clearing dominated on all sides by giant oaks and sycamores. In front her was a small log and limestone cabin with a tiny front porch and a wide picture window.

"Hang on," Quinn told her. "I'll come around and get you."

As he opened her door, another SUV pulled in behind them, and Quinn waved at the driver. "Let me get her settled," he called, "and we can sit down and talk."

"Who's that?" she asked.

"Nolan Hanks, from Nick's agency. Our backup. We need another pair of eyes so I can sleep once in a while."

Still foggy from the drugs, she was more than willing to let Quinn carry her into the cabin. Nudging open the door to one of the two bedrooms, he placed her on the rustic double bed with exquisite care.

"Where are we?" She had no sense of location.

"A place a friend of mine keeps for emergencies just like this."

"The same friend that helped us get out of the

Desiree Holt

hospital?"

He nodded.

"Will he get in trouble for this?" That was the last thing she wanted.

The corner of Quinn's mouth tilted up in an attempt at a grin. "Nah. He's pretty untouchable. He and his partner have too much clout."

"Good." Fear still had its fingers tightened around her. "Why are we doing this?"

"Because I don't want anyone—and I mean anyone—to know where you are until everyone in the cartel that's important is under lock and key." The lines on his face deepened. "And until I'm sure the target's not on your back anymore."

"Okay." She was too exhausted to think or talk any more at the moment. "I think I'd like to sleep some more."

"Sleep heals, you know." Quinn kissed her, a gentle kiss but one that held a great deal of promise. "We missed dinner. When you wake up, I'll fix you something to eat."

She closed her eyes and was out in seconds.

****

It was late when Kate awoke. The shade was up on the bedroom window, and she could see a sliver of moon and the glitter of stars in the inky sky.

She lay still for a few moments, orienting herself, remembering where she was. The cabin bedroom was compact and neat. Bed, dresser, bedside table, small straight back chair. Framed Texas prints on the walls. On the bed, covering her with its downy softness, an old-fashioned quilt that looked hand-stitched. Everything smelled sweetly of mountain cedar and sycamore, a fresh, clean scent.

Carefully, she maneuvered off the bed and onto her feet. There. Getting better and better.

Quinn was sitting at the small dinette table, drinking coffee and making notes on a pad of paper. He looked up when the bedroom door opened and leaped to his feet. In an instant, he had his arm around her, steadying her.

"Should you be out of bed? You had a lot of excitement today."

"I'm fine. Truly. Getting stronger every minute." She swallowed the tremor in her voice. "Where's Nolan?"

"Outside, checking out the area."

"Listen, I love this medical outfit du jour," she gestured at herself, still in the hospital gown. "But do you think we could find some real clothes for me? Even a big T-shirt will do."

Quinn reached behind him to the kitchen counter and grabbed a Wal-Mart sack. "Already taken care of. Sweats and a loose shirt. I figured those would be the easiest for you to manage. There's a few other things in there, too. I, um, guessed at the sizes."

"Please don't tell me Nolan went shopping for my clothes." Heat rose in her cheeks.

Quinn pulled out his little-used grin. "Nah. Nick sent his secretary out. You're safe. Bathroom's right there." He indicated a door to the right. "And there's a toothbrush and toothpaste lying on the sink in there for you. I think you'll find some other things you need in here, too." He handed her the sack. "Here, let me help you."

"I can navigate by myself. Really. I promise I'll

ask for help when if need it." She lifted her face and brushed her lips against his. "I'll be out in a minute."

She couldn't believe the difference a change of clothes and brushing her teeth made. "I feel almost human again," she told Quinn when she walked back into the main room.

"Looks like I guessed right on the sizes. So. What can I get you?"

"Some coffee. It smells divine."

"How about something to eat? We're pretty well stocked. Maybe some soup?"

"In a minute. Coffee to start would be great." And help clear her head of any leftover cobwebs. She was so tired of feeling fuzzy, even if it did take the edge off the pain.

"DeWitt said you'd been doing well," Quinn told her while he poured, "but just so you know, Nolan was a field medic in another life. Just in case we need help."

"I think getting out of that hospital will help me more than anything." She sipped at the hot liquid in the mug he handed her. "Tell me about the man who helped us. He must be a very good friend to do this."

Quinn gave her the short version of his relationship with Nick. "He and Jake are about the only people I'm close to. The only ones I really trust."

"He stuck his neck out for you on this one, didn't he?"

"Yeah, but Nick covers himself well. He'll be all right."

"What about Jake and the others? They'll have a fit when they find out I'm gone."

He shrugged. "Let them. They'll get over it. But I wasn't about to let you be used for bait or put through any more interrogation." He rubbed his hand against her arm, his fingers warming her skin. "Nolan and I will take turns on watch. Your job is to get better. Got it?"

"I'll work on it," she smiled. "And I think maybe now I could eat some soup."

Please, God, just let this be over soon and all of us be safe.

Hungrier than she thought, Kate finished the soup in record time.

Quinn made himself a thick sandwich and kept her company while she ate.

"Your appetite's getting better," he remarked, clearing away his dishes and Kate's.

"I'll look like a blimp if you keep feeding me like this." She patted her stomach.

"Not with a bowl of soup. And you could stand to add a few pounds, anyway."

"Are you complaining about my figure?" she joked.

"Not for a minute." He planted a soft kiss on her lips. "In fact, I can't wait until it's in fighting form again."

Kate's heart thudded and warmth filled her body. She wished her body wasn't in such a damaged condition at the moment and not in shape for what she really wanted to do. Despite her injuries, she still felt heat consume her whenever Quinn touched her.

He straightened. "Okay. If you're sure you're all right, I think I'll go outside and check the area with Nolan."

"I don't think a snake could get through with you two on alert, but go ahead."

****

Eva picked up the phone on the first ring, tension in every line of her body. The caller spoke briefly, the message short and to the point. When she put down the phone, she turned to her brothers who were standing near her.

"The girl will be ours before long," she told them, "and I believe Peter is finished."

"How long before we have her? And can we afford to wait any longer?"

"Soon," she assured them. "The wait is almost over. Esai, you need to contact our dealers one more time, then have everyone dispose of their phones. Miguel, make sure our supply route is re-established, then do the same. And be ready to leave when I give the word."

****

Nolan was sitting on a tree stump, smoking one of the thin cigars he enjoyed so much.

"What's up?" Quinn still worried that someone might have found them out.

"I called Nick." Nolan blew a smoke ring. "Lots of noise and activity going on out there."

"And?" Quinn figured there had to be something or Nolan wouldn't have been anxious to talk to him.

Nolan's lips curved in a tight grin. "They've got everyone except the National Guard out looking for you and Kate."

"Figures. What else?"

"Not much. Nick's watching the situation closely. He's got his sources, you know.'

Quinn gave a humorless laugh. "It sure isn't Kane Barton. He'd probably like to slice and dice Nick right about now."

Nolan shrugged. "He'll get over it. The DOJ needs a good relationship with Guardian."

At the moment, that was their saving grace. In the dark silence of the night, he cursed himself for allowing this to happen. For his stupidity, his cocksure attitude that he had everything well in hand. He did something he hadn't done for a long time. He prayed. He promised anything if only Kate would be safe.

"You have to keep it together," Nolan told him. "Kate's depending on you."

"I know, I know." He thought about calling Jake but didn't relish getting his ass reamed out. He also felt somewhat bad about deceiving his good friend, but sometimes in life you just had to make hard choices.

Quinn was already antsy. His original plan was to keep Kate hidden until the feds made their move and the Osunas were out of commission. If Kane was as good as he'd always been, that shouldn't be too much longer, but he was too impatient to wait. And too much had to be done in secrecy now that they knew about the payoff list.

But he needed to do something himself. He knew from experience how slippery these people could be, and the Osunas had more weapons than most. He didn't want to take the chance of them getting to Kate. He'd waited long enough. It was time to put Part B of his plan in motion.

He was positive all his old sources were still in place. Well, most of them, anyway. It wouldn't be that hard to find out where they were, make contact, get information. Then he could take care of this mess himself and be done with it once and for all. And Kate would be safe. He'd nearly lost her this time with his stupidity. He wasn't about to let it happen again.

Kate was lying down when he slipped into the bedroom, still wearing her comfortable sweats. The soft material outlined her body and round contours of her breasts. Quinn had lain beside her the past two nights, cradling her body against him, watching for signs of pain or discomfort and fighting his growing hunger. In just a few minutes, he was going to slip away, hoping to put this nightmare to rest once and for all, and he needed just a taste of her to take with him.

He stretched out beside her, studying her eyes, her face, whatever part of her body he could see.

"How are you feeling, darlin?" He stroked her cheeks and the slope of her neck. "We walked longer than usual today, and you were keeping up pretty good."

"Good. Getting better every day." She turned her face up for his kiss.

His lips brushed lightly against hers, a mere feather touch. But he was so hungry for her it was only seconds before the kiss became more urgent, his tongue pressing into her mouth and twisting with hers.

Kate lifted her hands and twisted her fingers in his hair, holding him to her. "More," she said against his mouth.

"I'm almost afraid to touch you," he told her when he lifted his head. "Although I'm so hard I think I might be in more pain than you are. God." He sucked in his breath. "I can't believe I almost lost you."

"*You* didn't do anything," she insisted. "I knew we were taking a chance going into town, and I agreed to it anyway."

"With me pushing you," he reminded her.

She frowned. "Listen. Neither of us expected anything to happen in the garage of the federal building. The attack was totally unexpected."

He ran his fingers over her face, loving the softness of her. "I feel like such a shit. I swore nothing like this would happen."

"Stop it," she commanded and lifted her hand to his cheek.

He kissed her and caressed her with gentleness, knowing she was still in pain, still healing, so hard from being next to her he was in pain himself.

He cupped his hand over her mound.

"One of these days, darlin', I'm going to stretch you out on my big bed and shave this thing so it's totally naked. Then I'm going to run my tongue over every bare inch of it and drive you crazy."

"You already do that." Her voice was unsteady. "You are now."

She was his. He'd told her that, and he meant it. No matter what happened. He bent his head and kissed her.

"Just remember," he whispered. "You're mine." He rolled off the bed and pulled the covers back up, rearranging her gown again. "You should get some rest."

"Where are you going?"

"Outside. Try to go to sleep, okay?"

He closed the door quietly as he left the room. He had things to do. Kane Barton and Dean Morgan and everyone else on their stupid task force were following the rules, trying to get warrants, putting their plan in place. Quinn wasn't bound by those rules anymore, and he was tired of waiting around. Every minute these people were still at large, Kate's life was in grave danger. It was time for him to move.

In the kitchen, he pulled the keys to his borrowed SUV from his pocket and checked to make sure he had some of the disposable cell phones with him. Then he went to find Nolan, who was doing his regular check of the perimeter.

"I need to ask a favor of you."

Nolan looked at him, his face expressionless. "What kind of favor?"

"I need to be gone for a while. Maybe overnight." *Probably longer.* "I want to make sure Kate isn't alone for a minute. Maybe Nick can send another man to work with you."

Nolan studied him for a long time. "And just what am I supposed to tell Kate? And Nick?"

"Nick will know what I'm doing. Right now Kate's asleep. When she wakes up, tell her…tell her I just had a couple of things to do to insure her safety. I'll be back before she even has time to worry. And I've got the number of the satellite phone you're using, just in case."

Nolan stared at him for a long time. "I hope you know what you're doing. Otherwise, you'll be the one in the slicing machine."

"Just cover for me, okay?"

"All right. Whatever. I'll keep an eye on the lady. No worry there. Just be careful."

"I will."

Not wanting to alert Kate he was leaving, Quinn pushed the truck part way down the drive before starting the ignition.

****

When Kate awoke, it took her a few moments to

realize where she was. Then she remembered. The stealthy exit from the hospital. The trip to this cabin. Quinn telling her no one knew where she was and he planned to keep it that way.

Quinn. Where was he? Had he left?

Moving slowly, her body still sore and stiff, she maneuvered out of bed and walked over to the window. When she pulled the curtains aside, she was stunned to see how dark it was outside. Still moving cautiously, she crossed the room and opened the door. Just as she walked into the main room of the cabin, she spotted Nolan, just clicking off the satellite phone.

"Where's Quinn? He said he was just going outside." She looked around as if he might materialize.

"He left to do a couple of quick errands."

Kate frowned. "At night?"

"He said he'd be back right quick. Listen, we've got a problem."

"A problem?" That feeling of fear slithered through her again, of something gone wrong.

"Yeah." He put the sat phone down on the counter. "I just got off the phone with Nick. He's trying to get hold of Quinn on one of those throwaways he gave you guys, and I was just coming in to wake you. Somehow, this place has been compromised, and I need to get you out of here."

"What?" *Oh, god! This could not be happening.* She raked her hair back from her face with an unsteady hand. "But I thought no one knew about it. That was the point." Quinn. She needed Quinn. "Can you get hold of Quinn? I want to talk to him. I *need* to talk to him."

"Calm down," Nolan soothed. "Nick will find him and let him know what's happening. But I have a new place to move you to. "He reached out to take her hand. "Come on. We have to get going."

Kate wished her brain was sharper or that she could speak to Quinn. But this was Nick's man and Quinn trusted Nick, so she needed to do what he said. "I don't know…I mean, is it a long drive? I'm not in very good shape."

"I'll take it real easy," he assured her.

"All right. Just let me change, make a pit stop, and get my purse."

"Do what you need to, but we have to hurry."

In the bathroom, Kate took care of business and changed into her sweats. She stuck her toothpaste and toothbrush in her purse, along with her pills. She saw her little gun nestled in the bottom of the purse and for some unknown reason, took it out and stuck it in the small of her back. She didn't know why. She was in a secure situation. But if she got separated from her purse for any reason…

She splashed cold water on her face and hands, dried herself with one of the towels and opened the door. "I'm ready."

"Okay. Let's go."

Chapter Twenty-Two

Kate hated to do it, but the jouncing in the SUV was exacerbating the pain. She popped two of her pain pills into her mouth and took a swallow of water from the bottle she'd snagged off the kitchen counter.

"Exactly where are we going?" she asked for the tenth time. "The signs say we're in San Antonio."

"That's right," Nolan told her. "There's a condo on the far north side where arrangements have been made."

"And Nick and Quinn know about this?" she asked nervously.

"Nick's the one who called me, remember? He'll get hold of Quinn, and they'll meet us there."

"But how did the cartel find out where we were?" she persisted. "I thought the place was so secret."

Nolan slid a glance at her. "Secrets slip out sometimes. Ah, here we are."

Kate sighed with relief as a huge, gated compound came into view. She could see low buildings rising behind a brick wall.

Nolan wheeled the big SUV up to the guardhouse and gave his name to the man on duty. "We're expected."

"Yes, sir. You know which building it is, right?"

"Yes. Thanks."

"Pretty fancy surroundings for a safe house," Kate

271

commented.

"We like to take good care of the people we're responsible for," Nolan assured her, a funny smile playing across his mouth. He opened the passenger door and held out his hand. "All set?"

"Yes. Thank you." She let him help her down from the big SUV, leaning on him as he guided her into the building.

The security officer behind the reception desk nodded to Nolan. "Go right on up, Mr. Hanks. They're expecting you."

Kate frowned. "They? Who are 'they'?"

"Just a few more people involved in this. We don't want any slipups. Come on. Here's the elevator."

The elevator rose smoothly, hissed to a stop, and the doors slid open. Kate stared at the woman she hadn't seen in ten years, not since her uncle had died and she'd disappeared like smoke in the wind. But she'd never forget what Eve Burke looked like. The black-hearted witch, her mother had called her.

Only…why was she here? What did she have to do with all this?"

"Kathryn, my dear." She took Kate's hands and tugged her forward. "My word, you look terrible. I understand you've been wounded. We're so sorry that had to happen."

"I don't understand." Panic griped her with icy tentacles. "Why are you here? How did you know I'd been hurt? What's going on?"

Eva looked over Kate's shoulder. "Thank you, Nolan. Good job, as always."

Kate turned to him, getting a very sick feeling in her stomach. "Nick didn't call you, did he?"

Of course he hadn't. They were all being played for fools. "And this is no safe house, is it?"

"It's safe," Eva assured her, "although not necessarily for you."

Kate clenched her hands, the pain of her fingernails digging into her palms helping her stay alert. She gave Nolan a look of disgust. "Nick Vanetta trusted you, and because of that, Quinn did." She swallowed back the bile rising in her throat. "How long have you worked for the Osunas?"

"Longer than you need to know about." His voice was hard, impersonal. "Vanetta has no idea how long I've been buried in his organization just in case something like this came up."

"What is this place you've brought me to?" she demanded. "And what's my aunt doing here?"

"Questions, questions." Eva shook her head, then reached out and took Kate's hand, gripping it in hers as she tugged her out of the foyer. "Come into the living room and sit down. There are some people here who will be very glad to see you."

Half a dozen steps into the room, Kate stopped and felt every bit of blood drain from her face. Two men, strangers, were sitting on a long couch, holding brandy snifters.

"I don't believe you've met my brothers." Eva's voice could have frozen fire. "Miguel and Esai Osuna."

"Brothers?" Kate was feeling very dizzy. Her heart was pounding so loud she thought it would shake her body.

"And of course—" Her aunt gestured toward the fireplace. "—you are well acquainted with this man." She gestured toward the man leaning against the

273

fireplace.

"Peter?" *God in heaven. What is he doing here?*

"None other." His face showed no expression, but rage burned in his eyes. "We've been looking for you for a long time, you know. We owe a lot to Nolan for bringing you here."

"Oh, my God." She made it to the closest chair and almost fell into it. If this was a nightmare, she wanted to wake up at once.

"I understand you and my son know each other quite well," Eva commented in her brittle voice.

"Your son?" God, she really *had* fallen into hell. She heard the words, but her brain couldn't process them. This couldn't possibly be happening.

Breathe naturally, Kate. Don't show them how terrified you are.

Eva nodded. "From a previous marriage. Your uncle was hardly the first to provide me the cover I needed, even if unwittingly." She smiled at Peter. "But as far as I'm concerned, he is mine."

Kate didn't dare pass out from the pain. If she couldn't figure something out, she had no doubt these people would kill her. The game wasn't over yet. Kathryn Burke would have folded like a wet napkin. Kate Griffin, even in her weakened condition, would find a way to fight back. It was only a matter of getting herself under control and figuring out what to do. She clenched her jaw, steadying herself, willing herself not to faint. The cold steel of her gun was a reassuring feeling at the small of her back.

Her eyes swept around the room. The two men on the couch, the brothers Osuna, were like bookends. In their early fifties, she guessed, with the same thick head of dark hair as their sister, but tinged with silver. Dark, almost swarthy skin, set off by the expensive light-colored silk shirts they wore. Cruelty lurked in the dark, hooded eyes that missed nothing. They watched her as if she were a lab specimen, waiting for the dissector's knife. She wondered which one was Miguel?

"You've been a lot of trouble to us, Kathryn." Peter straightened and shoved his hands in his pockets. "I have to say, I didn't give you nearly enough credit for smarts. Very embarrassing to admit you had me fooled."

"No more than you did me," she told him, more bravado in her voice than she felt.

"What a shame you were impetuous enough to steal something belonging to us." Eva's colorful skirt swirled around her as she turned toward Kate. "None of these stupid men seemed to have a clue how to track you down and retrieve it."

Eva's eyes were filled with contempt as she looked at each of them in turn. There was not one doubt who was in command here.

"Too bad for all of you." Kate lifted her chin, a gesture of confidence she didn't feel. "You have to know the U.S. Attorney's office has the flash drive now. And Peter? They've cracked your super secret code. I guess they're a lot better at it than you gave them credit for. They'll be here any minute looking for you." Her eyes traveled around the room. "All of you."

She had no idea if anyone even knew where she was or how quickly the DOJ would be able to move if they did. She just hoped her voice sounded more confident than she felt.

"Oh, but you're going to help us with that, my

dear," Eva told her. "And then some."

"I don't understand. What can I possibly do?"

"We've decided to move our operation to Mexico," she explained, "but we need to make sure we can leave here without a problem. That's where you come in."

"Me?" She frowned. What did they expect her to do?

"Simple. We're going to offer them an exchange. You for a clean exit across the border. Once we're there, we'll return you safely to them."

A hysterical laugh bubbled up from her throat. "You really think I'm important enough for the Department of Justice to trade for me? You're a fool if you believe that."

"No," Eva answered her. "But you are important enough to Quinn, and he is a man who can make it happen."

"I'm curious, Miss Burke."

Kate slid her eyes to the speaker. The initial M on his shirt cuffs identified this one as Miguel.

He uncrossed his legs and sat forward, his heavy ring and gold watch glinting in the light from the lamp. "What made you take the disk in the first place?"

"I was in the office that night and heard you and Peter talking about it." She gripped her hands together to steady herself. "Right after you discussed killing me. I thought I could use it in exchange for my life."

"Why the hell did you sneak in that way?" Peter exploded.

She turned her gaze back to him. "Does it matter now?"

"No." Miguel answered for him. "Now we're going to do the exchange, although not quite the way you'd expected."

Nervously, she wet her lips. "Could I have a glass of water, please?"

"Of course. Peter, please get our guest some ice water." She turned back to Kate. "I apologize for your injuries. You weren't our target, you know."

"Is that supposed to make me feel better?"

"If we had hit your friend, would you have grieved for him, Kathryn?" Peter asked, returning with the glass of water. "Just who is he to you? Protector? Friend? Lover?"

Kate drank slowly from the water glass, refusing to be baited.

"Let's make sure she's not carrying anything of importance," he said, grabbing her purse and upending it on the table. Her meds, her toiletries, and a handkerchief rolled out. Disappointment flashed across Peter's face.

"What did you expect?" she sneered. "A gun?" Thank God she'd moved it. Now she was even more conscious of the metal shape pressing against her back.

"We can't be too careful."

This whole scene is so surreal. Here I am, sitting in this lavish home, with murderers and drug dealers who want to kill me. Everyone is conversing so politely it's as if we're all at some sophisticated cocktail party.

"Nolan's going to call Nick Vanetta," Eva told her, handing her a slip of paper. "I want you to read exactly what's written here as soon as Nolan has him on the phone."

Kate watched him dial the sat phone, then nodded when the connection was made.

"I'm not calling to have a discussion with you,"

Nolan said in a flat voice. "That's over and done with. I assume by now you know what's happened. I have someone here you really need to talk to. And you'd better pay attention to what she says."

Then the phone was thrust at Kate, and she lifted it to her ear. "Nick?"

"Kate. Are you all right? Can you tell me where you are?"

She could hear in his voice how shaken he was but was grateful he was forcing his voice to be calm.

"I—"

Nolan grabbed the phone. "No discussion. Listen to her message. That's all." He gave the phone back to her. "Read."

Kate stared at the paper, the words blurring. She wet her lips with the tip of her tongue and forced the words out. "I am alive so long as you do what they ask. Follow their instructions, and they'll return me to you safely. They want a guarantee of safe passage to Mexico. They will call back in one hour."

Nolan took the phone back. "One hour. Get the word to your friends in the DOJ. If the answer is no, it won't matter to us if we kill her. But you might have some explaining to do to your friend Quinn."

He disconnected the call.

****

Quinn drove the SUV down the road that ran along the back of his property, keeping his headlights off. He parked in the underbrush and made his way through the woods. Entering the house from the front would leave him too exposed, just in case Kane Barton had someone watching.

On the way from the cabin, he'd run every

diversionary maneuver he knew, checking constantly in his rearview mirror. It took the better part of two hours, time he didn't have, but he was as certain as he could be that no one was on his tail. So far, so good. He'd get into the house, get what he needed and leave.

Getting his guns and a good supply of ammo wouldn't take long. He should have done that to begin with. At the same time, he would start digging for his old contacts and set about tracking down the key players in the Osuna cartel. At this point, he didn't expect them to be operating out in the open, so finding them would require some outside help. But someone would know where they were.

He'd use the same methods to convince people to talk as when he went after the Ramirez cartel. All he needed was one person to open up to him. And quickly.

Just in case Kane Barton—or worse, the Osunas— had someone watching his house, he left his car at a bend in the road and pulled in among a copse of trees. Hiking in through the prairie grasses that covered most of his acreage, he made his way to the back of his house and opened the side door to the garage. He was just about to pull it shut behind him when he heard a noise behind him. Yanking the .38 from his waistband, he whirled in crouch position.

"I should be the one doing the shooting, you asshole." Jake Garza materialized out of the darkness, slamming the door shut, and snapping on a flashlight. He held it up to his face so Quinn could see who he was.

"Jesus, Jake, you nearly gave me a heart attack."

Jake clicked off the light. "We need to talk."

"Where's your car?" Quinn made a supreme effort

to tamp down his fury. "I can see my driveway from the back of the property, and it's empty."

"I can be just as sneaky as you, Ace. I left it at the vacant property around the corner from here."

"How did you even know I'd be coming here?"

"I took a chance, knowing how your mind works. Your cell didn't answer; I figured you had it shut off so no one could track it. And Nick said you weren't answering any of the disposables he gave you. He called me in a panic when he couldn't reach you. And I called Dean. Come on. We've got serious problems."

"Why was Nick trying to call me? And why did he call you? What's going on?"

Jake shook his head. "Not out here in the garage. Go inside. We'll talk while you get whatever you came for."

Quinn led him through the utility room and into the darkened house. Not wanting to turn on any lights just in case he'd been followed by either Barton's people or, god forbid, the cartel, he motioned for Jake to follow him to his bedroom. The moon was full and gave them as much light as they needed.

In the closet, he slid back a panel to reveal his gun safe. "All right. Talk. I need to get my stuff and be on the way."

"We have a crisis. A bad one."

Quinn's heart almost stopped beating, and he couldn't draw a breath. He turned to look at Jake. "Kate? Has something happened to her?"

"I won't even go into the stupidity of the stunt you pulled," Jake ground out, "or the fact that I know you're out here ready to go hot-dogging. This isn't the time for it."

"You're right about that. So skip the lecture and get to the point." Quinn was ready to strangle his old friend if he didn't get to the point and damn quick.

Jake shoved his hands in his pants pockets as if he didn't know what to do with them. "Kate's gone. And so is Nolan."

Quinn thought he might pass out. A buzzing sound filled his head, and his stomach heaved. Gone? No, that was wrong. Kate was safe. He'd gone to great lengths to make that happen. He sat down before Jake could see how badly he was shaking.

"What do you mean, gone? Where the hell are they? I just left them a couple of hours ago."

"No one knows. Going through the list of the Osuna payroll, whose name should pop up but Nolan Hanks."

"What the fuck?"

"Kane called Nick who was already on the way to the cabin because he hadn't been able to raise anyone. I think he was afraid you and Kate were both dead. Nick's on his way to our office. I figured you'd come here, and Kane thought it would be best if I broke the news to you myself."

"Fuck, fuck, fuck." Quinn couldn't make his brain function, couldn't accept what he was hearing. "Damn it all anyway."

I promised to take care of her. To keep her safe. I've failed her twice. What a useless piece of garbage I am.

"There's more." Jake cleared his throat. "Kane's had a tail on Esai Osuna for a while, just to see if anything turned up. His guy called in to tell him Peter Fleming's in town and there's a gathering of the clan at a suburban condo. We may not be able to wait any longer to move against them. Besides, having everyone in the same place would be damned convenient."

Quinn drew in a ragged breath as he fought for control. "Jesus, can it possibly get any worse? I've got to find them, Jake. Where the hell could they be?"

He pulled out a duffel bag and began stuffing his equipment into it.

Jake stopped him with a hand on his arm. "Do everyone a favor this one time, will you please? Don't go off half-cocked."

"You can't expect me to just sit here," Quinn argued. "You know better than that."

"I do, but use your head. Come downtown with me. Kane's pulling out all the stops to get to her. I talked to Nick again, and he's meeting us there."

"Did it look like there was a struggle at the cabin?" Quinn asked.

Jake shook his head. "Nothing. For whatever reason, they just drove away. We can sit here and speculate, or we can go downtown and get some real information. Your choice."

"Let's go. I'll follow you."

But first, despite Jake's objections, Quinn went to his gun safe and took out his arsenal. Whatever happened, he'd be ready for it.

****

Kane Barton's office was not small, but tonight, with all the hulking men filling it, the room seemed unusually crowded. Five men Quinn had never seen before, dressed in suits identical except for their color, were having no luck trying to make themselves comfortable on wooden folding chairs. Other men leaned against the wall. Fluorescent lights bathed everything in their unforgiving glare, and the room smelled of stale coffee and sweat. Nick sat off to one side.

Nobody was smiling.

"Okay, I'm here," Quinn said, planting himself in front of the desk. "Tell me what's going on. How the hell did Nolan Hanks get by your vetting, Nick?"

"Let's just identify all the players first, okay?" Kane swept his glance around the room. "Nick can deal with that situation later. Right now, you'll need these men to do what needs to be done."

"This isn't a tea party," Quinn ground out. "And I'm not hanging around for bureaucratic bullshit."

"You never did. Just let me introduce you to the other men in the room." He nodded in their general direction. "Meet Special Agent Joe Tallmadge, Special Agent Aaron Hill, and Special Agent in Charge Noah Delaney of the FBI. They've been investigating the Osunas from the beginning of the Strike Force. And over there is Clay Peters, head of the district DEA office, and one of his men."

Quinn waved a hand in the air. "Nice to meet you all, but we can forget the social amenities. Where's Kate?" He turned to Nick. "And Nolan?"

Nick looked at Kane. "Why don't you fill him in? Then I can figure out how to apologize, if that's even possible, and we can get on with business."

Quinn ground his teeth. "Will someone please just tell me what the fuck is going on?"

Kane looked decidedly unhappy. "If you'd let us take care of her in the first place, this wouldn't have happened. Just keep that in mind."

"Damn it." Quinn's patience was gone. "Forget about who should have done what. I did what I thought was best for her. Can we get to the meat of this thing? I want to know what's happened to Kate?"

"First of all, you're right." Lines of tension were etched in Kane's face. "We've been working on that flash drive we got from Kate, cracking the codes one by one. Lots of good information there. Bank accounts. Dummy corporations. Suppliers. Buyers."

"And?" Quinn prompted, his voice rough.

"And a list of people all over the country taking payoffs from the cartel. It's far more extensive that any of us thought. They're into every area of law enforcement on every level, as well as private parties that could do them some good." He looked over at Nick, then back at Quinn. "As Jake told you, Nolan Hanks's name is on there."

Quinn looked at Nick, whose face reflected his own sick feeling.

"Jake said Fleming's in town, and they're all gathered at someone's condo for a sit-down," Quinn pointed out. "That's got to be where Nolan's taken Kate."

Dean handed Quinn a photo. "Let me introduce you to Mrs. Eva Gallagher. Wealthy respected San Antonio matron. Otherwise known as Eva Osuna Fleming Gallagher Burke. Sister to Esai and Miguel. Widow of Roger Burke. Mother of Peter Fleming. And according to the last of the codes we cracked, the real head of the cartel."

If Quinn had been panicked before, he was terrified now. For Kate.

Dean opened a folder he was holding. "The Osunas

284

came out of Mexico forty years ago dirt poor. Eva snagged herself a couple of rich husbands, who died not too long after their weddings. Of unidentified causes, according to the death certificates. She used her inheritances to set up the cartel." Briefly, he gave Quinn the rundown on how John and Roger Burke got caught in the trap.

"That's all wonderful information, but can someone tell me why we're just sitting here?" Quinn demanded, his patience long gone. He wanted to scream. To hit somebody. Anybody. Anything but having these conversations while Kate could be…*No. God, don't even think it.* "Nolan's taken her to the condo. We need to get going while she's still…all right."

Nick cleared his throat. "She's still alive, Quinn. Nolan called me just before you and Jake got here to let me know and tell me what they wanted."

"What?" Quinn thought he was hearing things. He pulled the tattered shreds of his control together and tried to pay attention to what Nick was saying. "The man has balls."

"Big ones," Nick agreed. "And I'll never be able to tell you how sorry I am about him. We have an excellent system in place to prevent just this kind of thing. I guess we'll have to look and see where the holes are."

Quinn gritted his teeth. "What. Did. He. Want?"

"They know we've got the flash drive, so their goose is cooked. Their only chance is to get away clean and start somewhere else."

"And?" Quinn made a motion with his hand to speed it up.

"They'll trade Kate for safe passage out of here into Mexico. A clean getaway. No cops. No arrests."

"So they can set up in another country," Noah Delaney put in, a bitter look on his face.

"Fuck." Quinn wasn't sure his legs would keep holding him upright. There was one empty folding chair, and he dropped into it. "What did you tell him?"

"I told him I'd have to get with the U.S. Attorney to get his approval on something like this."

"Did you get proof of life?" Quinn demanded.

"Yes. He put Kate on the phone to give us their demands." Quinn saw a look of admiration flash in Noah Delaney's eyes. "Your girl has more guts than most women I've ever met. We all know the ordeal she's been through, and still not even fully recovered. But she kept her cool. Just read the message they'd written out for her."

"When are you supposed to hear from him again?"

This is so much bullshit. I need to find out that address and get my ass over there.

Nick looked at his watch. "One hour from when he called, which makes it almost any time now. I told them it would take me time to get hold of Kane."

Quinn jumped up. "That gives us plenty of time to get there. If you guys want to sit around and gossip, have at it. Just tell me where the damn place is. I'm going to get Kate out."

"Hold on, will you?" Kane glared at him. "That's our plan, too, but can we at least get a few details together first?"

Nick's phone rang, and they all looked at each other. Nick pressed the Talk button.

"Yeah?" He listened a moment. "We got the okay

on it. It'll take about thirty minutes for them to type it up and get the AG's signature on it. Then we'll fax it to you. What? No, asshole. No one's going to do anything to endanger that woman's life. You just better get the hell out of town before we change our minds." He disconnected the call and looked at Kane. "Okay. We've got half an hour. Is that enough?"

Kane nodded. "More than."

"Unless they kill her first," Quinn pointed out with barely leashed anger.

"They won't do that," Kane told him. "They need a live body to do this. They know if they kill her first, all bets are off." As he finished speaking, the bell on his fax machine rang. He reached over and ripped out the paper as it fed into the tray. "This is what I was waiting for. A warrant for the condo and all its contents signed by Judge Harley. A man *not* on their payroll, by the way. It's our ticket in."

He stood up, rolled down his shirt sleeves and pulled on his jacket. "All right, boys, time to get the party started. Jake, you ride with Dean and me. Clay and Noah have their own vehicles."

"I'm coming, too," Quinn said, heading for the door.

"And me," Nick added. "It was my fuckup."

Kane hesitated only a moment, knowing they'd follow him anyway. He scribbled something on a slip of paper and handed it to Nick. "All right. Here's where we're going. Just remember who's calling the shots. And Quinn? That goes double for you. You wait for my call on everything. Got it?"

Quinn nodded, but he had his own thoughts on the matter.

Chapter Twenty-Three

Impatient with procedure, Nick and Quinn pulled around to the back of the complex, parked their SUV, and quietly went over the wall. With a stealth born of long years in the business and a connection that required little talking, they crept silently toward the targeted building.

The guard on duty in the lobby half rose from his desk when they entered. "Who are—"

That was as far as he got. Quinn gave the man's neck a pinch in the right place, and he folded. Nick pulled out the flex cuffs he'd stuffed in his pocket and trussed the man up.

"Elevator card?" Quinn asked.

"Right here." Nick held it up.

They opened the elevator doors, then flipped the card onto the desk for Kane and the others. Noiselessly, the car rose to the top floor.

The elevator doors to the Gallagher condo hissed open, and Quinn stepped out into the lavishly decorated foyer, Nick behind him. Both men had their guns drawn.

The living room was straight ahead, and for the moment, they were completely exposed. The sound of voices drifted out to him, but fortunately, no one was looking their way. In seconds, they were behind two tall cactus plants that provided some cover while they scoped things out.

The voices were louder now. A woman. A man. More than one man.

Quinn signaled to Nick with his hand. *You take the left side. I'll take the right. But wait until I know where Kate is.*

Nick nodded.

Quinn had to be able to see where everyone was, gauge their best chances. Cautiously, he slid forward to a giant schefflera plant and peered through its leafy branches.

"I'm not feeling well." *Kate.*

"Don't worry," A man said. Not Hispanic, so probably Peter. "Before long we'll be happy to put your out of your pain."

"But you said—"

"Peter, will you please shut up." That had to be Eva. Angry. No, enraged.

"How do you plan to do this?" Peter asked, sounding petulant. "What makes you think they won't just show up at the door with plenty of fire power?"

Yes, how do you plan to do that, you bitch?

"I know people like him. They won't want to risk Kathryn's life. The publicity fallout from something like that would be disastrous." Her voice was tinged with disgust. "As soon as that letter comes through on the fax machine we're leaving. I've already called Luis to have the helicopter waiting."

"What about packing?" Miguel asked. "Are we just supposed to leave everything?"

Eva lifted the briefcase Peter had given to her earlier. "Everything we need is in here. We have more than enough money to buy whatever we need, including houses. Traveling light is less complicated."

Able now to see everyone, Quinn memorized where each person was and stepped forward. "I think we may just change this situation a little."

"Quinn!" Kate started forward at the sound of his voice, but Peter grabbed her arm and jerked her back roughly.

Her face whitened and contorted with pain, and Quinn almost killed the man right then.

"How the hell did you get in here?" Peter's rage was unmistakable.

"Easy, if you know how. It would help if everyone sat on the couch." When no one moved, he fired his gun at Eva's feet and snapped, "Now."

Eva looked at him, her eyes shooting daggers. Everyone moved slowly, aware of Quinn's eyes pinning them.

"You're outnumbered, Quinn." Nolan Hanks rose from where he sat, a gun in his hand.

"You know, you are one lousy son of a bitch." Nick moved forward, also pointing a gun. "Surprised to see me, asshole?"

"Nah, I figured when I saw your friend here, you had to be somewhere nearby. Give it up," Nolan told him. "Back out of here, let us out of here as soon as that fax rings, and we'll let the girl live."

"Trusting you was my worst mistake," Nick spat, "but I won't make it again. No way am I just walking out of here."

Nolan raised his gun, and his finger tightened on the trigger.

"Bad idea." Nick shot him three times, once in the arm and once in each leg. "Anyone else? Okay, then.

Kate, come over here."

Nolan had collapsed on the floor, moaning and writhing. Nick stepped over and kicked his gun backwards, keeping his own gun trained on everyone while he picked it up.

Quinn was still covering the room.

Peter tightened his grip on Kate's arm. "Kate is it? Well, no matter what name she calls herself. She's not going anywhere."

"Kate." Quinn's voice was like a knife edge. "Walk away from him and come over here." His eyes swept over her for a brief instant.

It was like a tableau suddenly come to life, and Kate saw it begin to move in slow motion.

Eva pulled her hand from the pocket of her skirt, her fingers wrapped around a small pistol. Kate wrenched herself around, biting her lip against the pain, and shoved her knee into Peter's groin, freeing herself. She picked up a small but heavy statue from a display table and, gritting her teeth against the pain, heaved the statue at Eva's gun hand. The woman dropped her weapon, screaming.

"She broke my wrist," Eva screamed. "The bitch broke my wrist. Someone shoot her."

Esai was bent over, pant leg pulled up, reaching for a tiny Beretta in his ankle holster.

"Down!" Quinn shouted, and Kate dropped to the floor.

Quinn fired at Esai, hitting his gun hand. He wasn't quite quick enough for Miguel, however, who fired low at Kate.

She felt something sting her side, then a burning sensation flooded through her. She knew she was hit, and a searing pain told her she might also have torn something inside. She breathed through her mouth, willing the agony to pass.

Quinn swore at Miguel and shot twice, shattering his arm.

Kate looked up to see Peter pointing a gun directly at Quinn.

"That's it," he shouted, his finger tightening on the trigger. "You're done."

"Kill him, Peter," Eva screamed, cradling her broken wrist. "Shoot him now."

Kate, fighting not to pass out, forced herself to roll slightly. Sweat broke out on her body everywhere at the effort, and she was sure she was going to vomit any minute. Somehow, through sheer effort of will and overwhelming fear for Quinn, she pulled her gun from her waistband. Her hands were slick with sweat and blood, and she had time for only one brief thought.

Please God, let me remember how to do this.

Then she fired upward at Peter and kept firing, hitting him as his gun went off. She barely noticed the bursts of red that bloomed in the center of his chest, right where her bullets had hit so many times at the shooting range.

The shots had all come so closely together they might have been one, reverberating in the room, bouncing off the tall ceiling. Boom! Boom, boom, boom! Boom!

Kate heard Eva scream again, Miguel swear, glass break, and the thud of a body hitting the floor. Dizziness was overtaking her.

"Quinn?" She didn't know if she shouted it or whispered.

New voices. Running feet. And finally a vaguely familiar voice, heavy with authority.

"This is the FBI. Don't anyone move, or I *will* shoot you. And believe me, I mean every word I say."

Kate felt as if she were falling, but that was impossible. She was already on the floor, wasn't she? Someone was trying to pry the gun loose from her hands, but she put all her strength into holding on.

"Kate? Stay with me, Kate. It's Quinn. You can let go of the gun."

"Quinn?" She forced open her heavy eyelids to see him leaning over her.

"It's me, darlin'. Let go now. It's all right."

"Your shoulder." She saw the blood on his shirt.

"I'm fine. Hang on. The paramedics are on their way."

A babble of voices sounded in the background. Eva's, strident and imperious. Esai or Miguel, she didn't know which one, swearing in Spanish. Voices she didn't recognize. Someone giving orders. The pain was so unbearable this time she didn't think there was enough Tylenol to take the edge off.

Hands touching her, soft and gentle, but making her wince and cry out all the same.

"Dean." Quinn's voice, angry and impatient. "Where the hell's the damn ambulance? She's bleeding heavily. Tell them to get here *now.*"

"Was she shot again?" A voice filled with concern and worry. Whose?

"Yes, but I'm afraid to move her." Quinn's voice was shaky. He completely ignored his own wound. "All I can do right now is try to stop the bleeding."

"Quinn?" She could barely get the word out.

"Right here, darlin'." His face loomed over hers. "Kate, I am so sorry. I..." He stopped, and she wondered if she was fading away, but then he went on. "This is my fault. All my fault. I love you, Kate, and I let you down."

She tried to focus on his face, as movement swirled around them. "Am I dying?"

"Not a chance." He took one of her cold hands in his large warm ones, pouring the heat of his body into hers. "You told me you were a fighter. I'm counting on that."

Eva, her voice imperious, demanded that she be allowed to call her attorney. The Osuna brothers still cursed angrily in Spanish. There were sounds of token struggles and more strange voices, giving orders, making phone calls.

"Get them all out of here and take them down to the federal building." A strange voice, one she didn't recognize.

"Kate?" Jake Garza. Where had Quinn gone? "Kate, the ambulance is here. They need to check you over before they can give you something for the pain. All right?"

"Okay." Her lips could barely form the word. Her eyelids felt as if they'd been dipped in concrete, but as strange hands did things to her body, she tried to find Quinn. All she saw was unfamiliar legs and Jake crouching on the other side of the EMTs, his face pinched with concern.

"We're ready to roll," one of them said. "The wound in her arm busted open, and she's been hit again in the side, almost the same place as the last time. People need to stop using her for target practice."

"I'll ride with her." Jake.

"Quinn?" she croaked.

"He's here. They're fixing his shoulder." Jake moved away so the paramedics could fit her with the oxygen and hook her up to the portable EKG machine. As they lifted her she heard him swear. "Damn it, Quinn, let them patch you up. No, you can't…"

She forced one eye open. Jake, again.

"Quinn?" She could hardly get the word out.

"Being taken care of. You'll see him at the hospital."

"Hurt?"

"He'll be fine. I promise."

A hand grasped hers on the ride to the hospital. And then she faded, the shot they gave her dropping her into a blessed oblivion.

****

Kate felt the movement of the gurney along the halls, the *slap slap slap* of the rubber wheels on tile, the thudding of feet in surgical booties.

"Kate, can you hear me?"

"Mmm?" She was trying to swim up through inky waters, but something heavy kept pushing her down. She tried to breathe, and a pain so sharp it took away her breath altogether stabbed at her.

"Kate, remember me? Dr. DeWitt?" He was leaning over her, his mouth close to her ears. All around him nurses worked to complete their Strikes as his patient was wheeled toward the surgical suites. He took one of her hands in his. "If you can hear me, squeeze my hand."

She gripped his hand as hard as she could.

"Good, good. Listen to me. You've been shot again

295

and done some damage to your previous wounds. We have to do some quick repair work on you. Do you understand?"

Another squeeze.

"We ran a full blood panel, something we always do even if you've just been a patient. Things can change, you know." Pause. "We found elevated levels of hormones. There's a good possibility you're pregnant."

Pregnant? Really? Happiness flashed through her. She was having Quinn's baby? Then, as fast as it came, the feeling dissipated. What if Quinn didn't want it? What if… "Quinn…"

"He's being taken care of. They're removing a bullet from his shoulder, but he'll be fine."

She forced out the words. "Hope so." She tried for another breath. "Don't tell…"

"You don't want him to know?"

"Not…yet…please."

DeWitt shrugged. "It's your choice, of course. Well, we'll take good care of you upstairs and be extra careful."

She squeezed his hand again. "Thanks."

****

Quinn was still flat on his back in Trauma Three when Jake walked in. A massive bandage covered his right shoulder. He glanced at Jake.

"Come to claim the body?"

"Come to beat it back to life. How's he doing, doc?"

The ER doctor finishing up with him looked at Jake. "He refused anything but a local anesthetic. He's a wild man, even with all this pain. He absolutely has to stay here overnight. I don't know what to do short of handcuffing him to the bed."

Quinn shook his head. "Not going to."

Jake moved to where Quinn could see him better. "Kate's in good hands, Ace. She'll be fine. DeWitt just took her upstairs again. He said if you behaved yourself and stayed right here, he'd find us and let us know when the surgery's over."

"Go...check on her." The words felt as if he'd dragged them from the bottom of a barrel. "After."

"Okay. You'll be able to. But you won't do her any good if you kill yourself being stupid."

"Nolan?" he asked.

"Unfortunately not dead." Nick said, walking into the room at that moment and standing on the other side of the bed. "In the prison ward at University Hospital awaiting his own surgery. If I hadn't wanted him so badly for trial I'd have blown his head off." His face was twisted with pain. "Quinn, I don't even know where to begin to apologize for this. I can't—"

Quinn made a feeble hand wave at him. "Happens. Do...your best but shit happens."

He watched Jake exchange a look with Nick.

"Can you hang out here a while with me until we get news of Kate? This idiot thinks he's going to get up and go looking for her."

"It's the least I can do." Nick's eyes were bloodshot, and he looked as if he'd stared death in the face, but he had pulled himself together. "Why don't I go get us some coffee? Can the walking wounded have any?"

The nurse adjusting the IV drip in Quinn's arm nodded. "We'd just as soon he let this medication work on him, but with all he's been through, I don't guess a cup of coffee will do him any harm. If he's still awake to drink it."

Quinn rolled his head to look at Jake as soon as the nurse had left. When he spoke, his words were slurred. "I have to go home. Yank this damn needle out."

He reached for where the IV needle was taped to the back of his hand.

Jake knocked his arm away. "Are you crazy? They just dug around in your shoulder. You really ought to let them keep you here tonight."

Quinn shook his head. "Have...to get home."

"I thought you wanted to see Kate? Take a little nap, and by then, she should be in recovery."

He closed his eyes. "You...take care of her. I'm...poison. Just wanted...to see her...myself. 'Sall." Even saying the words, he felt as if a knife had carved a hole in his heart.

"What the hell are you talking about?"

Quinn made a supreme effort to rally and get his words out. "I...promised to take care of her. Keep her safe. Then I let her get shot, kidnapped, and shot again. Me, the big protector."

He should have been the one it all happened to. She was better off without him, even if letting her go was destroying him.

"Shut up," Jake ordered, worry lining his face. "Quinn, you look like shit. I'm calling the nurse back in."

"No." His eyelids fluttered shut, but he forced them back up. "Promised her, Jake. Made her a promise and look...what happened. Why would she even want anything to do with me? I'm better off out of her life. I can't keep anyone safe. Ever."

Jake stared at him. "That is just so much bullshit. I don't even want to hear it."

The door opened, and Nick walked in carrying a cardboard tray with three cups of coffee. He handed the cups around, and Quinn roused enough to take a healthy swallow of his, but Jake grabbed the cup as it started to fall. In seconds, he was asleep.

When Quinn awoke, for a moment he was disoriented. He had slept but was still edgy and unsettled.

"Nick." His throat felt as if he'd swallowed nails, and he had difficulty swallowing.

"Yeah, buddy?" Nick was there in an instant.

"Need you to drive me home." Nick didn't respond so Quinn looked at Jake. "I guess he won't do it."

"You're damn right—" Jake began.

"Home?" Nick stared at Quinn. "Are you crazy?"

Quinn sat up gingerly, testing his shoulder and wincing involuntarily. "Yes, home. Hand me my shirt."

"You're insane," Nick told him. "You're in no shape to go anywhere. And what about Kate? An hour ago you were ready to punch out anyone who wouldn't let you see her."

"Had…time to think. You…check her." He had difficulty getting the words out.

Jake looked at Nick. "The medication must have addled his brain. Now he's got this dumbass idea that all this is his fault and she's better off with him out of her life."

Damn right." Yet the thought of cutting her out of his life nearly split his heart in two. A pain such as he hadn't felt in a long time threatened to overwhelm him, smacking into him like a hard body blow."

"Don't tell me he wants to go crawl into his cave again." Jake looked at Quinn. "Dumbass."

"My…choice," Quinn insisted and started to pull on the tape over the IV needle.

"Wait, will you?" Jake grabbed his hand and reached for the call button. "At least let the nurse do it so you don't cause yourself any more damage."

But the pain from the intravenous needle was nothing compare to the emotional pain that invaded his entire body. He was sick with it, consumed by it, knowing how bleak his future was going to be.

When the nurse came into the room, she stared at Quinn first, then gave Nick and Jake a dirty look.

"Out," Quinn told her. "I want out. Right now."

She frowned. "You're not in much shape to be leaving."

"Don't care. Have to leave."

At last, she just shrugged her shoulders and set about disconnecting the IV. She placed a bandaid over the place where the needle had been inserted.

"Try not to kill yourself," she told Quinn.

If only.

"The doctor left a form for you to sign yourself out Against Medical Advice if you insisted," she went on. "I'll get it. Then you're free to go."

Quinn scratched his name on the clipboard the nurse brought back, then inched his shirt on with Jake's reluctant help.

"I'm going home." He groaned again, and his words were slurring. "You can take me, or I'll figure out how to get there myself."

Jake exchanged a glance with Nick, then nodded.

"Okay. If that's what you want. You sure can't go anyplace by yourself."

"And can you please just play chauffeur and keep your mouth shut?"

The nurse had given him a prescription to fill for pain meds, but he didn't think there was a pill in the world that could cure what was wrong with him. The light had left his life, the only thing that had brought him to life again. He closed his eyes, and Kate's face swam before his eyes, her gorgeous eyes filled with love for him.

That love had nearly gotten her killed. She was much better off without him. But her laughter wouldn't be echoing in his house any longer. He'd never feel her warm body cuddled up to him in bed again. Never cradle her breast in his palm as they slept or feel his cock harden against the curve of her ass. Never be able to sink himself into the lushness of her warmth.

Too bad the bullet had missed vital organs. The shooter would have done him a favor if he'd killed him, because his life was never going to be worth living again.

He leaned his head back against the seat and gave himself over to the tears coursing down his cheeks.

Chapter Twenty-Four

Kate looked up as the door to her room opened and Jake and Nick walked in. The heavy bandages were weighing her down, and the beeping of the machines drove her mad, but she was sitting up in bed. And no matter how bad she might look, she was wide awake and worried.

"Where is he?" she demanded. "He's hurt worse than you told me, isn't he? I want the truth."

Jake walked to the side of the bed and kissed her cheek. "He's a little banged up, but otherwise fine. He's home."

"Home?" Her eyes widened. "Why isn't he here?" When no one said anything, a sick feeling crawled up from her stomach. Something was very wrong.

Nick cleared his throat. "Kate, we have something we need to tell you. We don't understand it any more than you will, but here's how it is."

They told her what Quinn had said, and why he wasn't in her room, sitting next to her. And wasn't likely to be.

She just stared at them as they talked as pain rose through her body that beat any caused by the bullet and the surgery. She was afraid her heart would crack in two. But that was suddenly replaced by anger.

"What? Is he crazy?" A heavy breath rasped out of her lungs and she began coughing.

Jake pressed the call button for the nurse while Nick supported Kate with his hand and tried to prevent her from choking.

"What are you men doing to this woman?" the nurse demanded as she stormed in. "My God, she's not twenty-four hours out of surgery."

"We know," Jake answered. "We just had to…give her some news that wasn't too pleasant."

"I'm calling DeWitt. She doesn't look too good." The door swished shut behind her.

"How dare he leave me like that?" Even as weak as she felt, she knew they could hear the anger in her voice. "Doesn't he owe me an explanation?"

"Kate," Nick began.

"Wait." She let out a ragged breath. "He got hurt because of me. That's why he left, isn't it. I told him this was dangerous. That's why I didn't want him involved."

She blinked at the tears crowding her eyes, trying to hold them back, but a sob wrenched itself from her body and the tears streaked down her cheeks.

Dr. DeWitt breezed in at that exact moment, the nurse behind him. He checked Kate over, gave some orders to the nurse, then turned to the two men.

"All right. What the hell is going on here?"

Uncomfortable with what he had to say, Nick explained the situation.

"I'd think Miss Griffin might have something to say about that," DeWitt said.

The nurse returned with a hypodermic and injected something into Kate's IV line.

DeWitt picked up one of her hands with his. "Just try to relax, Kate. This will make you drowsy. You don't need to put stress on yourself this soon out of surgery."

"But—"

"No buts."

She didn't want to sleep. She wanted to get out of bed, crawl if she had to, find Nick, and kick some sense into his thick head. How dare he do this? He'd told her he loved her. Made incredible love to her. They had created a child together. What the hell was he doing walking away from her?

Now she knew what the term heartache really meant. But it was laced with anger at Quinn's thickheadedness and frustration with the futility of the situation. How could she get through to him? How could she live the rest of her life without him? The bed would be as empty as his future. She wondered if a broken heart ever healed.

She wanted him to slip into bed with her, hold her against his body, tell her everything was wonderful and they had a great future waiting for them. But when she reached out to grab him, there was nothing but emptiness…and the pain in her heart that threatened to destroy her.

****

When DeWitt told Kate she was ready to be discharged from the hospital as long as she had someone with her, she didn't know where she was supposed to go. The only place she knew was Quinn's, and apparently, he didn't want her.

"All taken care of," when she asked Kane Barton about it. "I'm moving you into one of the safe houses we keep, along with Sharon Langford and two agents to guard you."

They used three cars to do it, each of them switching direction back and forth to confuse anyone who might be trying to follow them.

Sharon grinned when Kate finally walked in the door. "This time I'm chaining you to the furniture."

"I don't think you'll have much to worry about," Kate told her in a quiet voice. "No one will be trying to break me out again."

Trying to hold in the tears that always seemed to be ready to spill, she let Sharon lead her to the bedroom where she'd be sleeping.

"I did some shopping for you," Sharon told her, pointing out the packages on the bed. "At least enough to tide you over until I can get you to store."

"Thank you. Really. Would you think me rude if I said I'd just like to lie down."

She tried to ignore the sympathetic look on the other woman's face.

DeWitt had confirmed the pregnancy before she left the hospital and made an appointment for her with an obstetrician. Two days later Sharon drove her to see the doctor and then to get her prescriptions filled. She forced herself to eat because of the baby and to begin an exercise routine. She walked around the backyard, swallowing tears because it reminded her of the walks she and Quinn had taken at the cabin. She made herself get in bed early each night, even though she was a long time falling asleep, knowing she needed the rest.

All the media was full of the story, and she couldn't turn on the television without seeing it on one channel or another. Jake came by with the latest newspapers for her to read.

"They're calling it the biggest cartel takedown in

ten years," he told her.

"Is…Is everyone still in jail?" She was almost afraid to ask.

"You betcha. The judge denied bail, and they're still screaming. They've got enough lawyers to fill the entire courtroom."

"At least they can't get to me."

"Oh, honey." Jake dropped onto the couch next to her. "They'll never get to you. They'll be lucky if they ever smell fresh air again."

Kate's eyes dropped to her hands that were fiddling with the bed covers. "You know, when Quinn taught me to use that gun, I wasn't sure I'd be able to handle it if I actually had to shoot someone."

"Most people have a hard time dealing with it," Jake told her. "It's not unusual. Even cops sometimes need counseling to get past it." He paused. "I could ask DeWitt to recommend someone for you to talk to if you like."

She sighed. "No, not really. Sometimes I have flashbacks and I feel physically ill, but I seem to be dealing with it a lot better than I expected. Am I terrible if I say shooting Peter gave me great satisfaction?"

Jake shook his head and smiled. "I'd say he deserved it. Sometimes ordinary people are forced to do extraordinary things way out of their comfort zone. Let it rest, Kate. You did the right thing."

He continued to stop by every two or three days, but it was hard to make conversation. They were both aware of the elephant in the room crowding them.

She had avoided the subject of Quinn, but finally, she asked, "How's he doing?"

Jake sighed. "Okay, I guess. No one's seen or

heard from him. I'm hoping he was smart enough to make his follow up appointment for his shoulder wound."

Kate felt tears dripping down her face again. "I just don't understand. Why can't he at least come to see me, talk to me? We have to hash this out." She plucked a tissue from her pocket and wiped her nose. "Maybe he decided he doesn't love me after all."

"That's a bunch of bull. I've never seen him this wild about anyone. Not even Lisa, God forgive me for saying that."

"Then he has to talk to me," she protested. "At least give me a chance to have my say. If he blames me, I can certainly understand. But none of this was *his* fault. None of it."

"I'll do my best, sweetheart. But you know what a stubborn man he is. He'll just hide up there killing himself with guilt."

"Thanks, Jake. And thanks for coming by."

She got up and walked him to the door, but as he was about to open it, she put a hand on his arm. It was time to play her trump card. She'd wanted Quinn to come to her without it, but he hadn't left her any choice.

"When you talk to him, tell him something for me, will you?"

"Anything, if you think it will help."

She wet her lips. "Tell him I'm pregnant."

Jake blinked. "Pregnant?"

"Almost two months now." She shredded the tissue in her hand. "I wanted to tell him myself, but it doesn't look like I'm going to get the chance. I don't know if he wants to be involved with the baby or not, but at least he should have the chance to make that decision."

Jake visibly pulled himself together. "I'll make sure he knows."

"One more thing, Jake."

His mouth curved in a lopsided grin. "I hope it's a little less shocking than the last one."

"I'll be leaving soon."

Jake stared at her. "Leaving? Leaving for where?"

"I don't really know yet. I have business still to wrap up in Tampa. My father's will was never probated. The remnants of the house are still sitting on the property so I've got to get it cleaned up and see about selling the lot."

"Don't try to do too much," he warned.

"I'll be fine. I plan to take good care of myself. But I also have to see what's what with my condo and decide what to do with my things." She drew in a long breath and let it out slowly. "And then I have to decide where I'm going to live."

"But not here."

She shook her head, a sad look in her eyes. "It would be too difficult for me." Then she brightened. "But I'm a damned good researcher. I thought I'd start my own business, advertise on the Internet. I've got more than enough money as a cushion until I generate some income."

"Don't try to tackle too much at once."

"I won't. But I've got my life back, and I don't intend to waste it by sitting around wringing my hands."

"Just don't leave too soon." He kissed Kate on the cheek and left.

****

"Pregnant?" Quinn felt all the blood drain from his face and shocked zapped his body. He wasn't sure he'd heard right. "Pregnant?"

Jake guided him to a chair and helped him sit down. "Yes. About two months."

"But how?" Quinn stared at the other man. "Is she sure?"

His friend chuckled. "I'm assuming the usual way, and yes, they did all the tests in the hospital."

"But she said she was on birth control pills." He rubbed his forehead. He had the weird feeling that he was having an out of body experience.

"Well, Ace, nothing is foolproof. And I'm guessing all the stress she was under probably worked to weaken their effect. Not to mention she may have missed a few." He watched Quinn. "So what are you going to do about it?"

Go to her and insist she marry me. Be a father to our child. Have a—

No, he'd lost the right to do that. But the sudden ache in his heart told him that wasn't going to be so easy.

"Nothing. All the more reason for me to stay away from her." He couldn't hide the pain in his voice.

Jake stood in front of him, hands on his hips, glaring at him. "Quinn, I don't usually get this angry with you, but if you don't pull your head out of your ass, you're going to miss out on another chance at life."

"But I—"

"Shut up. I'm, not done. Use your brain. She's safe. The danger is over. Bring her up here, and the two of you can live happily ever after." Jake walked over to the refrigerator and snagged himself a beer. "One more thing. She's planning to leave San Antonio for good as soon as she gets the okay. I'm not leaving here until you agree to see her before she goes."

For a long time after Jake left, Quinn sat, so many things running through his head. He couldn't seem to shake the guilt he felt about what happened. Yet at the same time, the thought of never seeing Kate again, of never knowing their child and raising it with her, nearly brought him to his knees.

For three days and three very long nights, he wasn't able to do anything but think of the whole situation. He'd never been so agonized about a decision in his life. He couldn't escape the fact he had fallen deeply in love with Kate or that he wanted this child. But could she forgive him for what had happened? Was that possible?

Finally, realizing hiding in his house wasn't going to give him any answers, he showered, shaved, dressed carefully, and headed into San Antonio, praying all the way.

****

Kate found she could handle a lot of things by telephone, set up appointments with people she needed to see. Both Sharon and the doctor had told her she was doing great and travel shouldn't be a problem.

"Just don't exhaust yourself," they both warned.

They figured two more weeks and she'd be good to go.

Jake had sent someone to pick up the laptop she wanted, along with a list of software, and deliver it to her. She was sitting at the dining room table setting up the computer when the doorbell rang.

"I'll get it," she called to Sharon. "It's probably

Jake, anyway. He said he was coming by with lunch."

But when she opened the door and found Quinn on the porch, she almost passed out.

Of all days for me to look like a slob.

She'd been anxious to get the laptop set up and just dragged on a pair of sweat pants and a T-shirt. Her hair was gathered in a messy ponytail, and she hadn't worried about makeup in a long time.

A swarm of butterflies were doing a tap dance in her stomach, and the pain in her heart was almost visceral. She was shaking in a way she hadn't since this whole mess started. Reaching for a control that seemed to have deserted her, she had to clench her teeth to keep from breaking into tears at the sight of him. She wanted so badly to pull him into her arms, but what if he had just come to say goodbye? Or to tell her he didn't want any part of the baby?

For a long moment, she just stared at him, unable to move. He looked thinner, his hair was longer, and lines of pain etched his face.

At last he broke the silence. "Hello, Kate."

She nodded, hardly able to speak. "Quinn."

"May I come in?" He held up a large brown paper bag. "I'm the lunch boy today."

"Oh, of course." Giving herself a mental shake, she stepped aside to let him enter. "Thank you for bringing the food."

He put the sack on the kitchen counter and began searching for plates in the cupboards.

Kate's body was so taut with nerves she was sure her body would snap and pieces would fly across the room like a broken rubber band.

He had brought lunch? Was that all? Okay, if that's

the way he wanted to play it, she could do the same, no matter the cost.

"Jake said you wanted a pressed Cuban from the Central Market," Quinn said over his shoulder. "I got some potato salad and drinks, too."

He unpacked the grocery bag, arranged the food on the plates with deliberate movements, all the while keeping his back to her.

"Here. Let me get the glasses out," she told him, proud that she was able to keep all emotion from her voice.

What is he doing here? Why the hell did he come? It isn't just to bring me lunch. Is it?

Ask him, her inner voice shouted. *No*, her other voice argued.

Oh, god, she was losing her mind.

She had to stand next to him to open the cupboard and get the glasses out. When their bodies touched, she was vibrating with such tension the glass slipped from her hand and shattered in the sink.

Quinn took her hand and turned it over. "You cut yourself."

"It's nothing. Really." She felt herself unraveling. Just being close to him, knowing he didn't want her, was almost more than she could bear.

"It's bleeding." He grabbed some paper towels from the roller.

"Everything okay?" Sharon Langford had come into the room. She couldn't quite hide her surprise at seeing Quinn. "I heard a crash."

"I've got it under control," he told her, blotting Kate's hand.

"Let me get the first aid kit." She was back with it

in seconds. "I can take care of that."

"I'll handle it." He grabbed the kit from her, cleaned the cut, and applied cream and a bandage.

"It's really nothing," Kate argued.

"Can't take a chance of an infection." Quinn said.

Sharon waited a moment before she turned to leave. "Okay. Call me if you need me."

"I'm okay, really," she protested, then proceeded to embarrass herself by bursting into tears.

"Oh, Jesus." Quinn wrapped his arms around her. "Oh, God. Kate, Kate, Kate. I'm sorry. I'm so, so fucking sorry."

The dam had burst, and he rocked her, holding her tightly against him as huge sobs wracked her body. She wasn't embarrassed at the way she clung to him, but she'd worry about it later. Right now she needed his warm strength. She held his shirt with both hands, her face tucked into the hollow of his throat. She couldn't seem to stop crying.

And all the while he rubbed her back, soothed her, and murmured in her ear. "Please don't cry, darlin'. It's not good for you or the baby. God, I am so damn sorry."

It seemed forever before the tears dried up and she could catch her breath. She waited for Quinn to drop his arms, but they were still wrapped around her. She tilted her face up to look at him, struck dumb by the pain in his eyes. What was that about? Had he come to tell her they were finished? Had everything reminded him too much of his other loss? Was it more pain than he could bear?

"Isn't this where you came in?" she asked with a watery smile.

He nodded. "I seem to have that effect on you."

"You didn't come to see me." She was trying to speak calmly, and it wasn't working. "I needed you so badly. Why did you stay away?"

"Didn't Jake or Nick talk to you?"

"I didn't want Jake or Nick. I wanted you."

"Kate, how could you even want anything to do with me after what happened?" His voice was laced with anguish and self-recrimination. "How could you ever feel safe with me again?"

She sniffled. "Listen to me. Nothing that happened was your fault. Nothing. And I don't want to hear any more of that. I was the one that dragged the cartel into *your* life, not the other way around. I'm the guilty party here." She tipped her face up to him. "Oh, Quinn. I want—"

Anything else she might have said was cut off by the crush of his mouth on hers. The kiss ravaged her, his tongue pressing against her lips to force them open, then pulling at her tongue with his own. The fingers of one hand threaded through her hair, holding her head while he drank from her with intense hunger. All the while she felt her breasts pressed against the hard wall of his chest, his heart thudding against her body, and the thick length of his erection hard against her mound.

She had no idea how long the kiss went on before he finally lifted his head.

"I shouldn't—"

"I'm glad—"

They laughed shakily as they stepped on each other's words.

"Me first," she said and clutched at his shoulders, afraid he might move away. "I have no pride left,

Quinn. Whatever it is, we'll work it out, but please don't walk away from me."

"Oh God, Kate. You have no idea how hard these past days have been." He rested his chin on her head. "It killed me to stay away from you."

"Aren't you the one who said we had something special between us?" she asked. "Do you want to throw it all away before we even know what it is, just because you're having a little pity party?"

He tightened his hold on her. "God, no," he said fervently. "But I just—"

"Just what? Are afraid? Don't you think it's time to get on with life again?" She bit her lip. "I was the one who brought the trouble here. I was the one who dragged you into this. So if you think any of this is your fault, just get that out of your head."

"Listen."

"No, you listen. I'm sorry you got shot. I'm sorry I messed up your life. And I guess if you don't want to take a chance on me, I can't blame you. But don't walk out on me because of some misguided notion that *you* caused all this. That's just plain stupid." Tears were threatening to spill down her cheeks again, and she swiped at her face. "I seem to have perpetual waterworks these days." She gave him a shaky smile. "Hormones, I guess."

"Kate, you don't understand."

"What? What is it I don't understand?"

"I made a promise to you." He moved her back from him just enough so he could look at her face. "To protect you, keep you safe, and instead, I almost got you killed. If I hadn't convinced you to go into San Antonio, you wouldn't have been shot the first time."

She smacked his chest. "That is such nonsense. Life is all about chances, Quinn. There are no guarantees, but I'd rather take chances with you than anyone else. If you can forgive me for dragging you into this mess, can't I forgive you for me getting shot?"

He studied her face, her eyes, as if trying to read every nuance. "What about Nolan? I left you alone with him."

She smacked his arm with her fist again. "Damn it. Nolan Hanks wasn't your fault, and you almost got killed yourself rescuing me." She pressed herself against him. "You told me we had a future. Was that some big fat lie?"

"No." His voice was soft. "But I just…"

"Just what? Was it easier for you to just go back into your hole and hide than try to live life again?"

"I thought I'd disappointed you," he said miserably.

"Oh, Quinn." She hugged him as hard as she could.

A discreet cough sounded behind them, and they both looked up. Sharon was standing in the living room with her purse. "I need to run some errands. I, um, expect to be gone a long time. Quinn, will you be staying?"

She studied the expression on his face, relaxing when his mouth curved into a hint of a smile.

"Yes," he told the other woman. "I expect I will."

"Fine, then. See you later."

"Now where were we?" Kate put her hands on either side of his face, pulling his head down to hers. "Oh, yes. I think we were here."

"No, I think we need to be someplace else."

He lifted her in his arms and strode into the short

hallway. "Which room is yours?"

She pointed, and he carried her into it, placing her gently on the bed. Then he smacked himself on the head.

"I should be shot. You're still healing, and here I am ready to ravish you. What an ass I am."

She grinned, albeit just a small one. "I'm fine. Really. Feel free to ravish away."

But still he hesitated. "What about…"

"The baby?" She placed her hand over her stomach. "The baby's doing just fine." She wet her lips. "I have two questions to ask you before this goes any further."

"Okay. You're certainly entitled."

A thread of anxiety wiggled through her. She had to be sure of something first, before she gave herself to him completely. She couldn't take the chance he'd walk out and destroy her all over again. "Are you okay about the baby? And did you come here today out of some sense of obligation?"

He brushed stands of her hair away from her face. "I'm ecstatic about the baby, and I came here today because I love you. I just thought…"

"Stop thinking. You can't know how much I've missed you."

She wanted to yank her clothing off, but she was shaking so badly she couldn't make her fingers work. Quinn sat her on the side of the bed and gently lifted her T-shirt over her head. When he saw the scars from the incisions, pain lanced across his face and tears actually threatened. "Jesus, Kate."

"Please. It's all right. I know they're hideous, but—"

317

He pressed his fingers against her lips. "You know that's not it. I just feel so…responsible. Look what I put you through."

She pushed his fingers aside. "Stop thinking about the fact I could be dead and think about me being alive. Which I am, thanks to you. So let's let that be the end of it. Please?"

He swallowed, hard. "I'll try. Oh, God, darlin'."

He dropped to his knees and buried his face in her lap, his shoulders shaking. Kate smoothed her hand over the silk of his hair and the taut muscles of his back, crooning softly to him until the storm of emotion passed. At last, he lifted his head and rubbed his hands over his face.

"Now," she said before he could utter another word. "Where were we?"

He loosened the drawstring on her sweat pants, leaned her back on the bed, and slowly drew the sweats and her panties down her legs. The heated look in his eyes more than made up for a lot of things.

He moved her so her head rested on the pillows, then knelt between her thighs and began to kiss every inch of her skin. The tip of his tongue pressed at the hollow of her throat where her pulse was beating hard enough to burst through the skin. His rough silk lips traced every scar on her body, trailing kisses over them as if he could magically heal them.

When he reached the lower part of her abdomen, the place where their baby was growing, he placed a large, warm, open-mouthed kiss on her skin, and she was sure she felt the wetness of tears falling on her.

Nothing escaped his attention—her thighs, the backs of her knees, her ankles, even her toes. She never knew what erogenous zones toes could be. By the time he'd covered most of her body, she was shaking with need.

"I want you naked, too," she whispered.

He moved off the bed, making short work of his jeans and shirt, and loomed over her again.

"Oh, my God." Her voice shook as the puckered scar came into view, and she reached up to trace its outline. "Your shoulder."

"It's fine, darlin'. All healed. Forget about it."

"How can I possibly? If it weren't for me, you'd never have been shot."

"Kate." He loomed over her. "We already decided that conversation's a done deal. Right?" His eyes flashed with need. "I have something else in mind completely."

"Touch me anywhere." She reached for him, closing her small fingers over his swollen shaft. "Touch me everywhere. And tell me again."

"Tell you…?"

"You know. What you said before."

His face softened. "I love you, Kate Griffin. With all my heart. I'm going to make love to you until you don't even know your own name. Then, if you can still walk, we're going to city hall to apply for our marriage license. How does that sound?"

"Better than you can imagine," she breathed.

He came down to her, kneeling over her, his hands following every inch of her body, as if learning her for the first time.

She moved her hands over his back, touched his shoulders, feeling the play of muscles under the skin.

"Make me better," she begged. "Make me whole

again."

When he reached the spot on her belly again where their baby was growing, he skidded soft, almost reverent kisses across her skin. Flashes of pleasure spiked through her, and she fisted her hands in the silk of his hair.

"Are you sure this won't hurt him?" he asked, his voice tense.

"It could be a her, you know." Her voice wasn't quite steady as a painful thought struck her. "Quinn? Would it be hard for you? You know, having another little girl?"

"Not as long as she looks like you, darlin'. I'm learning to look to the future and not live in the past." He lifted his head and flashed a wicked grin. "Now lie still, I'm enjoying myself."

He nudged her thighs farther apart and bent her legs, exposing her to him completely. He opened her labia, staring at it for so long she began to wonder if something was wrong. Then he lowered his head and his mouth closed over her throbbing nub while his fingers stroked every inch of her drenched flesh.

Heat flooded her everywhere. She had missed this so much and feared never to have it again. She pushed her hips against him, grabbing his hair and holding his head against her body. "Yes, oh, yes. Do that, please."

When he pushed two fingers inside her, she was so ready she convulsed around him immediately, her inner muscles gripping his fingers hard, milking them as her cream coated them. As she wanted to do with his hard shaft.

She reached down and found his swollen length, and as he shifted higher between her legs she guided him home, straight to the opening of her core. To her soul. To her heart.

One push and he was in, his hips rolling and thrusting almost immediately. Kate raked her fingers against Quinn's back as he drove in and out of her.

"Kate, Kate, Kate." He chanted her name like a litany.

As aroused as they both were, their climax rolled over them in seconds, no less intense because it caught them so quickly. Kate lost herself in him, everything disappearing except his cock inside her, throbbing and pulsing. Their bodies shuddered together, her liquid showering his shaft with velvet heat. His hands gripped her buttocks, pulling her tight against him, holding her until the last spasm faded away.

Still dragging air into his lungs, he slid carefully from her and rolled to the side, pulling her against him.

"I love you," he said when he could breathe again.

"I love you, too."

It was a long time before they ever got to eat their lunch.

Epilogue

Quinn leaned against the wall in the hospital room and watched his wife and newborn son. Kate was dozing, smiling in her sleep. John David Quinn—John for his daddy and David for his grandfather—nestled peacefully in her arms, replete from his recent suckling. The image caught at Quinn's heart.

It had been a wonderful year. Released from the terror that had dogged her, comfortable in a new environment, Kate had blossomed. Their wedding was small, with Jake as best man and Jake's sister, Julie, who quickly became a good friend to Kate, as maid of honor.

Kane Barton and the others who had been closest to Quinn were pleased to see him finally embrace life again. There had been much laughter and many toasts, and the guests treated Kate as a one of their own.

Quinn returned to the practice of law, but not with the U.S. Attorney. Instead, he opened an office in Windswept, and as Kate predicted, he was flooded with more business than he wanted to handle. Apparently, everyone thought a "local boy" should take care of their legal matters.

He'd had to hire a secretary and was thinking about a paralegal, especially now that the baby was here. He wanted to spend as much time with his family as he could. He felt so truly blessed. His life, which had been such a shambles, was richer than he ever could have hoped.

A light tap on the door drew his attention, and Jake slid quietly into the room. He smiled as he looked at Kate and John.

"You've certainly got it all now, Ace," he whispered.

"No kidding. Someone was watching out for me."

"I wanted to stop by and bring you the good news myself, make this a really good week for the Quinn family."

"What news?"

"Could you stop whispering so I can hear, too?" Kate's voice was soft. "Hi, Jake. Did you come to get another look at your godson?"

"Absolutely." He bent over and kissed Kate's cheek. "It almost makes me think of wedded bliss myself. I said almost." He grinned as they looked at him.

"So what did you come to tell us?" Kate asked.

"I thought you might like to know that the last of the plea bargains wrapped yesterday and everyone is gone for many years. I think after the first trial, when Esai got such a stiff sentence, Miguel and the others decided to get the best deals they could."

"So it's truly over?"

"You bet. And won't we be glad to see the last of them."

"Thank you again for arranging it so I didn't have to testify," Kate said.

"With that flash drive and the papers we were able to take from the offices, we didn't need you," he explained. "You can enjoy life with the monkey off your back."

Quinn had moved to stand beside the bed while they were talking. He touched his son's small head gently, awed by this tiny person he helped create, then took Kate's hand and held it tightly against his heart.

He didn't care how intense their feelings showed, how much his love for her shone. He'd needed redemption and never thought he'd get it. Then Kate had come into his life and everything changed. The two of them were so intent on each other and their child, he never knew it when Jake slipped from the room.

About the Author

Known as the oldest living author of erotic romance, Desiree Holt has produced more than two hundred titles in nearly every subgenre of romance fiction. Her stories are enriched by her personal experiences, her characters by the people she meets.

After fifteen ears in the great state of Texas, she relocated back to Florida to be closer to members of her family and a large collection of friends. Her favorite pastimes are watching football, reading, and researching her stories. She lives with her three cats, who love to sit with her when she writes.

Desiree loves to hear from readers.
www.facebook.com/desireeholtauthor
www.facebook.com/desiree01holt
Twitter @desireeholt
Pinterest: desiree02holt
Google: https://g.co/kgs/6vgLUu
www.desireeholt.com
www.desiremeonly.com

~*~

To chat with Desiree Holt and other Wild Rose Press authors of erotic romance, join us at
www.groups.yahoo.com/group/thewilderroses.

Also Available

Out of Control
By Desiree Holt
http://a.co/2lwmXpB

Twenty five years ago Carrie Nolan was the only victim to survive the killing spree of a pedophile. Her life has been frozen in time, and not even a move to a distant city and a name change has healed the wounds that left her emotionally and sexually scarred. Determined finally to reclaim her life, Carrie returns to High Ridge as multi-published crime novelist, Dana Moretti, in hope of asking the questions that would lay her nightmares to rest.

Sheriff Cole Landry, came to High Ridge to escape the horrors of Iraq and Afghanistan, but soon after the sexy author arrives and starts poking her nose into matters best forgotten, his town once again becomes the hunting ground of a ruthless killer. She's sure it's the same man, and he's not all that convinced she's wrong. Keeping Dana safe means keeping her close—very close—under his protection, under him.

Between her sexual need for Cole and the danger lurking behind every stranger's face, her world is spinning out of control.

Also Read

Trained for Seduction
Spy Games Book One
By Mia Downing
http://a.co/cTQ7fwI

Emma Walters didn't choose to be a spy, but when her crazy father was caught selling bombs to the wrong people, she was given a choice—become a spy or rot in jail. Her exciting new life as agent Kate Wells becomes more so when she discovers her new boss is the agent—undercover and investigating her father at the time—who took her to third base. Emma is already half in love with the dark and dangerous Chase Sanders. Kate wants nothing more than for him to finish what he started, but he's the devil incarnate. And one doesn't make deals or fall in love with the devil.

If someone had told Chase he'd fall in love with a certain virgin when he was on his last mission, he would have shot them dead, sniper style. She was nothing more than collateral damage, damn it. But watching the sexy new spy morph into a bombshell killing machine is too much to bear. So when the powers that be command him to train her in the art of seduction for her first—and possibly last—mission, he's scared witless. Making love to Kate means preparing her for sex with another man.

Somehow, Chase has to find a way to get Kate in—and out—of her mission without dying. And without falling in love.

Thank you for purchasing this
publication of The Wild Rose Press, Inc.
If you enjoyed the story, we would appreciate
your letting others know by leaving a review.
For other wonderful stories, please visit our
on-line bookstore at www.thewilderroses.com.

For questions or more
information contact us at
info@thewildrosepress.com.

The Wild Rose Press, Inc.
www.thewilderroses.com

Stay current with The Wild Rose Press, Inc.
Like us on Facebook
https://www.facebook.com/TheWildRosePress
And Follow us on Twitter
https://twitter.com/WildRosePress